I LET
HER IN

BOOKS BY MARIA FRANKLAND

Last Christmas

MARIA FRANKLAND

I LET HER IN

bookouture

Published by Bookouture in 2024

An imprint of Storyfire Ltd.
Carmelite House
50 Victoria Embankment
London EC4Y 0DZ

www.bookouture.com

First published by Autonomy Press in 2021.

ISBN: 978-1-83525-005-1
eBook ISBN: 978-1-83525-004-4

For Michael, fifteen books later, here we are! Thank you for all your support and belief in me.

PROLOGUE

Ten years ago

It was the party to end all parties. If you weren't invited, you were invisible, a nobody. I was that person. But I went along anyway, slipping in through the side door, as I had countless times before. I couldn't have stopped myself, even if I'd tried. Even if turning up was only going to be torture.

Nobody noticed as I stood in the corner, unwanted and unimportant. I tried to enjoy the dancing and the laughter all around, but all I could see was you flirting, with her. Jade. A rush of betrayal, loneliness and anger coursed through me – it was so powerful, it almost took my breath away. Clearly, you didn't give a toss about me anymore. You probably never had.

As the hours passed, I hid away, drowning in my misery. Then, suddenly, the mood around me shifted, jolting me back to the surface. Laughter twisted into shrieks, joy transformed into cries of anguish. The music died, and a cold dread hung in the air, suffocated by the weight of something terrible. Someone rang for an ambulance.

Everyone crowded around Jade, both desperate and powerless to help. I pushed my way to the front of them all and was the last one standing over her, calm, yet numb – a witness to her descent into unconsciousness. Paramedics buzzed around her like flies, demanding to know *who had done this to her*.

It was no surprise when accusing fingers pointed straight at me.

*

The police questioned *everyone* at the party. I was the final person to make a statement. Always, always last. It seemed as though they were eagerly waiting for confirmation that I was indeed the villain everyone was whispering about.

To begin with, they insinuated that perhaps I hadn't intended the ketamine to have such a devastating effect on Jade. Maybe I hadn't anticipated the nightmare of her gasping for breath on the floor. But in the end, there would be only one person held accountable for the nine agonising days she spent in a coma until her life support was switched off. Agonising for me, anyway – she wouldn't have felt a thing.

Only one person could be the scapegoat. Nobody cared that I was innocent.

PART 1

CASSIE

ONE

CASSIE

'It feels strange being back here,' Jon says as he parks behind the removal van.

'How do you mean?' I twist in my seat, first to look at him then to check on Teddy. He's still sound asleep in his car seat. He's slept for most of the journey to this new part of Yorkshire. This, with the strangeness of our new home, means we'll probably have a right time of it with him this evening.

Suki springs up behind him, her ears perked in anticipation. Initially, I adopted her to feel safer in our last home when Jon was working away, but she's quickly become more of an adored member of the family than any sort of protector.

'It's a *good* strange.' He's turned the engine off yet continues to hold onto the steering wheel. 'Only, part of me expects my mother still to be in there.' He exhales with a hint of resignation. 'I just wish things had been different – at the end, I mean.'

Reaching across the handbrake, I intertwine my fingers with his. 'Everyone handles death in their own way. It sounds to me like she didn't want a fuss made.'

'Perhaps I could have helped her. If she'd have let me in.'

His words are tinged with something that could be bordering on resentment.

Jon continues to stare at the house, his expression difficult to decipher. He might be feeling 'strange', but to me, the place is perfect through and through, with its stone-built walls and elegant shuttered windows. Even if it had needed gutting from the inside out, I'd have needed little persuasion to move in.

On the rare occasions we've visited, I've got the impression of serenity around here, while most importantly, that sense of being part of a thriving community. My sense of 'coming home' is possibly as strong as Jon's is.

According to the Need2Move website, Rawdale is an up and coming area, with lots going on; it's teeming with fellow millennials, and parents of young children. It will be a million miles away from the isolation I knew in and around our old house, especially with Jon working so hard and often being away during the week. I hated this sense of being a single parent when he wasn't there and I lived for his return at the weekend.

'So what's the plan?' I squeeze his hand, willing him to meet my eye, if only to offer reassurance that he's not descending into one of his funny moods where he goes quiet and into himself. He's as impossible to read as he often berated his mother for being.

'Well, they're bringing the sofa out.' He cranes his neck towards the van. 'That was one of the first things they loaded so they must be nearly done.'

I wave back at one of the removal men as he rests the sofa on the ground at the door.

'Let the unpacking frenzy commence.' I reach into the back seat and nudge Teddy. 'We're here, sweetheart. At our brand new house. Wakey wakey.'

Despite Jon's somewhat lukewarm reaction to our arrival at the start of our next chapter, excitement bubbles in my belly. I start my new job next week and I just know I'm going to love being part of this community. There'll be wine nights, book clubs and mum groups. It's going to be great.

Teddy stretches his legs from his booster seat and rubs his eyes, grimacing as Suki leans over the back seat to lick the top of his head with her slobbering tongue. 'Ugh! Suki!'

'Right, come on.' Jon opens his door. 'We'd better get on with it all.' Then, as quickly as he opened it, he shuts it again and leans over to my side to rummage in the glovebox.

'What are you looking for?' One minute he's getting out of the car, the next, he's desperate to find something.

'Erm, just some paperwork to do with the house.'

'Oh. Right. In the *glovebox*?' I press myself back into my seat and smile at a woman who emerges from the house next to ours. 'Oooh look, the woman next door seems to be around my age. Brilliant!'

Between the gap in our two houses, I watch as she unclips laundry from her washing line. She keeps glancing over at us – I expect she's wondering who her new neighbours are going to be. 'We should go and say hello.'

'Leave it for now, Cassie.' He glances up then back into the glovebox. 'We've far too much to do. There'll be plenty of time for all that later.'

'What's up with you?' Whatever he claims to be looking for doesn't seem to be in there. I continue to watch her. 'You don't know her already, do you?'

'I used to. A bit. But I've not seen her for ages. Mum never said she still lived here. Perhaps she's just visiting.'

Jon closes the glovebox and twists in his seat towards Teddy. 'Are you ready to see your new room?'

'Yes!' He flings himself against the back of his seat in excitement.

'How did you know her?' I'm definitely getting a sense of some history between Jon and this woman he seems to be avoiding. To look at her, she doesn't seem his type with her undyed hair gathered into a ponytail and baggy gym clothes. He prefers women – me – to look immaculate.

'Oh, she's no one really. She was just the girl next door.'

'*The girl next door?* Back in my day, that's how all the magazines used to describe a romantic interest. Should I be worried?' Great. Reading between the lines here, I bet we're moving next to one of his former girlfriends. This is obviously why he's all but climbed into the glovebox.

'Don't be daft. We didn't get on brilliantly as kids, that's all.' There's an edge to his voice that suggests there might be a story there but his closed expression says he doesn't want to tell it.

'Oh – right.' I'm certainly relieved that she's not a former girlfriend after all. Hopefully, the fact that she and Jon didn't get on well as children won't prevent me and her from becoming friends. Much as my husband likes me to spend time with him when he's not at work or on the golf course, I really miss things like girly chats, shopping and spa days.

She disappears back inside.

'I need a wee,' says Teddy.

'You tend to the boy.' I nudge Jon. 'I'll take care of the dog.'

'To be honest...' He pulls a face before opening his door again. 'I'm only stalling because I haven't a clue where we're going to start when we get in there.'

'We'll be absolutely fine.' I wink at him across the car roof. 'As long as we employ our teamwork strategies.'

I set Suki free from the boot. She promptly christens our new street by having her wee on the verge outside next door's garden wall. I glance up to see the shape of our new neighbour through the net curtain in her window.

'Sorry,' I mouth at her with what I hope is an apologetic smile but I can't see her reaction. That's not a great start, allowing Suki to toilet herself on the grass in front of the neighbour's house, rather than in front of ours.

'Can you remember her name?' I call after Jon. He's leading

Teddy by the hand up the steps to our new front door with the gorgeous stained-glass window in its centre.

'Whose name?'

'The woman next door.'

Perhaps I'll take something round there, a cake, or a plant, or something, by way of introduction. Even if it's supposed to be the other way around when someone moves into a new house, one of us should break the ice. First impressions tell me it's not going to be her.

'I can't remember, to be honest. You know what I'm like with names.'

As I get Suki on the lead, I observe my son and husband disappear into our new house. An unexpected sadness wells up in my chest as my mind drifts back to a time when Jon might have carried me over the threshold into our new home. But that was before he became a partner at his oil firm and Teddy came along. Before our lives seemed to swallow us whole and our relationship seemed to change.

Sure, he's a great provider as a father and husband, but if I'm truly honest, that spark we used to have has diminished. However, I'm sure this new chapter, and me making more of a life for *myself* here, will make him more interested in me rather than the perfect version of myself I often feel like I need to be.

I watch him at times, while he's knotting his tie in the morning or engrossed in the sport on TV. I try to see the boy he was, and the older man he'll become. But he's such a closed book at times that it's not always easy. Reaching his inner core has become almost like a project for me and I won't rest until I know every inner aspect of his being and what drives him to be the way he is.

Perhaps, returning to his hometown and living in his child-hood home will reveal other sides to him. There are bound to be people, other than the next door neighbour, who'll remain from his past. People who'll remember Jon the boy and Jon the teenager.

It's a pity he's got no siblings. It's also regrettable that all I've ever seen of his father are photographs. I attended his funeral just after Jon and I had got engaged, getting more of a sense of relief from Jon, as I stood beside him in the front pew, than grief.

It will be a shame if Jon were to follow in the distant footsteps of his own father. With our son, *or with me.* I hope this place changes things between us and we return to how close we used to be.

With these thoughts swirling around my mind, I take a deep breath. The street is silent apart from the rhythmic chirping of a bird and the rustling of the tree in our front garden. I'm ready to embark on our new adventure. This house holds so much promise – it offers not only the chance to rediscover ourselves but also to quell the longing for a place I can truly call home.

As I ascend the steps towards my new front door, the familiar feeling of being watched sends a chill through me. I look around to see the woman from next door, standing at her window, just staring at me.

TWO

CASSIE

Suki and Teddy bound from room to room, filling the house with their joyful footsteps. Jon and I cast our eyes over endless boxes marked 'kitchen'. I haven't a clue where to begin.

'Which one has the beers in?' He leans against the breakfast bar as he looks at me. Even in his worn-out jeans and a faded T-shirt, he still exudes a magnetic charm. He could probably have his pick of women, which is why I have to keep on top of my game.

'Good call.' I smile at him as my mind wanders to how I'd best conserve some energy for tonight. No doubt he'll want us to put our stamp on our new bedroom later this evening. At least now we're inside the house and the removal men have left, he seems far less uptight than he was in the car.

Suki's tail whips back and forth with excitement as she skids into the kitchen, her favourite squeaky pig clutched tightly in her jaws. She leaps into her basket, claiming her spot as the queen of our new domain.

Teddy races after her. 'Where's my room?'

'We'll show you in a minute.'

Teddy's eyes widen as he takes in his new surroundings. 'I want the blue one.'

'Come here, son.' Jon beckons Teddy to him and Teddy jumps up into his arms, keen as always for the attention he doesn't often get from his dad because he's often too busy. Jon swings him into the air. 'What do you think of our new house so far then?'

'I like it. Can I have new friends now?' Teddy looks over Jon's shoulder at me.

I smile. 'Maybe when we get a chance to go to the park.' I'm surprised he's not been nattering to go there immediately. 'And you'll meet some new friends when you start at Hazel's next week.'

Hazel won me over instantly. Her house reverberated with happy children engaged with each other and their games. It seemed full of fun. She's been a childminder for years which ticked a big box for me. The last thing I want is to be worrying whether Teddy's OK while I'm getting settled into my new job.

Moreover, Teddy will have two boys to play with who are nearly the same age as him. Sure, it's going to be a massive wrench leaving him with Hazel after having him by my side for just over four years, but it's time for me to get my career, and my life, back on track. Jon didn't want me to work – not really. His first argument was that he wanted me to wait at least until Teddy starts school in September. His second argument was his desire for another baby. He wasn't too happy when I went for the job without running it by him first, to say the least, but he seems to have accepted it now.

I need to reintroduce him to the woman I once was when we first got together – sometimes, I think he forgets. I need to be Cassie again, not just Teddy's mum and Jon's wife.

Teddy looks up at his dad, his eyes shimmering with curiosity. 'Did you live here?'

'I certainly did.' He lowers him to the ground and the fact

that he turns away from him conveys that he doesn't wish to elaborate on that.

I hack a knife through the edge of one of the boxes.

'Bingo. First attempt!' I unscrew a lid from one of the bottles and pass it to Jon, before opening one for myself.

I drink deeply, a sense of contentment washing over me with each gulp. We certainly deserve a beer after the manic day we've had.

The sun has begun its descent on our moving day, casting long shadows through the windows, and a soft evening breeze drifts in, carrying the laughter of children playing in the park.

I smile at Jon as I hoist myself up to sit on the worktop. Things feel different between us. Less pressured. Maybe it's me, now I'm away from the old place. I must have driven him mad with my constant paranoia that someone was hanging around outside – I certainly drove myself mad.

As I suspected, Teddy's been extra difficult to settle in bed. Even though he's completely exhausted from his big moving day, he's fractious and doesn't want to be left alone, saying he's scared of monsters. Jon's taken a turn to sort him out which is unusual but very welcome given how much we've got to sort out.

As I hang coats in the cupboard under the stairs, I hear his footsteps thump above me, and he appears behind the case I'm unloading in the hallway.

'How many stories has it been so far? It must be four between us.' He passes me a coat from the case.

'Well, I read him two.' I laugh as I take it from him and hang it. 'Bless him. It's strange enough for *us* being here. So imagine how he feels.'

'Yeah.' Jon's voice has a faraway edge. He's probably

thinking of his own parents. 'His eyes were drooping though. Hopefully, he's on his way.'

'I reckon it's wine o'clock.' I let my hair from its band and shake it down my back. 'We can make a start on the kitchen cupboards if you like. I've wiped them all out.'

Even though my mother-in-law has died, now I'm actually in here, I feel as though I'm invading her space. Hopefully, once we get unpacked, this feeling of being an uninvited guest will fade before too long.

'Right. One more hour at this then we'll call it a day. How do you fancy a takeaway tonight?'

I step towards him, encircling his lean torso in my arms. 'Sounds good to me. I think we're going to be really happy here.'

'That's good.' He brushes hair from my eyes then he looks up and around where we're standing. 'Once we've had the decorators in and replaced the bathrooms and the kitchen, the place should feel like somewhere we can invite people.'

Something inside me sinks. If there's one thing I hate, it's entertaining his work and golf cronies. Having to make myself up like a Stepford wife and cook like one too, while supporting Jon to schmooze and hold his audience captive. Just thinking about it makes my head hurt.

I just want to be *me*, instead of the wife I'm expected to be for these people. Now we're away from that old pretentious house that was three times too big for us, perhaps I can be less polished all the time and more down to earth.

'It's actually good to be back here.' He moves away from me and picks up his phone. 'Back where I belong.'

It's lucky for him that he feels like this. I wouldn't particularly want to live in my childhood home, especially after witnessing all the rows and being hostage to the chilly atmosphere between my parents as I was growing up. It's hard enough returning to visit Mum these days. I'm always pleased to get away again.

'We'll have a Chinese, shall we?' He raises the phone to his ear without waiting for an answer. 'Are we having starters? Or are you still on one of your diets?'

I laugh. 'Not today. I need the extra energy with everything we've got to do.'

He starts ordering for me without checking what I want. I start to protest but then clamp my lips back together. Really, I'm grateful that my husband knows me well enough to pre-empt what I want. And I certainly don't want to say anything that could mar the first night of our fresh start. I've got everything I could ever want or need here but most importantly, I feel safe now.

THREE

CASSIE

The chill of the tiles is comforting to my weary bare feet as I begin unpacking one of the boxes while Jon's on the phone.

'Let's get that wine cracked open, shall we?' His voice is suddenly behind me. 'It sounds like Teddy could have finally fallen asleep.'

But the same can't be said for Suki.

'What's up with the dog, Cassie? I can't believe she's at it again.'

I drop to her side. 'Hey girl, what's the matter?' She's making the same low growling sound that reverberates around the room and used to send shivers down my spine in the old house. The same sound that had me running many a night from door to door and window to window, making sure everything was locked and bolted. Stuck there alone with a small child, it had been terrifying when Jon was working away, though I'm sure it made him feel all-the-more-important and welcomed back, when he returned to end my isolation.

'What if there's someone out there Jon?' My voice is trembling with anxiety. A chill creeps over me, a haunting reminder of the fear and vulnerability I've experienced in the past. I dart to the kitchen window, cupping my hands against the chill of the glass as I try to look over the darkened garden. All I can see is my own reflection.

'Not all this again Cassie.' He lifts a box from the floor to the counter. 'Honestly, you need to get over this love. Do you really think this supposed person, who's been watching the old house for who knows how many months, has followed us here to lurk around this one instead?'

I pull out a stool to the breakfast bar. 'You've never taken this seriously. One day when you come home to find me dead, you'll wish you'd listened to what I've been trying to tell you for all these months.' I'm probably being completely irrational again and I hate myself for it but I can't help the way I feel. I've tried and tried to tell myself while at the old house that I'm imagining things but with Suki's reaction as well, it's difficult to convince myself.

Jon plucks a bottle of wine from the box and slides a stool up next to me. 'Of course I take you seriously.' He lets out a sigh. 'But let's be honest, it's not like we've ever *seen* anyone hanging around, is it?'

'You know what it's like though, when you can *feel* someone watching you.' The thought sends a tremor up my spine. Suki can certainly sense something again too. She's suddenly become really unsettled.

'I *don't* know actually. But listen to me, I really think it's all in your imagination. We've moved house, haven't we? You wanted to move here. You said you'd be happier and feel safer.'

'But what if...'

'Cassie. You've got to let this go. There's no one out there.' He gestures impatiently towards the back of the house.

'Can you just have a look for me?' I allow my eyes to meet his now, hoping to beseech him in the same way Teddy does with me. I can't relax until he's double-checked out there.

There's no way I can go through what I went through in the last house. I was always too wired to even relax in an armchair, let alone get any sleep.

He passes me the bottle and sighs again as he marches from the rear of the kitchen and through the conservatory. He unlocks the double doors then throws them open into the back garden.

'Hello?' He hollers into the darkness. He stands for a moment, first looking out, then back at me, with a look on his face as if to say, *I told you so.* 'There you go.' He closes the door. 'What did I tell you? It's nothing but a dose of your overactive imagination.'

'I'm sorry.' I twist the cap from the bottle, the rich aroma of the wine filling the air. I glug it into our glasses, feeling like I need a glass more than ever now. 'You're right. It might just take a while to get used to the creaks and noises of this place.'

I cast my gaze around our new kitchen. It's a waste of a good kitchen, us getting rid of it but Jon thinks that we need to put our own stamp on things. *It's not as if we can't afford it*, he's repeatedly reminded me even though it makes me uncomfortable to rip out a kitchen when there's nothing wrong with it. Since Jon bought into his company and his mum left him this place, I can't imagine money being an issue for the rest of our lives – not that it ever has been. I've wanted for nothing since we met. Nothing apart from Jon not having to work away all the time.

I jump as Suki growls again, more urgently this time. She arches her back before making towards the lounge door, yet she suddenly stops outside it. It's happening again, I know it is. I've been followed here, it's the only explanation.

'I'm sorry Jon. I know I'm probably being daft, but can you check at the front of the house as well?' I watch the expression change on his face. Shit. I know I'm putting a dampener on things but I can't help it.

'Just enjoy your wine for God's sake Cassie. And let's both of us enjoy our first night here, shall we? Like you've already said yourself – it's a creaky old house.'

'But Suki doesn't growl for no reason.'

Jon pulls a face. 'I beg to differ.' He takes a sip of his wine. '"Let's get a guard dog," you said. "I'll feel safer when you're working away," you said. Yet since we got her, you seem more scared than ever. I've got to be honest love, I do worry about the effect all this could be having on Teddy.'

'I know.' He's right. Our son's fear of monsters has come from *somewhere*.

'Listen, I could kind of understand Suki carrying on at the old house, after all, there was so much wildlife around that might have startled her, but here, well, there'll be nothing more than a bird or a squirrel in the garden.' He takes a big swig from his glass. 'Stop it now Suki. Get back in your bed.'

But she ignores him, and carries on growling, now even louder than before. Whatever's troubling her seems to be sensed more when she's near the lounge.

I march towards the lounge door, pushing it fully open. I stand back until I'm satisfied no one's hiding in here. Then I give myself a shake. Unless one of the removal men has taken up residence and hidden himself up the chimney for the last few hours, I'm being ridiculous. That said, I'd be better able to relax if every passer-by wasn't able to nosy in through our uncurtained windows. Yes, we've got shutters on the outside but, as I found out when we looked around after Jon's mum had died, the hinges are rusted beyond function. Replacing them is much more necessary than anything else Jon's got in mind for the house.

'Which box is the drill in?' I call out as I survey the yet-to-be-unpacked boxes stacked in the bay window.

'What on earth do you want the drill for?' Jon pokes his head into the lounge.

'I was hoping you'd put a blind up.' I'm back to my beseeching expression which he usually finds either endearing or irritating, depending what mood he's in. It worked before anyway. 'We must have something that'll fit that window.' I point at the front one. 'Until the blinds get delivered.'

'Cassie, I'm not drilling into the walls at this time of night. We'll wake Teddy up. Anyway, the food will be here soon.' He comes up behind me and rests his hands on my shoulders.

I look from the front-facing window to the gorgeous arch-shaped, side-facing one. 'Perhaps we could hammer some nails into some sheets to cover them?' I pick up the hammer which is poking out of one of the boxes. 'You've said you're wanting to decorate in here.'

Again, we don't need to redecorate any more than we need a new kitchen but I do understand Jon's need to make the house ours instead of his parents'.

'I'm not hammering any more than I'm drilling.' Jon grabs the hammer from my hands. 'You can manage without curtains for a few nights, surely? There's nothing to worry about around here. You've said yourself what a decent neighbourhood it is. It's not like the one *you* grew up in.'

'It's just—'

'Like I said before. You seem to be inventing things even more than Teddy and that's saying something.' His face breaks into a smile. 'Perhaps you've had a bit too much time on your hands lately. At least, now we've moved, I'm going to be around a lot more.'

Something within me sags. I'm probably taking it the wrong way but what he's just said about me *having too much time* feels like a put-down.

Well, I'll show him. From next week when I become head of human resources for my new company, he'll see, once again, what I'm truly made of. I'll become the *Cass with sass* he fell for, instead of being the diminished version of myself I've been since Teddy was born.

Though regularly stuck on my own, as I've been for several years, with only a dog and a young boy for company, it's no wonder I constantly hear noises outside and worry that some-one's watching me.

FOUR

CASSIE

Suki's lying against the front door, ears on full alert, her menacing growl continuing to resonate through the hallway. It sends shivers down my spine as I rinse the plates from our take-away. Jon won't take me seriously, so it's time to take matters into my own hands. I won't relax until I do.

Gripping her collar, I reach for the latch with my other hand. There's a soft squeak as it releases and I slowly open the door. The warmth of Suki's body pressed against my leg is a comforting presence. No one's going to come at me when I've got a German Shepherd at my side. Potential intruders aren't aware that Suki's more likely to lick them to death than pin them to the ground.

'Hello,' I call into the night as a cold blast of air hits my face. It's quiet out here apart from the distant sound of cars passing by. At least it's better lit than where we used to live. Stepping out of the door at night was like entering a void. I avoided it completely unless Jon was with me. Looking back now, I don't know how I lasted in that place for as long as I did without having some kind of breakdown.

I startle as there's a thud from my right, sending a jolt of fear through my body. Then I let my breath go. It's just the woman from next door, putting her bin out. Honestly, perhaps Jon has every right to be irritated by me. I'm as jumpy as a Jack-in-a-box.

What he's said is right, this is a decent neighbourhood and we're perfectly safe here. Though if being jumpy gives me the chance to say hello to our neighbour and suss her out a bit, perhaps it's not such a bad thing. I head down the steps with Suki hot on my trail. It'll be great if she and I become friendly, living in such close proximity. After all, any childhood disgruntlement between her and Jon is bound to be ancient history.

'Hi there,' I call out. The woman turns back towards her gate, her back slightly hunched, but upon hearing my voice, she hesitates, her eyes meeting mine. It's a fleeting moment, but I catch a glimmer of curiosity in her gaze before she fully faces me.

'I'm Cassie. I've just moved in – *we've* just moved in here.' My feet are cold against the stone slabs as I wait for her reply. I should have put my slippers on.

'Oh, right.' For a moment, I think she's going to continue into her house without saying anything else so I'm relieved when she steps towards my wall with her hand outstretched. As least she's acknowledging me, which is more than can be said for when we first arrived. She's still wearing her gym clothes from earlier. Perhaps she wears them all the time. I suppose I'd live in mine given half a chance. Now I've had a baby, I feel like I have to work extra hard on myself. I can never let myself go. Jon's occasional mentions of having a second child fill me with dread. Mainly because it was hard enough shifting the weight from Teddy.

'I'm Becca,' she says. 'I live next door with my mum.'

'With your *mum?*' My voice rises a notch without meaning it to. She looks a similar age to me, which is certainly too old to be living with her mum. I can't imagine a situation which would force me to have to move back in with mine again. I'd have to be pretty desperate and luckily, I can't ever imagine that being the case.

'I'm her carer.'

'Ah right. Well, it's good to meet you... Hang on, let me give my husband a shout. I've a feeling you might remember each other.' My voice bears the exuberance of a game-show host. She might not be the friendliest person on the planet but it's reassuring to suddenly have a neighbour after all those years of living well apart from anybody.

'I do remember him.'

'Oh?'

Her answer's too quick and her voice too flat. The two of them *must* have some sort of history. I suspected as much when Jon was so preoccupied with the glovebox when we first got here. I don't know why he wouldn't have just told me about it though. It's not as if I'd have minded. Not really. We've *all* got a past, after all.

'I noticed you arriving. That removal lorry would have been hard to miss.' She laughs, but it's forced. Maybe I shouldn't jump to conclusions. Perhaps she's just shy with new people.

'I wanted to say hello to you then to be honest,' I reply. 'But you looked busy. And we're *definitely* busy. It's chaos in there.' I gesture back towards the house. 'Jon – come out here a minute, will you?'

'Why's the door wide open? Are we suddenly paying to heat the street? Oh.' His tone changes as he stops at the top of the steps. 'Alright Becca. Long time, no see.'

Hmm, he said earlier that he didn't remember her name. She doesn't smile at him. She at least *tried* to smile at me. Nor does she offer her hand as he reaches the bottom of the steps like she did with me. But since they already know each other, that could *possibly* explain them not shaking hands.

'We've just opened some wine,' I say. 'Why don't you join us for a glass?'

'Cassie, we've got...'

'I can't,' she says quickly. 'Like I said, I look after my mum.' She jerks her thumb in the direction of her house.

'Is that why you're still living here?' Jon, also in bare feet, stands at my side. 'I'd have thought you'd be long gone.'

'Yeah, pretty much. Ever since she had her stroke – I've lost count of the years.'

'You can bring your mum round too, can't she Jon?' I look from Becca to Jon. 'It would be lovely to get to know one of your old friends. I bet you can tell a few tales.'

'I don't think...' Jon begins.

'My mum's bed-bound actually, I can't leave her on her own.'

'Oh, I'm sorry to hear that.' Here's me, able to spread my wings now I've found a childminder, while poor Becca's chained to her mother. 'It sounds like you've got your hands full.'

'You could say that. I work from home as well.'

'So it's twenty-four seven for you?'

'Yep. Apart from when she's sleeping.'

'Well if you ever want a break when she's fallen asleep, you're more than welcome for a coffee. I'm here for the next few days – until I start my new job on Monday.' I sense Jon bristling beside me. Hopefully he'll come to terms more with my new job once I've actually started and he realises it's not going to take anything away from us.

Instead of answering me, Becca looks straight at Jon. 'Your dad told us you'd moved away *permanently*.' There's a note of something in her voice that I can't put my finger on. I've known Jon since he was twenty but she's clearly known him a lot longer.

'I had.' His voice is low and I wait for him to expand on his answer. Both she and I watch as he seems to clam up. Whatever's going on here, she doesn't seem terribly happy about his return. Or is it because he's returned with *me*?

'Your dad said you were *never* coming back.' It's a rude question by anyone's standards and her tone has become almost accusatory. Why would Jon's dad have told the neighbours he was never coming back? I've always known something must have happened between Jon and his father all those years ago. He'll never talk about it but maybe, in time, Becca might be willing to shed some light on things.

I'm going to have to grill her as soon as I get the chance. He's always brushed my questions away like specks of dust on one of his designer suits. He's very good at changing the subject.

'Things change, don't they? Time moves on.' He's actually less defensive than I'd expect him to be, given the directness of her question. 'Besides, my mother left us the place.'

'Time moves on from *what*?' I look from him to her. There's evidently an unspoken knowing between them for a moment, even if their faces aren't giving anything away.

'Anyway, we'd better be getting back inside.' I feel the weight of Jon's hand on my shoulder. 'Come on Cassie – this unpacking isn't going to do itself.'

'Don't forget to pop round?' I shake Jon's hand loose. 'For that coffee, I mean. I don't know anyone or *anything* around here yet. It would be lovely to pick your brains about the place.' What I mean is, *it would be lovely to pick your brains about my husband and his family.*

'I'll try,' she replies, turning from me.

But if there's one thing I've learned in my twenty-nine years on this earth, it's that when a person uses the word *try*, it means they've no intention of ever doing so.

As we turn away from Becca, a mix of emotions swirl within me – doubt, curiosity, and a pervading sense of inadequacy. I wonder what lies beneath their shared history.

Jon's hand lingers on my shoulder as we ascend the steps. 'You don't have to try so hard with people, you know.' His voice is tinged with caution. I can sense there's more to their past than he's willing to reveal but at least he's snapped out of the strange mood he was in outside. 'Let them come to you for a change.'

'I'm not trying too hard, as you put it. It's just, she only lives next door. I thought it would be nice to get...' I slip my feet into my slippers to warm them up and shuffle towards the kitchen.

'I'm sure you'll make friends around here.' He nuzzles into my neck as I dry the plates from the draining board. 'Although you'd be more likely to make friends with other mums if you weren't going back to work.'

There it is – another remark about me going back to work. I feel guilty enough about leaving Teddy as it is. Maybe Jon's right. Perhaps it *is* too soon. But it's too late now – I've signed my contract, I've met people there and I've employed Hazel to look after Teddy. It's a big change but I'm sure we'll all get used to it.

'Anyway, there are far nicer people to get to know around here than Becca.' The way he says her name has a sharp edge to it.

'Why, what's so wrong with her?' I twist to face him and he lowers his hands. 'Did the two of you fall out? Were you, you know, really *together* when you were younger?'

He laughs as he steps back from me. 'She was just – oh look, let's not go on about the past. All I want to do is look to the future now. You, me, and Teddy.'

Suki opens one eye from her bed in the corner with a grunt. 'Yes, you as well, girl.' Jon laughs again as he bends to pat her. Then he stands and lets his gaze roam over the kitchen. 'Gosh, when I left here all those years ago, I never thought I'd be returning to live here as a married man with a kid and a dog. I guess, sooner rather than later, we'll be making it two kids and a dog, won't we?' He winks.

'Just let me get into my new job first.' Something inside me flips at yet another of his mentions of a second baby. He's clearly serious. But I can't let him believe that I'd rather work than us increase our family so I need to soften what I've just said. 'I wouldn't even qualify for maternity pay yet.'

'We don't even need your maternity pay,' he says.

'I know. We're very lucky, aren't we?'

'As long as we don't end up with a huge age gap between our kids. Nor would I want Teddy to grow up as an only child like I had to.' A strange light enters his eyes as he reaches for his keys. 'Anyway, you go up. I'll make sure everything's locked down here.'

As I ascend the spiral staircase, my feet sinking into the deep pile of the carpet, I can't help but feel grateful that Jon's an only child.

Selfish as though it may sound, if he'd had siblings, we'd have had to sell this gorgeous house and split the proceeds with them. As things stand, it's ours, all ours.

Nothing, and no one, can take it away from us.

FIVE

CASSIE

'Let's go on an adventure, shall we?' I reach for Teddy's hand, which is warm and soft against my own. The cool breeze brushes against my skin, carrying the scent of freshly cut grass from the park.

He skips as we head down our path alongside the stream which glistens like a silver ribbon being threaded through our garden. I can't wait to sit beside it with a drink on the patio when spring properly arrives. Another reason I wanted this house so badly is because it backs straight onto the park. Teddy won't even have to cross the road to get to it when he's older.

'Wow!' His eyes widen as I open the gate. 'Is there a troll under there?' We pretend to trip-trap across the footbridge over the stream, before looking around us.

'Well, this is rather brilliant, isn't it sweetheart?' The play area is a few yards in front of us, to our left is a cafe, and to our right, there's a path that leads to the river, where dogs can be let off their leads to play – according to the signs anyway. Teddy looks to be transfixed as he takes it all in.

'Let's throw the ball for Suki for a few minutes.' I delve in my pocket for it. 'We'll let her play first.'

'Then can I go on the slide?' He gazes longingly in its direction, to where the squeak of the swings and the noise of joyful children is clearly tantalising him.

'Course you can. Let's tire this one out first, then you can spend as long as you like on there.'

'OK.' He holds one hand out for the ball thrower and points towards the playground with the other.

As Teddy and Suki race around together after the ball, I'm more at peace than I've been for a while. I observe the bustling park and the presence of people. It certainly brings a newfound sense of belonging and ease.

Whilst I'm aware that it must be strange for Jon being back here, I'm sure it won't be long before we settle into the house and become immersed in the neighbourhood. Making some new memories here might go some way to cancel out whatever unhappy memories he's always been so reluctant to discuss.

'Ouch!'

'Oh no. I'm so sorry.' I dash over to the woman who's rubbing at her head. Teddy must have accidentally launched the ball at her. 'Teddy, watch where you're throwing that ball. Oh gosh, I should have been paying more attention. Teddy. What do you say to the lady?'

'It wasn't me Mummy.'

'Just say sorry.' I frown at him.

'It's alright, don't worry.' The woman stops rubbing and smiles at Teddy. 'It serves me right for hanging around in the dog walking area. Habit, I suppose.'

'Oh, right. Is your dog not with you today?'

'You could say that. He died.' A cloud of sadness crosses her face.

Me and my big mouth. 'Oh, I'm sorry to hear that.'

She shrugs away my sympathy. 'It means I'm always grateful for any chance to spend time with other doggies. You're beautiful, aren't you?' She drops to a crouch as she fusses over Suki. 'You remind me of my Milo.'

Suki cranes her neck, as always, enjoying the attention as Teddy looks on.

'Was Milo a German Shepherd too?'

'Yes, he was. He looked just like yours.'

We talk dogs for a few minutes. Teddy waits beautifully. He's probably subdued after managing to throw the ball at someone's head. However, it's not long until he starts tugging at my coat. 'Mummy, can we go to the slide now?'

'Come on then.' As I clip Suki's lead back to her collar, I'm reminded I need to get her identity tag changed to our new address.

'Are you new around here?' the woman asks as I turn to walk away. 'I haven't seen you before.'

'Yes, we've just moved in,' I reply as I turn back to face her.

'I can recommend all the best dog walking spots if you like? I'm not in a rush to be anywhere.'

'Oh, erm right, OK. Thank you.'

'Shall I walk to the playground with you?' She falls into step with me. 'I'm Amy, by the way.'

'Cassie.' I thrust my hand at her as Teddy bounds alongside us. 'This is Teddy and this...' I bend to pat her on the head. '...is Suki.'

As we watch Teddy go up and down the slide, over and over again, Amy shares details about the woodland walk, the scenic lakeside loop, and the track that locals amusingly refer to as The Giant's Bum. I've heard Jon mention that before as a place he went sledging as a boy. It's one of the very few childhood memories he's divulged. And that was to Teddy, not to me.

Amy and I then move on to other matters such as which hairdresser has the best reputation and I ask her about places to go out to eat.

'I know of a really good Chinese place,' she says. 'We'll have to try it sometime.'

I'm taken aback by her quick friendliness but there's no denying that we seem to chat away easily. It's the polar opposite to the indifference I encountered when attempting to ingratiate myself with Becca last night. Amy's as friendly as Becca was sullen.

'Mummy. Push me on the swing.' I hesitate, noticing the *no dogs* sign attached to the fence.

'It's OK, I can wait here with Suki if you like?' Amy holds her hand out for the lead. 'You go and give him a push.'

As Teddy shrieks with excitement and demands to go higher, I keep one eye on Amy as she throws the ball for Suki. It dawns on me that I've entrusted my dog to someone I barely know, *and* while she's grieving for her own, of the same breed.

However, it would take a very brave person to attempt to steal Suki away from us. I don't even think a large piece of steak would tempt her. I shake the thought away. I've got to start being more trusting of people – and less paranoid. But it's really difficult after what I went through in our last house.

'Let me treat you to an ice cream to say thank you.' Amy smiles at me as we let ourselves back through the gate.

'For what?'

'For letting me look after Suki, of course. It's done me the world of good to have some doggy time.'

'It should be me thanking you. She'd have only whined her head off if I'd left her tied to the fence. Isn't it a touch cold for ice cream?' I blow on my hands through my gloves.

'It's never too cold for ice cream.' She smiles as she hands Suki's lead back to me.

Amy looks like she could do with a few extra calories. She's painfully thin, her figure almost fragile, and her eyes, large and doe-like, hold a hint of sadness within them. She certainly seems like someone with a story to tell which is maybe why she's latched onto us. I'm almost envious of the fact that her face is completely devoid of make-up. Not like mine unfortunately – it would be nice not to have my face on at all times but spending ten minutes putting it on every morning has become an ingrained part of my routine.

'Suki's stealing my ice cream,' Teddy wails from where he's sitting, in between us on the bench. Amy and I laugh at the evidence smattered over Suki's whiskers. There's certainly no way she could deny it.

'Here, have mine, sweetie pie.' I swap ice creams with him. 'Lie down, Suki.'

'She's such a good girl.' Amy looks down at her and then around at Teddy. 'And your son's lovely too. You're very lucky to have them.'

'I need reminding of that when they're both under my feet and driving me potty.' I ruffle Teddy's hair. 'I take it you haven't got kids yet, Amy?'

A darkness enters her eyes, making me wish I hadn't asked. Before I had Teddy, it used to annoy me when my parental status was one of the first things people would enquire about. Like it's how we should identify ourselves.

'No.'

A heavy silence hangs between us for a few moments as I wonder what to say next.

'We should get together for a coffee sometime,' she eventually says. 'It would be lovely to get to know you better.'

'Yes – that would be nice.'

She brightens up again. 'How about now?'

'Sorry – I'm up to my eyeballs in unpacking.' I laugh. 'I've still not found the cafetière and the house is in complete disarray.'

'No worries.' She falls quiet again, making me hope she doesn't think I'm giving her the brush-off. I get the impression that she's had a lot of that.

'We just live over there.' I point across the stream, the new-house excitement probably evident in my voice. We might have had a larger house with more land before, but this house is more me. I don't need or want a big house and besides, this one's far prettier and with tons more character.

She lets out a long whistle. 'It's amazing. What's that building in the garden? It's not a summerhouse, is it?'

'It sure is.' I pull an excited face. 'I feel very lucky now, but it wasn't always like this.'

'What does your husband do?'

There we go. Yet another question that's asked in order for us women to identify ourselves among our counterparts.

'He's a partner in an oil company,' I reply, wondering if she'll ask what I do next. I'm so pleased to be going back to work at last and am definitely in no rush for baby number two where I'll be isolated at home again.

Her eyes become as wide as dinner plates and I can tell what she must be thinking. *They're loaded.* It's embarrassing really – and I want to be judged for *me*, rather than where I live and who I'm married to.

The fact that she's wearing thin leggings beneath an over-sized and rather shabby coat gives me the impression that life's possibly a struggle for her financially. It used to be for me when I was growing up so I know what she must be going through.

'So, how are you settling in Rawdale?'

'Not too bad.' I'm glad to change the subject. 'Slowly, but surely. You know how it is.'

She nods and smiles. 'You look like you're enjoying that ice cream,' she says to Teddy.

I reach into my pocket for a tissue. 'I think he's wearing more than he's eaten,' I say with a laugh, beckoning him to come closer.

He wrinkles his nose as I mop him up.

'Shall we arrange that coffee then?' Amy says. 'How long do you think it'll take you to find your cafetière?'

'Erm, at least a few days. But from next week, I'll be home after seven if you'd like to call in then?'

Her smile fades to a frown. 'As in seven in the evening?'

'Erm, yes. Or I could be around on Saturday. Jon, that's my husband, will no doubt go playing golf and leave me to carry on sorting out the house.' I laugh. 'Are *you* married?'

'No.' Her voice is flat again. 'How about Sunday? Do you have Sundays free too?'

Maybe she can't do Saturday – or maybe she's wanting to meet Jon. 'Jon likes us to keep Sunday as a family day.'

'Nice. OK, I'll probably come on Saturday then. Evenings can be a bit tricky for me.'

'Really? Why?'

'I've just got a lot on.'

'Oh right.' Something in her expression and her tone seems to suggest she doesn't want to discuss this any further. Or maybe she's just more reserved than I am. *Just because I like wittering away about my life doesn't mean everybody else wants to.* My enthusiasm falters for a moment. Jon's told me many times that I can be too much of an open book, as he puts it.

'Can I have your number?' she asks as she fishes around in her bag. 'Then I can drop you a text before I set off.'

'Yeah, sure.' I take the pen and scrap of paper from her and place it on the bench so I can write. 'There you go.'

She glances at it and drops it into her pocket. 'Thanks, that's great.'

'I'm so pleased to have met you Amy.' My hand brushes the wool of her coat sleeve as I rise to my feet. 'But we need to get going – I've so much to do.'

'I'm pleased to have met you too. Whenever you're ready you'll have to let me show you around the town.'

'Erm yes – I guess so. Perhaps you'll be able to introduce me to some of your friends too. It was so quiet where we used to live and we were out on a limb there. It's great to have moved into a proper community.'

'I bet it is. I hope you'll be really happy here.' There's a note in her voice which I can't put my finger on. I want to ask her about her home but I've probably asked too many personal questions already.

We say our goodbyes and Teddy and I return home the way we came, over the stream and back through the garden gate. As I turn to lock it behind us, my attention's averted to an upstairs window next door.

Becca stands framed within it, watching again. I don't know why, but I get the impression she's been watching for a while. As I wave up at her, instead of waving back, she drops the curtain and disappears from view.

SIX

CASSIE

'It's never-ending, all this.' I open yet another case and glance at Jon, sprawled out on our bed in his joggers and a T-shirt, scrolling through his phone. It must be nice to dress so casually. I'm not sure he realises just how tedious and time consuming it is to always have to have blow-waved my hair, applied a face full of make-up and swan around wearing the designer clothes and shoes he often buys me. Perhaps I should be grateful but I'd be so much more comfortable if I could be like Becca next door. How I envy her leggings, T-shirt and ponytail.

He grins as he shrugs his shoulders. 'Sorting it all out might remind you of what you've got.'

'I won't be able to fit it all in the wardrobes here.' I look around the room. 'It's not as if I've got that walk-in wardrobe anymore.' I don't add that I'm pleased about this.

'Just use the extra cupboard space in one of the spare rooms.'

'Perhaps it's time to let go of some of it.' I try to sound mournful but I can't think of anything better than bagging up some of this stuff and letting a good cause have it. It's always felt stupidly indulgent to possess this amount of clothes. Especially when Jon's chosen most of them. 'Perhaps I could donate some of the stuff I haven't worn for ages.'

'Whatever you think,' he replies. 'Though let me check through what you're getting rid of first. I love to see you in some of those dresses.'

'Perhaps I should go through Teddy's old outfits and toys as well.'

Thomas the Tank Engine music echoes across the landing from his room. I must spend some time with him soon. We've subjected him to quite enough of the 'electronic babysitter' over the last few days while we've been packing at the old house and then unpacking here.

Jon frowns. 'I thought we were hanging onto his things. In case we have another boy.'

He's back onto this again and I resist the urge to say *that'll be months, if not years away.* Instead I say, 'I reckon baby number two will be a girl when the time comes. I'm outnumbered here, as it is.'

'Not entirely.' Jon laughs as, right on cue, Suki trots into the room.

'Which reminds me,' I say as she drops at the side of me, right onto a pile I've created. 'I've got Teddy sorted with the childminder, but I need to find a dog-sitting service sharpish, or at least find someone to call in and walk her for us.'

'You know Cassie, you really haven't thought all this through, have you?'

'What do you mean?' I silently berate myself for mentioning anything about starting my new job. I'm perfectly capable of sorting something out for Suki myself without needing to whinge at Jon about it. What I need to do is make sure nothing really changes in his world – be at home when he leaves for work himself and then when he returns. Once he sees that my new job will hardly affect our family life, he'll be far happier about it.

'Well firstly you wanted a baby, then you wanted a dog.'

'We both wanted a baby.'

'Yes and I didn't want to leave it with strangers.'

'Him, not it. And he's not being left with a stranger. Hazel's lovely. You seemed to like her when I introduced you both.'

'And then you wanted a job,' He doesn't acknowledge what I just said about Hazel. 'But then suddenly, who's going to look after the dog when you're putting all your energy into a job you don't even need.' His voice has taken on the sarcastic edge that I have to stop myself becoming defensive against. We've been getting on so well since we moved in here that I don't want anything to spoil that.

'I know I don't need it Jon. And I'm grateful more than you know for how you provide for us. But I want this job – it'll do me so much good to properly get my brain into something again.'

He tilts his phone screen back towards himself. 'I'll have a look on Facebook for a dog-sitter, shall I?'

Phew. At least he's trying to help me with the situation. It's the most acceptance he's shown about me working since I first mentioned it.

'Do you think Becca next door might be interested? It might do her good to have an excuse to go out each day and have a break from looking after her mum.'

'You heard her.' Jon looks up from his phone. 'She's already tied up. Besides, you'll need to find someone who can give Suki at least an hour in the middle of the day.' He looks at her. 'I *still* don't know why we had to go for such a big dog.'

'Of course you do – to protect your wife and son in your absence.' I try to load something of the damsel in distress into my voice and expression. It usually thaws him towards me. I look up at him, then back to the clothes. 'What I might do is put a couple of cards around,' I continue. 'There must be lots of dog-walking businesses in a little market town like this.'

'So you're thinking of bringing a complete stranger into our home? I don't think so.'

'Of course not. I'll check out exactly who the people are first.'

'Just don't be bringing anyone dodgy into our home, for God's sake.'

A heavy sigh escapes me as I cast my gaze over the garments strewn across the carpet, feeling overwhelmed. One human being does not need this amount of clothes and shoes. I can't wait any longer to start offloading some of them. 'Can you amuse Teddy for a while?' I get to my feet. 'Get him away from the TV?'

'Why, are you going *now*?'

'I won't be long, I promise. I'm going to find a charity shop in town and drop off some of this stuff...' I start shovelling some of the clothes into a pile. 'Then I'll put some cards for dog walkers up in a shop window or two while I'm at it.'

'I've got a meeting at half three.'

'I'll be back before then.'

'I don't fancy your chances of finding someone for Suki in time, you know.'

'Well I've got to try.'

'Just make sure you ask for references on the card.'

'Yeah – yeah.'

'Oh and you haven't forgotten about Saturday, have you?'

'Saturday?' Something inside me sinks. What on earth have I agreed to that I've forgotten about?

'The dinner that's being hosted for me at the golf club.'

'Oh gosh, yes.' *Damn!*

'I can't believe you've forgotten. You know how much being elected for president of the club means to me.'

'I hadn't forgotten – it's just – you know, what with the move and everything.'

'More like you've been getting wrapped up with thoughts of

this new job. I really hope it won't get in the way of our home life.'

'It won't, I promise,' I say quickly. And I really mean it.

As I'm carrying bags from the house to the car I notice Becca watching me over our dividing hedge.

'Hi there,' I call as I'm returning to close the front door. 'How are you?'

'OK,' she replies.

'How's your mum?'

'The same as always.' Then she closes her door behind her. In spite of whatever history may or may not exist between her and Jon, I feel really sorry for how they're living in there. Becca, trapped in her house, and her mother, trapped in her bed. It's no life for anyone and it's no wonder she seems down in the dumps. It probably explains why she's always so offhand with me.

There's certainly no shortage of charity shops here. I drive up and down the high street looking for a space, before easing my Mini into one right outside the Animal Rescue shop. There's a ton of designer labels amongst the little lot I'm donating and I'd much prefer them to be raising money to help animals. The back of the Mini is stuffed with as much as I could fit into it. Really, I should have driven Jon's car down but I feel so pretentious swanning around in a Range Rover that I avoid it at all costs. Jon's request to go through my donations thankfully didn't come to anything as he got sidetracked with a phone call from his work.

As luck would also have it, my chosen charity shop seems to be the only one on this side of the street with a load of cards and notices displayed in their window. With what I'm donating here, surely they'll be only too happy to display a card for me?

As I step onto the bustling street, the air fills with the scent of the bakery combined with the fish and chip shop, making my belly rumble. Chatter drifts from every direction, mingled with the soft melodies escaping the open doors of the shops either side of where I'm heading. It won't be long until this street is totally familiar to me.

I squeeze myself through the door of the charity shop, the aroma of used books filling my nose as I balance my handbag on my shoulder and the bulging black sacks in each hand. I'm so pleased to be getting rid of this little lot – I wish I could have done it ages ago.

An assistant rushes forward to help me as though I'm the most important person in the world.

She looks familiar. I have to look twice to start with. Then I even have to glance at her name badge, just to make sure. But yes, it *is* her!

'Amy!' She looks different out of her coat and woolly hat. 'You never said you worked here.'

'Well, I'm a volunteer,' she replies as she shifts from foot to foot. 'Just three days a week.'

'Oh, so is this your, um, job?' I stop myself from using the word *proper* as that would sound terrible and isn't how I'd want to come across. Maybe she's not as poverty-stricken as I suspected she might be which makes me feel better. After all, if she can afford to take on charity shop work... It's what I'd like to do eventually but now's not the right time.

'Kind of.' She glances at the bags between us. 'I take it you've been having a sort out then?' She raises her eyes back to me and smiles. 'We can certainly take this little lot off your hands.'

'Great. Thanks. Oh, and also...' I slide one of the cards from my handbag. Another outrageously priced monstrosity bestowed on me at Christmas. I wish Jon would realise that I'd be more at home with something costing twenty quid. 'Would you mind putting this in your window for a week or two?'

She takes it from me and studies it before raising her eyes to meet mine. 'Do you need a walker for Suki? Is it for every day?'

'Just weekdays. But it's such short notice – I should have thought about it earlier. It was only when I was talking about it to my husband earlier that—'

'Did you say it was this coming Monday,' she cuts in, 'when you start your new job?'

'Yes.' I pull a face as if to say *eek!* I'm really excited about it. The people seemed lovely when I went for the interview. They offered me the job there and then. Everything to do with this house move has fallen easily into place. It all feels so right – as though it's absolutely meant to be. All I need now is for Jon to get used to me working again. I'm sure he'll be fine when he sees me happier and more fulfilled with my life. I'll have so much more to focus on than the noises I may or may not have been hearing from outside.

'I'll do it for you.'

'What? Walk Suki? Every day? *Really?*' She can probably tell from the elevated pitch of my voice how surprised I am. But it's a *nice* surprise. After all, I've already got to know her a little; I've seen how good she is with Suki. It'll be far easier giving *her* the job than sifting through people I don't know a thing about and having to chase references down. 'But what about your work here?'

'I promise them a certain number of hours each week.' She briefly averts her gaze to a lady behind the till who is busy serving a customer. 'They're pretty flexible with me – so long as they know in advance what I can and can't do.'

There's a hungry look in her eyes. She doesn't say the words but I'm certain she's thinking them. *I could do with the extra money.* And I'd much rather give it to her than to someone else.

If she's working here, in a charity shop, she's obviously been checked out as well.

'I'd really love the dog company,' she adds. 'I miss walking one so much – ever since I had Milo...' Her voice trails off. 'It's like a dog-shaped hole has been left in the centre of me.'

That does it. She's a fellow dog person, she's already told me that Milo was a German Shepherd like Suki, so there's no doubt she'll be able to handle Suki's strength and impulsiveness.

'Would you be able to start as soon as Monday?' I take the card from her and drop it back into my bag.

'Sure thing.'

'This is brilliant.' I clap my hands together. 'What time do you finish here?'

'Today? But I thought you weren't free until Saturday.'

'I wasn't. But now I've discovered that I've got to go to some dreary golf dinner and I'll need to spend the best part of the afternoon getting ready for it.' I roll my eyes.

'I can do later today if that's any good? Have you found your cafetière?'

'I can go one better than that. We've got our coffee machine up and running now.'

'Very posh!'

'So we can sort the key and the alarm code and then cele-brate with a cuppa.'

'Is half past four OK?'

'Perfect. Can I take your number?' I grapple in my bag for my phone.

She reels it off. 'While you've got your phone out, are you on Facebook?'

'Isn't everybody?'

'Do you want to add me as a friend on there?'

'Sure. What's your surname?'

'Jarvis,' she replies. 'Though there's not a great deal on there right now. I haven't been bothering with social media all that much but I plan to improve. Starting with adding you as a friend.'

'I'm glad to hear it,' I reply. 'Jarvis. Jarvis. Is this you?' I scroll through the names then hold my phone towards her.

'That's the one.' She grins at me as though we've been friends for years.

'Fabulous. You just need to accept my request.'

The woman at the till has finished serving. Amy turns to her as she comes up behind us, looking at the bags I've brought in. 'No, it's fine,' Amy tells her. 'I'll handle this. I'm just working on another batch in the back so I'll sort through these straight after.' She gestures towards the back room from where can I hear the spin of a washing machine. I'd love to have a look around in here. As a perpetual lover of bargains at heart, I used to buy nearly all my clothes second-hand. I can only imagine how Jon would react if I turned up back at home with a charity shop haul.

'You're a star.' I resist the urge to give her a hug for saving the day with Suki. I'm over the moon everything is coming together so easily. Life is really, really looking up.

SEVEN

CASSIE

'Come in – thanks for coming round. Suki, no.' I tug the dog back into the hallway. She's evidently pleased to see our guest. Her tail wags like a windscreen wiper.

'Amy!' Teddy springs down the stairs, stopping just short of where she stands on the doormat. A shy smile spreads across his lips, mirroring his excitement at the rarity of a visitor to our home other than Jon's work colleagues or golf friends. And usually by then, Teddy's in bed anyway.

'You remembered my name!' A wide smile lights up Amy's face.

'Have you remembered mine?'

'Of course I have: *Teddy*. How could I possibly forget?' She turns to me. 'Is it short for anything?'

'Theodore,' I reply. 'But he only gets called it when he's in trouble.'

She laughs.

'Can I show you my new room?' Teddy tugs at her sleeve. 'It's not got a curtain yet, but I've got a car park for all my cars and there's my train set, and...'

'Is that alright?' Amy slides her coat off as Teddy draws breath.

'Of course. I'll make us a drink while you're up there.' I take her coat and hang it on one of the pegs. 'Coffee or tea?'

'Coffee of course. Since you've told me all about your posh coffee machine.'

As I stride into the kitchen, there's a thundering of feet and paws up the staircase. Suki has clearly tagged along with them.

'Have a seat.' I point at the table where I've laid out some biscuits on a plate. 'And help yourself.'

'Thank you. These look like seriously good biscuits.'

She sits and Teddy clambers into the seat beside her. Any other person being here in the daytime is a real novelty for him. Before long, hopefully, he won't be able to recall a time when we didn't have a constant stream of visitors. He puts a biscuit in each hand and Suki lies at the side of Amy.

I admit to myself as I pour the coffee that it makes a refreshing change for *me* to have someone around here too. I can't recall the last time I made a drink for someone besides myself, Jon or one of his posh dinner guests.

I place the cup in front of her. 'Have you always lived in Rawdale?'

'Pretty much.' She brushes biscuit crumbs from the side of her mouth. 'Though I did move away for a while. Once.'

'Oh?'

'Ah, it was nothing exciting.' She hooks her finger through the cup handle. 'It was just to do with work and stuff.'

'And stuff?' I'm probably being nosy but it makes sense that I should know more about the woman who's going to be looking after Suki. I haven't mentioned anything to Jon yet. The best way to deal with him is to organise it first and then tell him when it's too late for him to get involved – much like I did when applying for and accepting my new job.

'Again, nothing exciting. It's a decent place to live – around here, I mean. It pulls you in very quickly.'

'I know what you mean.' It's true. There's a charm and a homeliness everywhere I've been so far. 'I'm so glad my husband wanted to come back here.'

Pouring milk into her coffee, she asks, 'Did he used to live around here?'

'Can I have a drink please Mummy?'

'Of course you can.' I tug one of his beakers from the dish-washer and hold it next to the dispenser in the fridge door. 'My husband, Jon, he's called, actually grew up in this house.'

'Really?'

'He hasn't actually said this to me, but I reckon that he feels as though it's still his parents' home, even though they've both passed away. He said as soon as we pulled up behind the removal van that it felt strange.'

'Yeah – I can imagine.'

'He seems to be settling here though.' I place Teddy's drink in front of him and sit at the opposite side of the table from them. 'He's got a ton of plans for the place.' I sweep my gaze across the kitchen. 'By the time he's done, it'll be unrecognis-able, by the sounds of it.'

She twists around in her seat and sweeps her gaze over the room. 'It looks pretty perfect as it is to me,' she says.

'I completely agree with you. To be honest, I'd rather he left things the way they are but he doesn't seem to be taking any notice.'

'I'd give my right arm for a house like this.'

I feel my face colour up – I hope she doesn't think I'm some sort of show-off. 'Where do you live Amy? Are you fairly close by?' It's best if I try to shift the focus onto her.

'Yeah, I guess so. I've got nothing like this though. But

there's just me, so it'll do. It's somewhere to live, for now anyway.

She's not nearly as guarded in her answers as when I was asking her about husband and kids the other day so I'm probably OK to continue. 'So is it a flat, a house, a—'

'A flat. One bedroom.'

'Oh. So you live on your own then?'

'Yes.'

Gosh, I feel like I'm interviewing her here – but I suppose I should find out at least some basic information before I hand over the door key and the alarm code to our house. If I don't do my due diligence, as Jon will describe it, he'll have my head on a pole!

I expect Amy's short answers come from her feeling as embarrassed at being less well off than we are, as I am about having what we've got. I want to assure her this way of living isn't how things always were for me, having grown up with a father that preferred to spend all our money on booze; it might even give her some hope of how life can change for the better just when you're least expecting it. But I don't really know her well enough to start down that line of conversation.

'You should do some before and after photos of the place.' She picks up another biscuit. 'Thanks Cassie. These are great.'

'Yes, I suppose we should. And you're very welcome.'

'It's been ages since I've had a friend invite me round for a cuppa.'

I smile, even though to refer to each other as *friends* feels a little premature. Nice, but I don't feel as though I know her well enough.

'So, are you going to give me a guided tour?' She places her cup in front of her and I notice how chapped her hands are. They look like hands that have known hard graft and I feel just as sorry for her as I felt when I noticed Becca earlier. 'Tell me about your plans for the place? Besides, I'll need to know where the loo is, for after the long walks me and this one will be having.'

She looks down at Suki, who wags her tail. It's the word *walk* that's done it.

'They're Jon's plans really.' I fold the tea towel I've been fiddling with into quarters. 'Like I said, I'd prefer to leave things as they are.'

'I'd still love a look around.' She jumps to her feet.

'Oh, OK then.' I slowly rise from my seat as well. 'I suppose you'll be the very first person I've been able to show around.'

'OK, let's start with the conservatory, shall we?' She steps towards it and we both follow. Teddy first, then me.

The sunlight streams through the windows, warming our skin and casting a golden glow on our faces. The gentle breeze through the open window carries the distant sound of birds chirping, lending a peaceful ambiance to the room.

'Wow. I love it in here. If I had a house like this, I'm not sure I'd ever want to go to work. I'd just sit in here, drinking coffee and reading books all day. What could you possibly do to improve it in here? It's lovely.'

I feel so uncomfortable about this. Here's Amy, probably quite hand to mouth with her finances and I'm talking about frittering away unnecessary money.

'Go on. I'd love to know,' she continues.

She seems genuinely interested so I'm probably safe to continue without offending her in any way. 'Jon's thinking of getting new furniture in here, and those blinds have got to go. He thinks they're very nineties. Like there's anything wrong with that.' I pull a face. Jon's mother evidently took the same care of this house as I'm going to. No wonder she lived here until death took her. I plan to do the same.

Her eyes widen as she looks outside. 'Does the stream actually run through your garden?'

I clap my hands together. 'Yes. It's the thing I love most

about the place.' I don't mind showing the stream off. After all, it doesn't cost money – we're just lucky enough to have it running through our garden.

'I bet it's amazing sitting out there in the summer.'

'We've obviously yet to try that out.' I fold my arms and follow her gaze.

'Did you not spend much time here with your in-laws? When they were still alive?' She gestures towards the summer house with the same edge to her voice that I picked up on the other day.

'Not really.'

'Why's that then?'

'Well…' I hesitate. I'm not sure how Jon would feel about me divulging his family history to someone I don't know all that well so I'll tell her the bare minimum. 'From what I can gather, there'd been some sort of big falling-out in the family.' I glance towards the old box of photo albums. Jon can't have noticed them yet or I expect he'd have shoved them straight into the loft. I'll be getting stuck into them as soon as I have the chance.

'Really?'

'It was years ago.'

'What was it was about?'

My reluctance continues to tug at me. She's being weirdly pushy to find out more about our background, especially when she doesn't want to talk about her own.

'All I know is that if it had been up to Jon's dad, we wouldn't have got this place – he'd have left it to a charity or something. It was actually his mother who left the house to him.'

'Oh, right, that all seems extreme – it must have been some falling-out between them.'

'I don't know too much about it to be honest, but it was a shock when we found out the house was ours – we hardly *ever* spent time with his mum. She was so aloof that on the occasions I saw her, I honestly thought she didn't like me.'

'Well she must have thought *something* of you to pass on a place like *this*.' She looks around again.

'I guess so. But it's all on the proviso that Teddy eventually inherits it, which he would anyway.'

'Did you have all your mother-in-law's belongings to clear out before you could move in?' She looks around again. 'That can't have been easy.'

'Jon pretty much took care of that side of things. Anyway, however this house has all come about for us, I feel very lucky to be here.'

'Well, be sure to invite me around for a glass or three on that patio. When it's patio weather, that is.'

'Yes – of course.'

'I'll look forward to it.' She clasps her hands together.

Jon's been on about throwing a house-warming party once we've got everything as he wants it. The idea fills me with dread. Whilst it would be a good opportunity to meet local people, Jon will be meticulous about every inch of the place, and probably me, looking absolutely perfect. But perhaps even Becca from next door will thaw out if we invite her.

'It's bigger in here than it looks from the outside,' Amy remarks as we go back inside, through the utility room to the dining room and then across the hallway to our lounge. 'No wonder you both need to work full-time.'

It's on the tip of my tongue to tell her that we don't as the house is completely ours but I stop myself.

'You're very lucky. Especially since your husband wasn't close to his parents and yet they've left him this – lock, stock and barrel.' She swings her arms around herself as she speaks.

I can feel the heat rising in my face again. 'Yes I know.' I wish I'd never agreed to show her around – the admiration, if it can be called that, is starting to feel uncomfortable.

'I take it your husband's an only child? To have been left *all* this?'

'Yes. Anyway, it's probably for the best if we get all the dog-walking formalities sorted out now. I've got so much to do before Jon gets home.'

Without acknowledging what I've just said, she stands in the centre of the room which now, thankfully, is starting to resemble a lounge since we rescued the sofa from beneath a pile of bags and boxes last night.

'I can see why you'd love it here.' I feel guilty for wanting her to leave when I hear the pang in her voice. In fact, there's a sadness about her that I can't decipher. I'm getting the sense of a loss of something or someone. She certainly doesn't look to have had life nearly as easy as I have since I escaped from my child-hood home. Not that I didn't graft to be able to afford to go trav-elling. Without that I'd have never met Jon.

'Are you going to show me upstairs now?'

I try to search for an excuse why I can't but she's already heading for the door.

EIGHT

CASSIE

'I've already seen Teddy's room, haven't I?' She looks back over her shoulder as I follow her. 'But I'd love to see the rest.' As if it's *me*, following *her*. I can't believe how keen she is to look around.

At the sound of his name, Teddy darts out of the kitchen, his little feet padding eagerly on the hardwood floor.

'I hope your room was tidier than it was earlier, young man.' I give him my best stern look then ascend the second set of stairs. As the steps creak under my feet, I look behind to see if Teddy is following me. He is, and so is Suki.

'Oh my goodness, how many bedrooms do you have?' Amy's hair flies out behind her as she twists her head from right to left then back again.

'Five.' I say the word quietly. Obviously we don't need five bedrooms. This is so embarrassing. I'm just glad she didn't see our last house.

'Gosh, is this one en suite?' She pokes her head into one of the spare rooms.

'Yes. Anyway it's a bit of a mess up here. Maybe we should

go and get another coffee.' I step back towards the top of the stairs.

'*Five bedrooms*. Wow! And you were having to get rid of some of your clothes because you didn't have enough space for them. Your last place must have been enormous.'

I ignore her remark, not even wanting to think about where we used to live right now – I was so anxious and uncomfortable there. I only want to focus on the present and the future. That is all that matters to me.

'Is that room your bedroom?'

'This is the bathroom.' I steer her away. Her looking around our bedroom feels like a step too far. Besides, it's still a tip in there.

'Obviously I'm not at all jealous of you.' Amy laughs as she turns a circle in the centre of the bathroom then comes back out again.

I've no idea how to respond to this so I stay quiet.

'So this must be the *master* bedroom,' she says with a mock grandiose as she pushes the door open before I can stop her.

The fragrance of the lavender candle I was burning last night greets me as I push the door open. It feels oddly intimate, having this woman I've only met three times within my personal sanctuary. If I'm honest, it's almost as though she's encroaching on our private space. I don't know what Jon would make of it either. I watch as she casts her gaze around and my breath catches as her eyes linger on our bed for a fraction longer than is comfortable.

'I'll show you the guest room.' I gently grasp her arm, leading her out of the doorway and across the landing.

'It's gorgeous in here. And what a lovely view across the park. I'd choose *this* room to sleep in if I lived here. I'll pre-book this one for when you have your house-warming party.'

I laugh as I follow her gaze to the window. She's right about the view. The park stretches out before us like a painting.

As I head to the top of the stairs, she calls me back. 'What's in the other rooms?'

'Just boxes and cases at the moment. There's nothing much to see.'

'But I'd still love to see them.'

Without saying anything I push the doors into the last two rooms as though to prove what I've just said, that they're full of boxes and cases. One which will eventually be a nursery, and I do mean *eventually*. And the final room which will be my office. My desk and new bookcase are on order. I don't tell her any of this of course – she's learned enough about our family as it is.

Jon's already bagged the best downstairs office space off the hallway – not that he really needs an office at home. He never seems to actually work in there, it's more of an escape room for him when Teddy's being noisy. I can't grumble, after all, I've got the summer house to retreat to now.

'You're incredibly lucky,' she says yet again as she follows me back downstairs. Now that she's seen everything, at least her voice has lost its excited edge. 'It's funny how things turn out, isn't it?'

'How do you mean?' I pause at the bottom of the stairs and turn to face her as she catches me up. Her words feel loaded with something. I hope I'm doing the right thing, taking her on. Though I'm sure I am – as usual, I'm probably being over-sensitive.

'I only mean that if your in-laws hadn't died, then you wouldn't be living here.' She reaches the bottom step and follows me back to where we started, in the kitchen. 'Some things that seem really good come out of something that's been a nightmare for someone else.'

'Erm yes, I guess so.'

She's possibly thinking she could fit her flat, wherever and whatever it is, inside this house and garden several times over which sends a wave of guilt washing over me again. But I *do* count my blessings and know that living here is a far cry from the poky mid-terrace I grew up in, complete with rowing parents and my hostile older brother.

'Let's pour another coffee, shall we?' It's time to return to the main reason I invited Amy round. Now I'm returning to work and have this place to organise, I don't have *all the time in the world* like I used to in the old house. 'Then I'll talk you through Suki's routine and the alarm code.'

'If you have any problems on Monday, give me a call.' I open the front door to a fine mist of rain.

'We'll be fine, won't we Suki?' She reaches behind to pat her on the head. 'Bye Teddy.'

'And don't forget to text me your bank details.'

'I won't and thank you.' Amy flips her hood onto her head and follows me down the steps towards the gate. We seem to have regained our earlier ease from before I showed her the house.

'No, thank *you*. You don't know what a huge weight off my mind it is that I've sorted something out for Suki.'

'You're welcome.' Amy smiles and glances in the direction of the screech of the gate next door, from where Becca emerges. She's carrying a bag so must be managing to escape from her mother for a while. Her smile fades as quickly as it appeared.

'Hi Becca.' I wave like she's an old friend though I suspect she won't want to talk to me now any more than she did earlier. 'How's things?'

'Erm, fine thanks.' She pauses as she gets to us, but for some reason, she seems more interested in looking at Amy rather than at me. It's a similar look to what she gave Jon when we first arrived here.

'Do the two of you already know each other?' I gesture from

one to the other. 'Of *course* you must do, living in a close-knit place like this.'

'I don't think we do actually.' Amy bends to fuss Suki, who's followed us from the hallway. Teddy's clearly taken the opportunity of my being occupied to turn the TV back on. The strains of the *Thomas the Tank Engine* theme music echo from inside.

'Just to let you know, Becca, you might notice Amy coming and going after Monday next week. She's going to be walking the dog for us.'

'What's that got to do with me?' Becca's gaze lingers on Amy before she haughtily turns and strides away.

'I really don't know what her problem is.' Shaking my head, I nudge Amy as we stare after her. 'She's been funny with me every single time I've tried to speak to her. *Do* you know her?'

'She looks vaguely familiar,' Amy replies. 'Perhaps we once went to the same school, but no, I don't think I do.'

I look from Amy to the corner which Becca disappears around. There's a wobble in Amy's voice – a wobble that suggests she's lying about her history with Becca. But whatever it is, somehow I'll get to the bottom of it.

NINE

CASSIE

It's unusual for Jon to ring me from the golf course unless he's checking up on me. He's normally too immersed in hobnobbing with his golfing counterparts to bother with what I'm up to.

'This is the third time I've tried ringing you this morning.' I can hear what could be exasperation in his voice. 'Why haven't you been answering?'

'I've been at the park with Teddy and we've been to the shops, and...'

'None of that stops you answering my calls love.'

'I'm sorry. I left my phone behind.' It's lame, I know it is. I know it concerns him when he can't reach me. Mostly because of the states I've managed to get myself into when he was working away when I felt there was someone outside.

'Well in future, try and remember it, will you? They were making jokes on the course as to why you might not be answering – I felt like a right prat.'

'I'm sorry. It's just I plugged it in on charge, and—'

'Never mind that anyway,' he stops me. 'I'm ringing to check you've remembered about this evening – my presidency function.'

'Of course I've remembered.' I want to say *how could I forget?* He's been banging on about it for the last couple of days. I glance in the mirror. At least he hasn't video-called me. Knowing he's out for the day means I haven't worn a scrap of make-up for going out this morning. And I'm wearing my comfy gym clothes for a change.

'I'm going to shower here after play, then I'll swing by at six thirty to collect you, if that's OK? If you could dig out a black bow tie for me, that would be great.'

'Sure, but what about Teddy? We can't expect a four-year-old to sit through such a formal meal?' I don't even know how *I'm* going to sit through it. The thought of an endless evening with a lifetime between each course while having to make small talk with people I barely know is already sending me out in hives.

'I've arranged for the club's receptionist to babysit Teddy,' he replies. 'I'll drop her off when I pick you up.'

My hackles rise. It's not the first time he's arranged a babysitter I don't know. 'I could always try calling my mother, you know.' I check my watch. 'I might just about be able to fit in driving him over there.'

'You'll need to spend your time getting ready, won't you?'

'But I don't even know your club receptionist, Jon. And I haven't asked my mum to have Teddy for a while – I'm sure she'd jump at it.'

'*I* know her. She'll be absolutely fine. She's expecting a baby herself if that makes you feel any better. Just make sure Teddy has been fed and that he's in his pyjamas so he won't be any trouble for her. Oh, and Cassie...'

'What?'

'Make sure you're looking your gorgeous best, will you? Your *very* best. This is such an important evening for me.'

It's the nearest thing I've had to a compliment for a while from him. I glance into the mirror. *Let the transformation begin.*

. . .

It's not the first time I've attended a function in this room. With ten people to each of the eight tables, I imagine the caterers are going to have their work cut out for them this evening. Especially to produce food and service that will live up to Jon's high standards.

He's already sent me back into the house to change my dress and shoes. He'd expected me to wear my little black dress and heels so was disappointed when I ran out to the car wearing a floaty number and flats. I'm sure he didn't mean it but the expression on his face when I set off down the steps from our front door didn't do a lot for my confidence levels. Really, it's my own fault. The fact that he mentioned his black bow tie had already suggested what I needed to wear. And I've always known he prefers me in heels. He reminded me as we were setting off that I should want to wear them. What woman doesn't feel more dressed up when she's wearing heels?

I find my name card next to Jon's and stand behind my seat – as everyone else is doing. Each table is laden with wine but judging by some of the ruddy faces gathered around me, many of the people here have already had more than enough to drink. As I wait until we can be seated, I study the pristine white tablecloth while vowing to drink white wine. If I were to spill anything, at least it won't stain. I can be quite clumsy when I'm nervous.

'Ladies and gentlemen,' announces the woman who must be the maître d' for the evening. 'I'd like to present your host for the evening, our new president of Rawdale Golf Club, Mr Jon Hemingway.'

I try to look as enthusiastic as the others when my husband sweeps into the room, smiling at the applause that greets him. I know this golf club and this presidency means the world to him and I want to support him. As he reaches my side, he takes a bow and stretches his arms out. 'Thank you.' He casts his gaze over everyone. 'Please be seated.'

As waiting staff bustle around to fill everyone's glasses, Jon leans over to me. 'You look so much better now.' He winks at me. 'Just as I like you.'

I shrug off his 'compliment'. I'm more pleased I can still squeeze myself into this dress, although I won't be able to breathe after I've eaten the starter. And now I'm sitting down, at least I can slip these ridiculous heels off. I sink my stockinged feet into the pile of the carpet. That's better.

'I don't think we've met.' The man to my left thrusts his hand at me. 'I'm new to the club. Miles Brompton.'

'Jon's wife, Cassie.' I return his handshake while trying not to focus on his huge red nose.

'He's a good sort, your chap,' he continues. 'He's got so many improvements planned for the place. He plays a good game as well.'

'Well, he's had plenty of practice,' I laugh. I joke about being a golf widow but I don't mind really. I quite like the space on a Saturday, now that we've moved house and I've got so much to do. I didn't like it quite so much in the last place though.

I cast my gaze around the table to see whether there's anyone who looks like I could hold a half-decent conversation with them for the evening – someone who isn't obsessed with golf and nothing else. Jon's tried to get me involved in the past but I don't know a tee from a bogey. There's only two other wives on our table. One looks as bored as I already am. I smile across at her, knowing our opposite positions at the table will make it difficult to converse while the meal is in progress. And the other wife is a golfer herself.

'I'll be back in a moment,' Jon says. 'I see you've met Miles.' He smiles from me to him. 'You'll look after my wife for a few minutes, won't you?'

I listen peripherally as Miles regales some story about how Jon helped him perfect his swing while I watch Jon out of my other eye. I can see why he enjoys being here – he's treated like he's some sort of celebrity.

As he makes his way around the room, saying his hellos and giving people his attention, they're practically eating out of his hand. A younger blonde woman throws her head back in laughter at something he's said, as her much older husband looks on. She's wearing a dress similar to mine. Jon looks over at me and winks as if to say, *don't worry, it's you I'm coming home with.* I should be used to playing second fiddle at this sort of thing – there have been enough functions and meals with his business associates and partners that I've been forced to attend over the years. Jon loves them – he's that sort of person. I hate them with a vengeance.

We've been here over an hour now and have only just finished the starter.

'I'd just like to say a few words before the main course.' Jon rises to his feet. It's all I can do not to roll my eyes as he launches into his spiel about how much the evening means to him, how much everyone here means to him, what he's going to do and how things are going to change. Looking around at the nods and smiles, it's clear everyone is hanging on his every word. Everyone apart from me, that is. He's always been able to hold court with any crowd and is totally at home with it. Personally I'd give anything to be at home in my PJs, with a glass of wine in my hand, watching *Strictly*.

'And finally.' He puts his hand on my shoulder. 'I'd like to thank my good lady, Cassie. She gives me the solid base from which I can do all my wonderful things. We're very excited to return here to Rawdale and to embark on our next chapter.'

He lowers back to his seat and the applause is even more

enthusiastic than before. He's as popular as this at work as well. Or perhaps there's more than popularity feeding into it. He practically oozes status and power. He's certainly charming, there's no denying that – but sometimes when I watch him, I can see that it has a superficial edge.

He turns to me again and I'm just about to thank him for giving me a mention in his speech when he murmurs into my ear, 'Cassie, get your shoes back on – I don't see anyone else having taken their shoes off in here.'

'I'm sorry. You know I'm not a fan of heels.' I smile at him.

'And I hope you don't mind me saying I think you'd better go to the ladies. You've got lipstick on your teeth and your hair could do with putting back up.'

My face burns as I rise from my seat. This is so embarrassing. I was in such a rush to change my dress before that I hardly bothered to check my hair. Who knows what everyone here must be thinking of me.

The blonde woman at the table at the other side of the room is watching as I scuttle away to the toilets. I glance back as I leave the room, just in time to notice her heading to the seat I've just vacated.

PART 2

AMY

TEN

AMY

The best thing about this time of year is the time dusk falls. Not too early, and not too late. Most households don't close their curtains until after it's fully dark, which is a wonderful opportunity to nosy in as I walk by each house.

Sometimes, it's a really enjoyable pastime, where I can study the pictures on people's walls or see what's flickering on their TVs. As I walk past each house, I can't help but wonder about the lives of the occupants. Do they ever feel the same emptiness I do? The longing for something more?

In the wealthier homes, I can pretend I'll have their lives one day. Maybe I would have had their lives already, if my own life had taken a different direction. But I can never allow myself to linger on that thought for too long. All it does is cloud my plans and upset my judgement.

On other days my pastime brings me misery, to the point of making me feel bitter, yet I still can't seem to stop myself from doing it.

Here I am, at the age of twenty-eight, alone, broke and barely able to dream about leading a comparable existence to the kinds of lives these people take for granted. People like Cassie and Jon.

Cherry Tree Lane snakes around the perimeter of three sides of the park, providing the perfect route for my evening strolls. It's a path I often take when I have half an hour to spare, like tonight.

I pause outside a house where a family of five are eating their dinner, seated in their huge bay window. The soft glow of candlelight lights up the dining table, casting dancing shadows on the walls. I catch glimpses of their faces, illuminated by the warm flickering glow, as they enjoy their meal. It's as if I'm peeking into a scene from a movie. *How very civilised.* Far more so than the ready meal I usually pick at from a tray in my lap.

I move on to next door where a couple are tucked into each other, a cat beside them, as they watch TV from their sofa. Mugs steam on a table in front of them as they bask in their togetherness. I'm aware that in the scheme of things, it's such a normal way to spend time, but how I envy them.

Sometimes I worry I'll be on my own forever. With no one to ever hug me, to want to spend time with me, or believe in me. I must have been really awful in a former life to have ended up as I have.

I shrink back as the woman appears to notice me looking in. She says something to her partner. He rises from the sofa and strides to the window. I drop to the ground, pretending to be adjusting something on my shoe. He twists the blinds until they're impenetrable, shutting me out in a darker and colder world than ever.

Loneliness settles over me like a heavy fog as I trudge further along the street, wondering if I'm ever going to find their sort of security or whether things will always be like this for me. Then, with or without really meaning to, I find myself outside Tolbeck Cottage.

If I could choose where I would want to live, this house

would always be my first choice. As a teenager, I passed it on my way to school, and often imagined living here one day. With its fairy-tale shutters and stained glass in some of the windows, it's no wonder Cassie's so happy to have made it her home. Even the driveway's pretty with its crazy paving and the rows of daffodils which border either side.

When I was there the other day, she was moaning about her husband's lack of time to fix the rails for their curtains and blinds, or fix *anything* for that matter, then she was going on about how she's having to get someone in to do it. *First world problems*, I wanted to say but obviously, I don't know her well enough to joke about something like that just yet. Although – I'm getting there.

Light beams from every orifice of the house, so by the looks of it, she's still not managed to sort anything out to cover the windows with. Never mind. It looks like she's put some pictures up in the lounge though. There's a blown-up canvas of their wedding day on the back wall and an even bigger one of a slightly younger Teddy on the side wall. He's a pleasant kid, is Teddy. I've never had the opportunity to be around kids but I've warmed to this one.

Light floods from the window, but there doesn't seem to be anyone occupying the room. They must both be in the house *somewhere*. There's a huge Range Rover on the drive, a symbol of his affluence and success, and a gleaming Mini Cooper tucked up behind it. They've really fallen on their feet, both of them.

When drawing comparisons between myself and Cassie, it's impossible not to feel bitter. But I try to swallow it as I carry on walking, my footsteps loud and rhythmic in the silent evening. I usually hate Sundays – the day when nothing can happen – a day that stretches out even longer than the other days of the week. I reach the snicket which runs by the far side of their house, leading towards the park.

There's a pervading scent of earthiness here after an earlier downpour today. It's hard to reconcile the silent and eerie space I find myself standing in, with the shrieks and laughter of normal daylight hours and I'm reminded of the day I met Cassie and Teddy here. It couldn't have gone better really and opened doors more quickly than I could have anticipated.

I need to keep moving; the darkness around me feels like it could swallow me up. For a moment, even in this salubrious neighbourhood, I feel quite vulnerable walking along the edge of the park behind the houses. Anyone could be lurking in those bushes. But this a decent area – at least *this* side of the river through Rawdale is. At the end of town where I'm forced to live, personal safety is not quite as guaranteed.

There's slightly more light filtering through the trees as I approach the back of Cassie and Jon's house; their garden is lit up like a Christmas party and I have a clear view through the gaps in their wooden gate. I spot Teddy in one of the upstairs windows, his arm dangling over the edge of his cabin bed while his TV flashes in front of him. If he was my son, I'd spend every waking moment enjoying his company. I'd play games with him, I'd draw with him – I'd talk to him. So many parents are the same these days – they don't appreciate what they've got. Often, it can take a threat to their child's safety or wellbeing to make them realise how blessed they are. Hopefully, it won't need to come to that for Cassie and Jon.

My gaze moves downwards to where Cassie's sitting alone, nursing a glass of wine in the conservatory. All is clearly well in her world – she's moved to a lovely house, she starts her new job tomorrow and she's got what she thinks is a stable family life.

Then a hulking male figure appears in the frame within the doorway.

Jon. My breath catches.

Slowly taking the glass from between her fingers, he places it on the coffee table and reaches for her hands, drawing her from the sofa up to meet him. She seems reluctant and first but then yields into him. Of course she does. In the three times I've been in her company, I've gained more than just a sense of Cassie's subservience to her husband.

He cups her chin in his hand and they begin kissing, softly at first, so it appears, then more frantically. He seems to be driving it.

He moves his lips to her neck and he reaches for his belt. Then Suki trots into the conservatory and Cassie springs back from him; clearly the mood between them has been broken.

The conservatory is plunged into darkness, then a few seconds later, another light appears in the room directly above it.

Perfectly framed in the window, Jon pulls Cassie's blouse upwards and over her head before tugging off his own top. Then they continue kissing, her breasts pressed into his chest until they disappear from view.

It's not fair. None of it's fair. I don't feel like this just because it's *them*; I could feel this way after watching any couple. No one's ever cupped my chin in their hand, then led me up to the bedroom. And I've never had a real home, a proper family, or the sense of belonging that comes with any of these things.

I'll probably always be on the outside, looking in from the shadows, having nothing but envy for the lives of others and the injustice of it all.

Things could have been different for me. So different. I should have had a life like Cassie's. *Her life could even have been mine.* But knowing what I know about her and her family, would I have really wanted that anyway?

My attention's caught by a twitching curtain in the house next door. Becca. She's standing statue-still and I'm certain she's spotted me. Hopefully, in the gloom, she won't realise who I am. That would go down a treat if she were to say to Cassie, *oh yes, I spotted your new dog-walking friend stalking the back of your house in the dark.* I drop to the ground while shrinking myself back into the shadows. I need to get away from here sharpish before she either comes out to investigate or calls the police. Glancing at my watch, I can see it's time I got going anyway. It will take me a while to get back over the river and across town.

She lingers in the window for a few more minutes, so I remain crouched in the same place, willing her to move. I can't go until she does.

I've still a chance of her just blaming my presence here on a trick of the light and perhaps this is worth being late back for. I've done incredibly well to land this dog-walking job in such a short space of time and I don't want anything to jeopardise it.

Eventually she drops the curtain. Letting a long breath out, I hurry away in the opposite direction to which I arrived, glancing back the whole time in case Becca suddenly emerges from her back gate. As I'm about to venture down the snicket at the other side of the playground, I steal a final glance back at her now-darkened window, knowing our paths will cross again and eventually, she won't have the opportunity to just dismiss me like she did before.

Yes, I think to myself. *I know exactly where I know you from Becca. And in time, so will Cassie.*

But for now I've just got to get back – if my whereabouts this evening are discovered, it could ruin *everything*.

ELEVEN

AMY

She's harder work than I envisaged, this damn dog. I practically had to drag her along the street after collecting her. Any neighbours who happened to see us must have thought I was trying to kidnap her. The only one I noticed was Becca, messing about in her garden. I fought back the urge to speak to her, realising that I've got to bide my time.

Every time I've let the dog run free in the park, she's bolted back towards the snicket, clearly wanting to return to her familiar place, and back to her perceived safety. I guess she doesn't know me all that well but even though she's just a dog, there is still an echo here of when I'm judged and sidelined by other people. Other dog walkers keep looking at us, as if to find out what's going on here – they're probably thinking I've stolen her.

After only ten minutes, I can't stand Suki's behaviour any longer. I need to get her home before I lose my temper. I clip her onto the lead, trying to keep a lid on my fury as she attempts to, or so it feels, wrench my arm right out of its socket.

Of course I lied to Cassie when I told her I used to have a

German Shepherd. But I wanted the job. I *needed* it far more than she could ever have guessed.

I was, however, even more economical with the truth when I led her to believe that the loss of Milo had been a recent one. But how's Cassie ever to know that Milo was, in fact, my grandparents' Yorkshire Terrier who died around eighteen years ago?

'Suki. Stop bloody pulling, or I'll...' I try to yank her back. 'Heel – stay – or whatever it is they tell you to do.' The weight of anxiety presses down on me as I struggle to control her.

'You've got your hands full there.' An elderly man chuckles as he passes.

'You don't say.' I pull a face at him. My arms are trembling with the exertion of keeping hold of this stupid animal; I don't know if I'm more incensed about her apparent rejection of me or the lack of training that's obvious here. She certainly didn't seem this out of control when I first wheedled my way into Cassie's life last week. She seemed to have her exactly how and where she wanted her. But then Cassie has everything. For the moment.

As soon as Tolbeck Cottage comes into view, the dog deploys her entire body into dragging me in its direction. It takes all I've got just to keep hold of the lead – my hands are slick with sweat. I can't let her go; if she runs off or bolts in front of a car, I'll ruin everything I've begun. I'll have to speak to Cassie and find out what strategies, if any, they use to control her. As long as she doesn't get any inkling that I can't cope.

No, on second thoughts, I'd better keep my mouth shut. After all, this job means far more to me than just the money.

Hopefully, it'll all be fine if Suki gets used to me. It should only take a few days, surely. And that might be long enough. Or perhaps I'll just have to bribe her. Yes, that's it. Tomorrow when I arrive, I'll fill my pockets with bits of cheese and ham. Before the week's out, she'll end up being happier to see me than her own family.

I release the lead the instant we get to the gate, noticing
Becca in the window as I pursue the dog to the foot of the steps.
Does that woman have nothing better to do than gawp into the
street all the time? Her life must have turned out even worse
than mine. Judging by the amount of time she seems to spend
inside that house, it's not far off.

I slam the door behind me and throw my coat onto the
bottom of the banister, pausing for a moment as I try to get my
breath. Suddenly, the reality dawns on me of where I am.

I'm *inside* Tolbeck Cottage. The house I've coveted for so
long. It's not a material longing either; it's something so much
more than that.

I push the door into the first room off the hallway. The scent
of freshly polished pine infuses the air as I run my fingers along
the bookshelves. *The Golfing Professional, Bridge for Winners,
The Range Rover Owner.* He evidently holds himself in high
esteem.

Sunlight filters through the slats of the blind, creating a
dance of dust particles that swirls in the air. I tug at the drawer
of the filing cabinet in the corner. It's locked. Damn – I try the
desk drawer for the key. Also locked. My curiosity rises to the
top of its range – he's clearly got things he doesn't want 'prying
eyes' seeing. I'll have to keep trying in here; he's bound to slip
up and leave something unlocked sooner or later. My gaze falls
on a framed photograph of the three of them when Teddy was a
baby. Such a happy-looking family with the kind of life anyone
would aspire to. Especially me.

I peer into the kitchen which is silent apart from the hum of
the fridge and Suki. She's stretched out in her basket, still
panting from her efforts of dragging me back here. The last time
I was here, she followed me around like a lost soul; now she
doesn't want to know me. The thought settles in my chest like a
lead weight.

After trudging up the stairs, I wander around the unpacked

boxes and cases in each room, shaking my head at the amount of stuff they've got. At first I wonder if some of it could be the packed-up belongings of the house's former occupants but it's evident it's theirs, all theirs. Some people have it all while others have nothing.

Their bed is unmade and there are clothes strewn across the carpet. Her bra. Jon's T-shirt. I lift it to my face and inhale deeply. Expensive aftershave. And *him*. Apparently, everyone has their own unique scent. His is almost intoxicating and I hate myself for this realisation.

Next, I head into their en suite and open the door to the cabinet. Tampons. Condoms. Insulin pens. Paracetamol. There are pots of expensive cream in here that would probably cost me the equivalent of a month's groceries. I unscrew one of the pots and plunge my finger into the centre. Its fragrance fills the air as I rub a generous amount onto my face. Its smoothness wakes my skin but can't quell the longing that won't stop simmering within me. The longing for a life I can only imagine. I resist the urge to drop the pot into my pocket. It's too much – too soon.

The huge double shower in the corner displays more examples of their wealth and fulfilment. Buttons which change the colour of the lights. Hairdresser-sized pump bottles of designer shampoo.

How can they have so much when I have so little?

The need to pee distracts me from my comparisons. I glance at the toilet with its cushioned seat, then I look back at the shower. I hitch up my skirt and tug down my knickers as I head towards it. Then I squat as I take a piss in there. Just because I can.

It's one of those pisses that feels as though it's never going to end. Until I hear a creak on the stairs. My breath quickens as I clench my muscles to stem the flow. I rush to the door, wondering how I'll explain what I'm doing up here. I let a long breath out as Suki appears on the landing. If that had been one of them returning, I could have been in serious shit. I'd better go back downstairs.

I've worked the morning in the charity shop, so have nowhere to be this afternoon. No purpose, nobody caring where I am – the story of my life really. I wander into the kitchen to make a drink, first peering into the fridge which is full to bursting. I've never seen anything like it. It's obscene that a family of three could need so much food and drink. There's another box full of insulin pens. I take it from the shelf and study the label on which Jon's name is printed. I say it out loud, turning his name over in my mouth like it's a boiled sweet.

Running my thumbnail down the centre of a KitKat, I pop half of it into my mouth. It tastes of childhood as the chocolate melts onto my tongue. I resist the urge to spit it out.

Heading into the conservatory with my tea next, I seat myself where Cassie was when I watched her the other night.

Casting my eyes over the perfectly manicured lawn, daffodil-filled borders and summer house, I can almost pretend it's really *my* home for a few minutes. Then I take in the more immediate surroundings. I'd love a conservatory – I always used to say *I'd kill for one.*

I remove my trainers and sink my feet into the plush rug, as I settle back into the chair. It's like resting them on a cloud. Even with bare feet, it feels warmer in here than anywhere else in the house. Fighting the sudden urge to take a snooze, a box marked *memories* jolts me back into the present. Interesting. *Whose memories?* I tug the box towards me and begin rummaging. It's just full of photo albums. I pull one from the bottom and begin leafing through it. The paper separating each page is smooth between my fingers.

Jon, aged 2, Tim's birthday party – Jon, aged 4, Christmas at Nana's – Jon, aged 7, Minorca. Jon, aged 9, Cub Camp. And on and on.

A lump the size of a lemon emerges in my throat. No such

album exists of my life because no one took any pictures of me. No one gave a shit.

There aren't quite as many of him as he was getting older. Presumably, he either spent less time in the company of his parents as a teenager, or just didn't consent to them taking his photo anymore. There's one of him sporting a floppy fringe and an assured smile. He's wearing the awful bottle green uniform of Rawdale High. I turn it over. *Aged 16*, it says. Its frame bears the school logo and there's an aching familiarity about so many aspects of it that tears burn at the back of my eyes.

'*Stupid woman*,' I mutter to myself as I drop it back into the box. Stupid, stupid woman.

I reach into the box next to it and pull out another album. *Dating days*, it says on the title page, in curly blue handwriting. They both look far fresher-faced than in the frame sitting on the office desk. As I turn through the pages, Cassie's clinging to Jon's arm as though she's fearful of losing him. He sports that grin in every image – the one that says *look at me*.

In those days they probably believed they knew everything there was to know about one another as they looked forward to the uninterrupted togetherness of getting married. But now I'm here. It's better late than never.

I continue to leaf through the pages, my emotions dancing between envy, sadness and hatred. Each image is a testament to the life I've always longed for but have never been granted. I'm overwhelmed by resentment as the photographs continue to taunt me.

I drop the album at my feet as the door slams, causing me to take a sharp inhale of breath.

Simultaneously, what sounds like a bunch of keys drops to a table in the hallway.

TWELVE

AMY

I shift the album from the floor to its box, plunge my feet back into my trainers, and spring from the chair.

'Hello?' It's a male voice. Shit. Shit. Shit. He clearly knows someone's in here. 'Cassie? Are you back already?'

I pour the remainder of my drink into a plant and shove my cup behind a cushion. What should I do? Hide? Get out through the back? Is there time? I glance at the door. There's no key in it. My eyes flit around. Can I get out of the window? Footsteps click closer. I'm going to be forced to face him. In any case, I've left my coat in the bloody hallway. I rush towards the kitchen, praying he doesn't recognise me. It's not the right time and I didn't expect us to come face to face. Not yet.

He stops dead in front of me in the kitchen, his eyes widening and his mouth forming the shape of an O. Time stands still for a moment as we eyeball each other. I search his eyes for a flicker. There's something but clearly, it's not enough. After what feels like forever, he breaks the silence. 'Who the hell are you?'

Phew. He hasn't recognised me. And clearly, I don't present

an immediate threat being in his home or he might have something more threatening in his hand than his mobile phone.

'I'm waiting.' His voice bristles with accusation and his gaze becomes more piercing. I look down at my feet. Any minute now he's going to realise who I really am.

'I'm, erm, I was walking the dog.' I point at the empty basket. 'We've, we've just got back here.' Well, this is great. I don't even know where Suki is, yet I'm claiming to have only just returned with her. 'We, we went to the park.' I need to stop stammering – but I often do when I'm guilty of something.

I stare down at Jon's immaculately polished shoes, wondering if it's Cassie who irons the impeccable creases straight down his trouser legs. Perhaps he gets her to shine his shoes as well. *Get a grip*, I tell myself. This is no time for idle thinking.

'You were walking the dog.' He strokes his chin with his free hand. 'In our conservatory?'

'I was just looking for the loo, actually.'

'Well you won't find it in there.' He steps back and points behind himself towards the hallway, his voice filled with irritation. 'Be quick, will you? I've got work to be getting on with.'

'Thanks.' My voice is a mumble. 'I'll be out of your way in a minute.' I step forward but he doesn't move. Nor does he take his eyes off my face as I walk around him. My face burns with the humiliation of being caught like I have. But in with that is the relief that he hasn't recognised me. I need to get out of here before he does.

Locking the door behind me, my anxious breath comes quick and shallow. I try to steady it in case he can hear me – after all, I can almost feel his presence out there. It's so close, he's probably pressed up against the door.

As I pull my knickers down again, every instinct is screaming at me to hurry up and get out of here. I lower onto the toilet, conscious of every sound outside the door. Obviously, there's nothing left in my bladder to release.

There's a rustle from outside. *Right outside.* He's still out there, and he'll be expecting to hear me wee, yet I can't do *anything*. Instead I cough, but even that probably sounds forced so I rattle the toilet roll holder before reaching forward to the tap and letting the water trickle down the plughole for a few seconds. Then I flush and rake my fingers through my hair before making a song and dance of washing my hands as audibly as I can.

I emerge back into the hallway where he's *still* standing. Clearly he's making sure I've left his house before he gets on with his work or whatever else he's arrived back early for. I make towards where my coat's hanging but he steps in front of me. It's a sudden move but I get the sense he planned it while I was in the toilet.

'Was the dog OK for you?' He tilts his head to one side, his sharp jawline accentuating the shadow of a beard. I notice how blue his eyes are. I swiftly look away – I can't think about him in these terms.

'I guess so.' I'm hardly going to tell *him* the truth. That I had no control over her whatsoever.

'And what about the alarm?'

Surely the fact that it isn't wailing into the silence of the street should answer his question. It's probably because he didn't need to reset it again that he realised someone was in the house as fast as he did.

'It was fine. Anyway, thanks for letting me use the loo. I'd better get going.'

Or it might have been my coat that gave me away. I can't imagine Cassie would be seen dead in a coat like my charity shop special. He finally steps aside and watches as I reach for it.

But he's still not taking his eyes off me. My hands fumble to locate the arm holes, nerves betraying any attempt at composure.

'Do I know you from somewhere?' His voice is soft, though it bears an accusatory edge.

I shrug myself into my coat, making a concerted effort to keep my gaze downwards as I attempt to fasten my buttons. 'No, I don't think so.'

'Perhaps you—'

The handle to the front door is depressed and the front door springs open. I've never been so pleased of an interruption in all my life.

In shoots Teddy. 'Hey! You're back again.' He looks from me to his dad, grinning widely. 'And you're here too.' He flings himself at him as Cassie ascends the steps from the front garden. Behind her I see Becca jump back from where she looked as though she might have been coming up the path behind her. Perhaps she's seen me – perhaps she's seen Jon. Who knows? But clearly, something's stopped her following after Cassie.

'What are you doing back so early?' She looks straight at Jon as she closes the door. At least she's not asking me why I'm here so late. If she does ask, I'll say I was held up getting away from the charity shop.

'I needed some papers. And to make some calls in peace. But don't mind me. I only live here.' With a final glance at me, he turns on his heel and strides towards his office.

As the door closes behind him, Cassie looks at me. She's done up like a dog's dinner and looks more like she's having an evening out than going to the office. 'Sorry Amy. Take no notice of him. He's always a bit grumpy when he first comes in from work. He reckons he needs time to *adjust* to being back at home. Anyway, how was Suki for you?'

'Brilliant – we had a great time.' My voice is possibly a bit too enthusiastic. I need to change the subject from the wretched dog. 'How did your first day go?'

'I *loved* it, thanks.' She slips her jacket off and unwinds her scarf. 'They've let me go early today as we got through all the induction meetings ahead of time.'

'That's good.' How anyone can say they've *loved* a day at work is beyond me. She clearly doesn't even need to work. I bet she could do anything she wanted with her time.

'They're sending me down to London in a couple of weeks to meet the *big* boss and they're even going to train me to manage one of the other departments. It's all very exciting. Nerve wracking too.' She pulls a face.

'Well, I'll leave you to tell your husband all about it, shall I?' I edge towards the door.

'Oh he'll be shuttered up in there for ages now. Nor will he really be interested. He's still getting his head around me being back at work. Why don't you stay for a coffee?' She gestures towards the kitchen. I recall my cup stuffed behind the cushion. Hopefully they'll just blame each other for it being there when it's discovered. I could stay a bit longer, try and move it myself, perhaps? Then again, I don't want to be around when Jon emerges from his office.

Which might be sooner rather than later if he gets wind of me still being here. He makes me very uneasy. It's the way he looks at me – *what can he see?* Under normal circumstances, I'd be taking advantage of this unexpected opportunity to deepen the friendship me and Cassie have begun but coming face to face with Jon has totally unnerved me.

'Sorry no. I really need to get going.' I make it sound as though I've got some sort of full life or someone waiting for me. She doesn't know that either notion is ridiculous.

'Well, thanks again Amy. You don't know what a godsend it is, having you take care of Suki for us. I'll get your money over to you later this week.'

'That would be great, see you soon,' I say, before clicking the door shut behind me.

As I turn left from their gate, Becca springs up from behind the bins next to her garden path. *What's she doing?* I keep my eyes on her as I continue to walk past. And she keeps her eyes on me as though her life depends on it.

I feel in my coat pocket to make sure I picked up the key for Tolbeck Cottage and heave a sigh of relief. After disabling the alarm, I must have dropped it straight back into my pocket. For a moment, I feared I'd have to go back in for it.

I didn't like the way Jon peered at me when he said *do I know you from somewhere?* Though I really can't imagine how *anyone* from my past would recognise me these days or be able to equate the person I am now with the person I once was. I catch a glimpse of myself in the window of a van that I pass. My once dimpled face is now gaunt and pale. The blonde hair I previously wore in a swaying bob now hangs brown, lank and lifeless down my back and instead of figure-hugging colour, there's nothing in my minuscule wardrobe that isn't navy, grey or black. For now, anyway.

I wish I was more like Cassie. But wanting to *be* like her is not why I'm back.

THIRTEEN

AMY

I've been relishing the prospect of this activity for days. It's not really part of my overall plan but it's a welcome distraction. Occasionally, I've peeked into the black bags I snuck from the charity shop when my supervisor's back was turned. On other occasions, I've taken one or two items from the top of the bag and passed them from one hand to the other. The clothes carry a faint whiff of their previous owner's expensive perfume, mingled with the subtle scent of a well-used leather wallet.

After so much anticipation, I can no longer resist how I'm going to spend the next couple of hours. I tear open one of the bags and empty its contents onto my floor.

I sift through the pile one garment at a time, pausing to bring a midnight blue jumper, in extra-large, to my face. I burrow my nose and cheeks into its softness. All I can smell is soap powder. Then a women's jumper, size ten, green in colour. It's well-cut and unlike anything I'd ever be able to afford. I carefully fold it into quarters and stack it to the left of my single bed. That can be the *yes* pile. Then I make a *no* pile and a pile I call, *I'll keep it. Just because I can.*

The growing mound I've said yes to could have just been

bought from a designer boutique. Some of the pieces still have tags on. Cassie must shop for clothes on a whim, then decide she doesn't really like them, or determine they don't look right on her as soon as she gets them home. Or perhaps it's Jon who casts the deciding vote. Still, her loss is my gain. I really can't understand why she'd even be getting rid of them.

I poke my feet into a pair of luxury jeans. Cassie's at least two dress sizes larger than me after all the weight I've lost so I'm forced to thread my shabby belt through the loopholes. At least I can cover it with the sparkly, crimson top she's donated. It's the first time I've worn any colour in years. There's no such thing as a mirror in here so I preen this way and that in front of my window, managing to catch my reflection in the darkened glass. I'm so enamoured with the result of my new appearance that I even drag a brush through my lifeless hair.

Then, twisting the key in the lock of my room as I leave, I head into the shared area to see if I've got anything left to eat in there. All this clothes trying on has made me hungry.

But there's not a lot. Some selfish arsehole has finished my bread *and* my milk. I can't even make myself a drink. I'd gone to the trouble of labelling what was mine but that doesn't matter a jot in this place.

A vision of Cassie's brimming fridge emerges in my mind, causing anger to spiral in my gut like a fireball. Thank God I get some money tomorrow. More rifling around the fridge uncovers a box containing three fish fingers, and a tub of some leftover but rather dried-out baked beans. I pinch a potato from whoever occupies shelf number three since taking other people's food seems to be the culture around here. At least I can make a few chips out of it.

'Ooh, look at you.' Right on cue, Vicky from room three saunters into the kitchen, seeming, luckily, to be more interested in what I'm wearing, as opposed to the potato I've begun to peel for myself. 'Levi jeans.' Her voice is sing-song. She steps closer and smooths her hand over my sleeve. 'That's cashmere, that is.'

'How would you know?' Vicky's no better off than me – none of us who live here have much.

'My gran used to wear it.' She smiles, flashing her discoloured teeth. 'Have you come into some coin then, or what?'

'I get first dibs at the charity shop, don't I? It's one of the perks.'

'Well, with clobber like that,' she says, running her hands down her hoodie and joggers, 'you can get me a job there as well.'

Now that Cassie and I are connected on social media, one of my favourite ways of passing the time, after my neighbourhood nosying each evening, is to trawl through her social media which she updates frequently.

New job drinks is her latest post, captioned against a large glass of wine. I hit the like button. After all, technically, we're now *friends*, so I can. Perhaps I should comment as well but witty comments are not my forte. It's probably best in any case, not to draw attention to myself, just in case anyone around here knows them. Well Jon. Or me.

Had I stuck around earlier when she invited me to, I may well have been the recipient of an identical glass of wine. But after Jon's reaction to my presence, it was best to scarper.

She's changed her work status to show off her posh new company and her flash new job title. Lastly, she's snapped a picture of Jon on the sofa, concealed behind his newspaper. She's captioned it, *anyone for a conversation?* I don't 'like' that post. Really and truly, how could I ever 'like' anything to do with *him?*

I scroll back through Cassie's well-curated social media

feed, where every picture with Jon portrays a picture-perfect life. They're in Cape Verde, tanned, happy and *everything* I'm not. Everything I will probably never be.

Scrolling back further, I stare at a photo of a somewhat younger Teddy posing excitedly by a Christmas tree. There's enough presents around him to open a toy shop. As a family, they appear happy enough but it's all on the surface – I know this and it's the main reason why I can't just walk away. Not until I've achieved what I've set out to.

I continue to rewind through Cassie's timeline, which reveals holiday after holiday, and night out after night out. Eventually, I reach photographs of her sporting a huge pregnant belly. Jon's standing behind her, his hand caressing her bump as though proving ownership of it. Everything with him is about ownership. The bump becomes smaller as I turn back their time.

Then follows the ultrasound picture, him carrying her over the threshold through a door, their wedding, their engagement and yet more holidays.

Jon smirks from nearly every picture, looking confident and assured, in the belief that he doesn't have a care in the world. He can clearly do whatever he wants to in life. His grin says *life is good. I don't have to worry about a thing.*

Yet.

I swallow back the indigestion from my earlier meal. If it can be called that. I bet Jon and Cassie never have to eat soggy fish fingers and a sprouting potato for their dinner.

My phone's shrill ring jolts me from my jealousy. Oh my God, it's *her*. Cassie. She must be telepathic. It's as though she's somehow sensed that I'm scrutinising every inch of her life in all its glorious perfection, while also wearing her cast-off clothes.

'Hello?'

'Hi – I'm really sorry to bother you Amy, I just need to ask you a favour.' Her voice has a slight wobble to it. Evidently, she's had more than that one glass in the picture, or maybe it's something else. Jon was clearly in a less than favourable mood when I left the house.

'It's fine – there's no need to apologise.' I load my voice with friendliness. 'Ask away.'

'I was wondering if there's any chance you could come *twice* for Suki tomorrow? It's just that my new office has rung up and—'

'*Twice?*' I pause, as though deliberating a hectic schedule. I was kind of hoping she'd be asking for help with something else. The pause between us is filled with her anticipation. 'Well, I'm not back at the charity shop until Wednesday morning so I guess I *could* do.'

'Thank you, what *would* I do without you? You won't believe it but they've piled an extra meeting onto me, in my first week as well. It should have been today, but anyway, never mind all that – I won't bore you with the details.' Her words might be light and airy, but her voice is somewhat flat.

'Are you OK?' I ask as though we're lifelong friends.

'Yeah – I'm good. Why wouldn't I be?'

'Did you get to tell Jon all about your new job?'

'Erm no. I expect I will later.' Her voice dips and becomes more echoey as though she's moving away from his earshot. 'I hope he wasn't off with you before I got back home earlier? I got the impression you were hurrying away.'

It's clear she's waiting for me to put her mind at rest. 'Well, erm, I could tell he didn't really want me there but that's fine – I understand he was busy. In any case, I was only dropping Suki back home and nipping to your loo.'

'Well take no notice of him; like I said, he can be a grumpy git after work.'

'Can't they all?' I laugh as though I'm an expert on the males of our species.

She doesn't laugh back.

'He doesn't take it out on you, does he?'

The silence from her end suggests my question is a step too far. I wonder for a moment if she's even going to answer it.

'No, of course not. It's all fine. We're good.'

But something in her tone doesn't ring true. I'd hazard a guess that she's living under more of a shadow than her Facebook feed conveys. It looks as though I'll have to step up my game.

'Oh, and there's another thing Amy...'

'What's that?'

Cassie hesitates before answering. 'Can I ask you to make sure Suki's shut inside the kitchen when you bring her back in tomorrow?' Her voice is tinged with concern.

'Yeah sure.'

'Hopefully it's just a passing phase.'

'What do you mean?'

'She's probably just unsettled with the house move and so much change.'

'What's up?' Though I know exactly what she's going to tell me.

'She's never done *anything* like it before, bless her, in fact, she's been totally toilet trained in the house since she was six months old. She was so easy to train as German Shepherds are.'

'What's she done?'

Cassie pauses. 'For some strange reason, she decided to use our shower as a toilet.'

'Oh dear.' I run my hands down the folds of my cashmere sweater. 'It definitely sounds as though she *is* unsettled. And of course I'll shut her in the kitchen from now on.'

'You're such a star Amy. I can't thank you enough.'

'What time do you want me?' It certainly feels powerful being the only person she can ask these sorts of favours of for the moment.

'Shall we say once in the morning and again in the afternoon? Is that OK?'

'Perfect.'

'How about eleven o'clock and three o'clock? That should do her nicely.'

'No problem at all.'

'Phew – you're a lifesaver. What with us not knowing anyone else around here yet and my mum living miles away, and...'

'Honestly, I don't mind at all. I'm happy to help if I can.'

'I knew you were a good'un as soon as we met at the park,' she tells me before we ring off.

Ah, I say to myself as I drop the phone into my pocket, *but it's evident from who you've married that you're not exactly the best judge of character, are you?*

FOURTEEN

AMY

I look behind myself as I unlock the door into Tolbeck Cottage. Any casual passers-by will naturally assume it's *my* home. After silencing the alarm, I step into the hallway, noticing the kaleido-scope of coloured shapes the stained-glass windows cast onto the hallway wall. Stepping into the warmth is like entering a cocoon of comfort, a stark contrast to the chilly breeze outside.

My first port of call is to fill my pockets with bribery treats for the dog. While I'm at it, I make myself a sandwich. I could call it extra payment for having to walk such a strong-willed and disobedient dog. After all, I'm going to need the extra energy. The bread is soft, the cheese is smoked and the ham looks to be the best money can buy. There's no economy brands in this house.

Having a constant supply of ham and cheese was a smart move as Suki trots obediently at my side today. Every time I say *heel* and offer her something in return, she slows down. There's no tugging and pulling, which enables me to let her off the lead in the park. I do notice her looking longingly towards the back gate of the house, but she doesn't try and bolt towards it like she did yesterday. Perhaps she got a telling-off for toileting herself in the shower. Maybe Jon rubbed her nose in the yellow-stained corner – I somehow imagine that's the sort of thing he'd do. Suki's spirit definitely seems more subdued than it did yesterday. Whatever's caused her mood, I hope it remains. At least then, for as long as it lasts, this dog walking lark should be more bearable for both of us.

The first thing I notice as I turn the corner back towards the house is Becca's in her garden, looking as though she's fiddling with the latch of her gate. Perhaps it's just an excuse to be out here, watching my every move. We eyeball each other for longer than is necessary, as I open the gate at the foot of the steps to Tolbeck Cottage. She opens her mouth as though she's going to speak but suddenly turns away. She must have thought better of it.

From what Cassie's told me, the two of them are not exactly on friendly terms, so I shouldn't have to worry about her reporting back to them when I remain inside the house until the next scheduled dog walk at three. Why would I possibly want to go anywhere else when I can bask in the lap of luxury here? It's much more fun to be actually inside here than merely observing from the street as dusk falls. Perhaps I should be offering dog walking as a service to other households too. That way, I'd only have to return to the place I'm forced to reside at to sleep. 'Home' is far too pleasant a word for it. Only I know too well that I shouldn't really be letting myself into *any* households. Or walking dogs. Especially *this* household.

To be on the safe side, I won't sit in their lounge as it still has no curtains up. It's a shame, as really, I would have preferred to sit in front of their TV. Perhaps I'd have put a film on. After all, it's the size of a cinema screen.

Instead I opt for daytime TV on the smaller screen, yet still larger than necessary, in the kitchen. The chatter of the show participants echoes through the kitchen, creating a comforting hum to keep me company while I make another sandwich and a cup of tea.

I chuckle at the phone-in: *Do you feel your partner or friend is invading your privacy? Share your story and seek our panel's advice.*

As I listen, I kick my shoes off and potter around the kitchen, pausing to leaf through the letters in the rack. The energy statement from their old home is eye-watering, as is the figure at the bottom of the bank account statement in Jon's name. I've seen shorter telephone numbers. I stare at it until the numbers blur in front of my eyes.

The words *miscarriage of justice* don't begin to cover it. What on earth has Jon done to deserve the fortune he's had falling into his lap like this? It's certainly not difficult to see what Cassie sees in him – no doubt she constantly thanks her lucky stars that she's the one he ended up with.

Suki opens one eye at me from her basket as I slam the letters back where I found them, then promptly closes it again. She appears to be as comfortable with me today as Cassie is with me being in her house. I've given them no reason not to be.

Bored of the kitchen, I head upstairs again, my bare feet sinking into the thick pile of the carpet.

I reach the top of the staircase as if I own the place, which I really should, of course. Naturally, I find myself back in their bedroom which is tidier than it was yesterday. A sheet now hangs at the window, pinned into place with drawing pins. I wonder if they somehow knew they were being watched at the weekend.

The floor is clear of clothes, revealing a pristine oatmeal carpet. It's a far cry from the stained and threadbare thing I have to put up with. The bed has been made too. With its carefully assembled cushions and padded headboard, it looks very inviting.

I perch at the edge of it, opening and closing the drawers

beside me as I get comfy. The top drawer is piled high with lingerie. Top class, grade A lingerie. I envisage it beneath the prim dress Cassie wore for work yesterday and wonder if Jon buys it for her. Then I visualise it against my own skin, replacing the shapeless multipack shite I'm forced to wear. It's all I can afford. Sometimes it feels like all I'll *ever* be able to afford.

Feeling braver, I shuffle myself back so I'm leaning against the pillows. Plump and feather-filled, they couldn't be more different than the flat grey things I'm forced to rest my head upon every night. It's only natural I should make comparisons about what they've got with what I've got – who wouldn't?

I stare at the ceiling as I become aware this is Cassie's exact view when they're having sex. I wonder if she stares at the rose light surround and the ornate coving around the top of the wall, or whether she's too caught up in the throes of her husband writhing around on top of her to pay attention to anything else. She's living a lie – an absolute lie.

I know which of the two it would be for me. The thought makes me feel lonelier than ever. Without really planning to, I unbuckle my belt and lower my hand until it finds itself between my legs. For several moments, I imagine I'm Cassie, with her life, with her...

Bang.

It's the front door. *Shit.* I leap from the bed, hurriedly zipping my flies as I hurtle back towards the landing.

'Amy? Are you in here?' Cassie's voice has a puzzled note. Doors open and close beneath me. Footsteps tap from one end of the kitchen to the other. 'Go and lie on the sofa sweetie pie.'

I loiter on the landing, trying to gain control of my breathing. *I can't believe she's come back.* Is she trying to catch me out? What am I going to tell her? Then I realise that I've got no choice other than to make my presence known. The longer I hang around up here, the dodgier it looks.

'What are you doing upstairs?' Cassie narrows her eyes as I reach the middle of the staircase. I was hoping she might be in the lounge so I could pretend to be coming out of the toilet. But no. Luck is not on my side today. She tilts her watch towards her. 'What are you even doing here at this time?'

'Erm, why? What time is it?' I display what I hope is my most nonchalant face, especially in light of what I've just been doing.

'It's only half past one. I thought we said eleven and three when we arranged things last night?' Her words are laced with suspicion and her tone is in complete contrast to the gratitude in it last time we spoke.

I rack my brain for a convincing excuse. 'Did we? Oh, I must have got mixed up then. I thought you said ten and two.' I laugh. 'Sorry to be so early. But I need to be somewhere at three, that's all.'

'Oh.' Her voice is flat and she looks disappointed, as though her faith in me has been temporarily displaced. 'But that still doesn't explain what you were doing upstairs.'

She jerks her head upwards as I search myself for an answer.

FIFTEEN

AMY

'I, erm, I heard a noise up there, that's all, while I was in the loo. I thought I'd better check it out before I took Suki for a walk. Just in case.'

'What sort of a noise?' She stiffens as I stand in front of her.

She believes me – her former accusatory expression has become one of mild panic.

'A sort of creaking noise. If I'm honest, it was pretty loud. It sounded as though it was coming straight from above us.' I point at the ceiling.

'Are you really sure?' I might be imagining it but I'm certain there's a slight tremor to her voice.

'Yes, but don't worry.' I reach out and lightly touch her arm – her skin is warm beneath my fingertips. 'I was certain I'd heard something but there was nobody there. I looked in all the rooms, just to be sure.'

'It's such an old house.' She shuffles towards the lounge and though she doesn't invite me to, I follow her. 'I love living here and all that, but the creaks and knocks are taking some real getting used to.' She sits beside Teddy and strokes his blonde head. 'You lie here and I'll put *Thomas the Tank Engine* on for

you,' she says. 'That Calpol will start to work soon, I promise.'
She points the remote control at the screen.

'Aww, is he not well?'

'No – that's why I'm back so early. The childminder called
me out of work.' She turns her attention from Teddy back to me.
'You're absolutely certain that you thoroughly checked up
there?' She rises from the sofa. 'Shall we go and make doubly
sure together? Maybe we should look in all the cupboards?'

'I already did.' Then noticing her strange expression, I add,
'It was just a quick glance.' Her shoulders have visibly slumped.
'Look, are you OK Cassie? You seem really unsettled by this.'
No matter what, she's clearly believed what I've told her.

'It's just—' She glances at Teddy then jerks her head in the
direction of the door. 'Come through to the kitchen, Amy, this
isn't for little ears to hear. I'll tell you all about it in the kitchen.'

'Are you not very well, Teddy?' I lay my palm across his
forehead as his mother reaches the door.

He shakes his head and clutches his monkey closer to his
chest. He seems even more vulnerable now he's poorly, adding
weight to why I'm doing what I'm doing in the first place.

'I hope you feel better soon,' I say as I follow Cassie from
the room. I know I will.

'He's a bloody messy sod, my husband.' She sets about
wiping up the crumbs I've left sprinkled across the counter.
'You wouldn't think he'd leave this sort of mess to look at his
perfect hair and pristine suits, would you?' She grins as she
shakes the dishcloth over the sink. 'Right, I'll make us a drink,
shall I? Is coffee alright?'

'Perfect.' She fiddles with coffee pods and buttons on the
espresso machine that looks as though it should be in a coffee
shop rather than someone's private kitchen.

'Does he always expect you to clean up after him?' I'm
never going to pass up a chance to steer the subject to Jon,
particularly when there's a negative undertone. But we

certainly need to return to the subject of the noises in the house. A scared Cassie is going to need me more than a Cassie who's just having a moan about crumbs on the counter.

'No – it's very unusual actually. With Jon, things are to be *just so* as a rule.'

'In what way? Here, in the house, you mean?'

'I guess so.' She tugs at her hair band which allows her hair to fall in waves around her shoulders.

'Or does this extend to *you* as well? I did think at the park that you were very dressed up to be walking the dog!'

'Oh, really?' She looks almost offended.

'Just an observation – honestly, I'm not saying it's bad to make an effort. Maybe I should, a bit more.' I laugh, trying to cut through the tension that's found its way into the room.

'Sugar?' She's evidently trying to change the subject.

But I'm not done yet. I need to find the chink in her armour. 'No thanks. So long as you're OK. I'd hate to think he was trying to control how you look or how you keep the house in any sort of way.'

'Jon's alright!' Her voice rises. 'He's not violent, controlling or *anything*, if that's what you're trying to get at?' She looks outraged. 'I don't know what you've been used to in the past but Jon's a decent man. God, how on earth did we get onto this line of conversation?'

I need to be careful here – she's bound to be defensive of him. 'Some men don't need to be violent.'

'What's that supposed to mean?'

'You don't need me to tell you that physical violence isn't the only thing that can happen when someone's being abused.'

'I'm not being abused in the slightest. Whatever gives you that idea?'

'That's alright then. It's just, I saw your face when he was home early yesterday. Let's just say that you certainly didn't seem as pleased as Teddy to see him.'

'You're reading into things that aren't there Amy.'

Her tone has completely changed with me and if I'm not careful she'll be asking me to leave. I can't really continue this line of conversation without giving things away. And it's still too soon for that. For now, I'll change the subject back to where it was. Though I already suspect what she's going to say.

'What was it you were going to tell me about before anyway? The thing which you couldn't talk about in front of Teddy?'

SIXTEEN

AMY

Cassie turns from the coffee machine to face me. 'The noises you've mentioned hearing – they've been going on for a while. Jon thinks it's all in my imagination but if you've heard them too...' Her voice trails off.

'But you've only just moved in here.'

For all the previous bravado in her voice when we were discussing Jon, she's now gripping onto the counter as though she needs to steady herself. 'It happened in the last house and I'm scared it's happening again.' Her voice has become almost a whisper.

'What's happening?'

'I've been followed here.' Her face is suddenly paler than I've ever seen it. 'I'm absolutely *sure* I have.' She reaches for a cardigan hung over the back of one of the chairs.

'*Followed?* By who?'

Her expression darkens. 'I don't know. But it's all exactly the same as it was before. It's the main reason why we got the dog...' Cassie points to Suki. 'And why I was so keen to move here as soon as we could. Jon was too – he knew how much I was struggling.' Tears are pooling in her eyes. 'I can't cope with it all over again. I just can't. It's been going on since we moved in.' She tears off a piece of kitchen roll and dabs at her tears.

'Hey.' I jump from the breakfast bar stool and rush to her side. 'There was no one up there when I checked.'

'There could have been though.' She rolls her eyes upward. 'It's always been *outside* the house before – never inside. I've got a son to keep safe, for God's sake.'

'I thoroughly checked everywhere – I promise.'

'Maybe Jon's right. Perhaps it's just the floorboards creaking and it'll be fine once I get used to the house.'

I daren't say any more but I suspect that Cassie's fear will both empower yet irritate Jon. Another side to her definitely came out when I mentioned the noises. This could give me something to work with. An irritated Jon will, without a doubt, eventually snap. The more I talk to Cassie and watch from the fringes, the more I get to read between the lines to what could be the areas of rot in their marriage. Without actually getting in here like I have, these chances would be taking much longer to present themselves.

'Have you actually *seen* someone out there?' I nod towards the window. I know what her answer will be – I've been very careful to remain in the shadows so far.

'No – it's more of a *sense* of someone. It's not just me, even the dog has sensed it as well. It's being going on since our first night here.'

'Have you thought about involving the police?' I already know what the answer will be to this.

'I've thought about it but Jon says they'll think I'm going daft. Or they'll think that he isn't doing his job as the "man of the house" properly. And I don't want anyone thinking bad of him.' She gives me a look as if to say, *including you.*

'Did you actually *see* anyone hanging around where you used to live?' I reach for her shoulder and look her in the eye now. I can do the concerned friend thing very well indeed.

Especially when it's my concern too. I reach for the coffee she's made me.

She sniffs, and nods. 'We had a huge garden, five times as big as this.' She stretches her arms out – not that she needs to demonstrate it to me. 'I'd often see a figure hanging about around the trees. Suki would growl her head off. You know how perceptive dogs can be. And it's not just her growling – it's the feeling it all gives me when it happens, like a cold creeping up my spine. It's exactly as I felt it before.'

'It sounds really scary for you.'

'When Jon was away, I hardly dared to go to sleep.' She hangs her head, as though ashamed of declaring such vulnerability. Perhaps I should give her a hug. After all, it's what a friend would do. But I can't bring myself to. I can't remember the last time I hugged someone or someone hugged me. Instead I touch her arm again.

'Thanks for listening to me – I must sound...' Her voice trails off. 'I'm definitely being stalked again – I know I am. Either that or Jon's right – I *am* going crazy.'

'Why would someone be stalking *you*? It's not as if you're a film star or anything.'

'I've no idea. Maybe it's money they're after. Or Teddy. Or someone with a grudge against either me or Jon.' She sighs deeply and turns back to the coffee machine. 'I can't imagine what either of us could have done.'

My arm falls back to my side. 'What could someone possibly have against you or Jon?'

Cassie presses a button. 'Bits and pieces.' She raises her voice above the whirring sound and takes a steadying breath. 'Anyway, let's talk about something else, shall we? Something more positive.'

'Things will settle down for you both, I'm sure. Moving home is up there as one of the most stressful life events, isn't it? It's even ranked alongside death and divorce.'

She laughs but it's a hollow sound as she places a cup in front of me. 'There you go.' She gestures to the stool I vacated at the breakfast bar. 'Have a seat. Anyway, I hope neither of those things come to pass. Death or divorce, I mean.'

'You'll be fine.' I'm playing my part beautifully even though I know only too well that she won't be.

She sits opposite me. 'What you were saying before Amy... you know we *are* happy enough.' She hesitates. 'Jon and me. But he has been a little distant with me lately but...' Her voice relaxes. 'I'm sure it's just the pressure of his job and our big move.'

'How do you mean, distant?' At last, she's finally opening up a little.

She has a faraway look in her eyes and takes more than a moment to answer. 'It's nothing serious – it's just as if I can never sense what's *really* going on in his mind,' she replies. 'Like there's always part of him that's concealed from me. Perhaps it always will be hidden away.' Her voice fades and for a moment, it's as though she's forgotten that there's someone else in the room. 'Oh I'm sorry Amy.' Her voice sharpens again. 'I don't mean to go on like this. You're clearly easy to talk to.'

'I don't mind at all. You talk away if it helps.' I really can do this friending stuff. Perhaps in another life, had things been on a different and more equal footing, we genuinely might have been friends.

'I'm hoping this move will be the making of our family – when we properly settle in.' Her voice brightens as she glances at the photo of the three of them pinned onto the fridge. She laughs. 'I've just got to get his attention – all I ever see is the top of his head behind the laptop screen or the sports pages.'

'Most men are like that, aren't they?' Here speaks the world expert.

'Have you got a boyfriend Amy?' I could swear she's looking me up and down as she asks this question, probably thinking the same thing that I always feel. Inadequate and invisible. There's only me that can change this which is why I *have* to continue doing what I'm doing.

I stop myself from snorting in reply. I mean, who'd want me, with the way things are anyway? 'No. Life's simpler staying single.'

'Don't you ever get lonely though?'

Meaning *she* would if she was on her own. I'd hate to be like that. To be someone who *can't* be alone and needs to be with someone more than needing to eat, sleep or breathe. I'd like to see how Cassie would handle the life *I've* been forced to live. She's probably *never* had to manage on her own.

'Not really – people can be far lonelier when they're married if you ask me.'

'Yeah – I know what you mean. I *do* get lonely now and again – especially when Jon works away.'

Cassie sweeps her gaze over the kitchen. 'It felt like fate, getting this place, I mean, after Jon's mum died. I thought it would be the new start I needed. But this feeling of being watched won't go away, no matter what I do.' She places her cup on the table. 'Jon's mentioned that perhaps I should see a doctor if I can't shake it.'

'I don't think that'll be necessary,' I tell her. 'Besides, you've got me to talk to now.'

'I know. And thanks – it makes such a difference.' She reaches for my hand and raises her eyes back to meet mine. 'I'll sort it all out Amy. Whatever it takes to shake all this anxiety away. *I'll do anything.*'

Her hand over mine feels uncomfortable but I allow it to linger while I consider what *anything* might be.

SEVENTEEN

AMY

'Are you still at the charity shop?' Cassie's speaking in a whisper, as though she doesn't want to be overheard on the phone.

'No. I left at lunchtime.' I won't tell her that I'm lounging in her lovely conservatory with coffee and a croissant after enjoying a shower in her guest room en suite. I've never used shower gel and conditioner with such a luxurious feel.

'Have you walked Suki yet?'

'No, not yet. I'm just about to take her.' A bird lands on the table outside. I watch as it pecks at the seed left there. 'Is everything alright?'

'It's just – I'm on this course today – I might have already mentioned it to you – I can't remember. Hang on a minute.' I listen as there's some shuffling and a banging of a door. 'That's better. I can talk normally now.'

'Where are you?'

'I'm at the head office in Manchester. On an induction course and I can't get back.'

'What do you need to get back for?' I was looking forward to my afternoon here. Anything to avoid that godforsaken place

I'm forced to call 'home'. No one can blame me for only being there when I have to be.

'It's Teddy.' She sighs deeply. 'I should *never* have sent him to Hazel today. Instead, I dosed him up with Calpol and just crossed my fingers.' She pauses as though deliberating whether to say what I already suspect. 'I don't know what I was thinking of; really I knew he wasn't well enough to go. But it's my first week here, I couldn't...'

'Could Jon not have taken care of him?'

'We've kind of got an unspoken – spoken – arrangement that I pick up the slack on the domestic front. To be honest, it's not as though we *need* me to work. I'm here for my sanity more than anything.'

It can't be bad, I want to say. Instead I say, 'But surely he'd pick him up if you can't get back?' I'm just testing the waters here. I glance at the clock, knowing if there's an inkling of Jon getting back while I'm still around then I'm out of here. It's Cassie I need to work on for the moment which is far easier if I keep out of Jon's way. If he's going to come back, Suki will have to sacrifice her walk for today. He's been too close to recognising me as it is.

'He probably would if he knew Teddy was poorly, but that's the thing.' Her voice appears to crack slightly. 'I can't reach him. I've been trying for the last hour. Even his assistant can't tell me where he is. Or *won't* tell me.' Her voice hardens.

'Maybe he's just in a meeting? Or his phone battery has died.' I have to sound like I'm *trying* to reassure her – at least to start with.

'No – he *never* lets his phone die. And I'm sure his secretary would have mentioned a meeting if that's where he was. I told her that our son's ill and needs picking up, but she didn't sound very sympathetic.'

'I'm sure he wouldn't go in for the boss and his secretary cliché.' It's time to start feeding things back to her.

'I'm not suggesting he would, but—'

'You do need to trust your gut Cassie. That's what I've always done.' A vision of him lifting Cassie's blouse above her head enters my mind again. For Jon, perhaps one woman will never be enough.

'Sorry – I don't mean to moan about it all. I'm just not myself at the moment.'

'Do you need me to collect Teddy? Is that why you're calling me?'

'Would you, Amy?' Her voice relaxes somewhat. 'I'm right over in Manchester. It's at least a ninety-minute drive and I really could do with staying for this training and getting it out of the way.'

'Of course I will.' I lower my legs from the comfy pouffe I'm resting them on. 'Just tell me where I need to go.'

'You're an absolute lifesaver.' Gratitude floods her words. 'At least now, I can stay until the end. Damn Jon though. He's as much Teddy's parent as I am. Whether we need me to work or not.'

'Look don't worry about any of that. I'll pick him up and take care of him. You just concentrate on your training.'

'Ah, you must be Amy. Come in, won't you? This little lad needs to be tucked up warm in his bed.' She throws her hands in the air. 'Not putting up with all this mayhem, the poor mite.'

I follow the homely-looking woman into a bustling room stuffed from corner to corner with toys, art and books. The giggles and clatter make it sound like there's a playground full of children in here but there's only actually four of them. Two of them are fighting over a train, one's smashing cars together and the other is stacking blocks of Lego. 'Teddy's mum's just called to let me know you'd be coming. I don't know why she even gave me his dad's number if he can't even be bothered answering – I've tried him several times.'

'Maybe he's just in a meeting.' I've got a part to play here which is playing dumb in front of this woman.

'You walk their dog, don't you? How do *you* get on with Cassie's husband?' She pauses and cocks her head to the side. I get the inkling that she's really interested in my reply. However, I'm more interested in what *she's* got to say.

We reach another door, as we leave the worst of the noise behind us. 'He's OK, I suppose – I don't know him all that well.'

She turns to look at me. 'He might be a good-looking man, but he's a little aloof, isn't he?'

'I guess so.'

'I'm glad it isn't just me. In fact, he made me feel quite self-conscious when he came to give me the once over. I wouldn't like to be on the wrong side of him, that's for sure.'

'Oh, I see why you called Cassie.' Teddy's in exactly the same position I saw him in yesterday on his own sofa.

'She shouldn't have really left him with me to be honest.' She tuts as she shakes her head. 'I'd already sent him home yesterday. But she said he was feeling better when she dropped him off this morning.'

'That's kids for you.' I half laugh, like I've a clue what I'm talking about. I've got to show my loyalty to Cassie here – it's what's required.

'Do you need a hand carrying him out to the car? I've got all his stuff together.'

'Car? Erm no. I don't drive actually.' It suddenly doesn't seem appropriate to tell her that I was planning to walk him home.

'You don't?' Her jowls wobble as her voice rises. She reminds me of our old school headmistress and the memory knocks me off centre for a moment. I don't like uninvited memories.

'So how are you planning to get him home then? He certainly isn't well enough to walk.' She folds her arms across her ample bosom as she looks at me. She's the typical earth mother type – everything that the grandmother who brought me up wasn't.

'Could you call a taxi for us?' Damn it. It's going to take the last of my money to pay the fare. I can hardly ask Cassie for a refund and risk her discovering just how on the sharp edge I'm actually living. To build on our 'friendship', I need to position myself in as elevated a way in terms of social standing as I possibly can. She needs to view me as a near-equal, rather than as her hired help. I'm doing everything I can to make more effort with my appearance. Just so long as she doesn't get wind of where I live. If she does, it's game over.

EIGHTEEN

AMY

'Do you want to get yourself back onto the sofa when we get in Teddy?'

He nods against my shoulder as I carry him up the stone steps. He's heavier than he looks, though it's oddly comforting to have another human so close to me. It's a very alien feeling.

'We can put the telly on, can't we? That'll make you feel better.'

'*You've* got your feet well and truly under the table, haven't you?' Becca calls from the other side of the wall as I get to the door. Her voice is dripping with sarcasm.

'What's it to you?'

'I'm watching you – that's all you need to know.' Then she slams her door behind her before I can throw anything back in retaliation.

I balance Teddy on my hip as I unlock the door, expecting Suki to come bounding out at us, before remembering she'll be locked in the kitchen.

I've half a mind to go back out there and bang on Becca's door about her snide remarks, but something stops me. It's not the wisest thing to do. Not yet anyway. I'll let her think and say what she wants for now.

I lower Teddy onto the couch. 'Get yourself laid down. I'll get you something to drink.' I lay my palm on his forehead which is warm and clammy.

'When's Mummy here? Soon?' His lower lip trembles as he glances around. He must have expected her to be here. It's probably the first time he's been in this house without her. But I can't help but feel a bit hurt that he isn't happier to have *me* looking after him.

'I'm not sure.' I sit beside him and smooth my hand across the softness of his hair as he lays his head on the cushion. I really should have been a mother. If he was my son, I'd never have sent him to a childminder when he's sick.

'Can I watch *Thomas?*' He points at the TV.

'Yes, of course you can. If I can work out how this TV works, that is.'

He reaches for the remote on the arm of the sofa and presses a couple of buttons. It's almost criminal that a four-year-old boy should be able to operate technology better than a twenty-eight-year-old. It shows how much time he must spend in front of the thing.

'I'll be back shortly Teddy. You settle yourself down.' I head into the kitchen where Suki is right behind the door, wagging her tail as I enter. 'I can't walk you now, I'm afraid.' I continue past her and throw open the conservatory doors. 'You'll just have to make do with the garden. I've got Teddy to look after.'

But as the doorbell suddenly echoes through the hallway, Suki flies to the door, barking for all she's worth.

'Shhh, Suki, Teddy's trying to rest.' Like she can understand what I'm saying. I grab for her collar as I throw the door open. 'Hang on a second,' I tell the young man standing on the doorstep. 'Just let me put my dog in the kitchen.' I drag her back in there, quickly shut the door, followed by the lounge door, and then return to him. 'How can I help you?' I lean against the door frame with my arms folded.

'We were wondering if you'd like your paths cleaning – all ready for the spring?' he suggests, his eyes bright with anticipation as he waves the wand of his pressure washer in the air.

'I'm sorry but not today.' I shake my head.

He looks disappointed. 'But it's a one-time offer. It's now or never.'

'I can't be having the racket of one of those things outside the window. My son's trying to sleep.' I gesture behind me. 'He's not very well.'

'Oh right. I see. Maybe next time then.'

'Maybe. Thanks for calling anyway.'

The dog's nosing around in the garden when I return to the kitchen. I put some cheese on toast under the grill for myself then pour a drink for Teddy. I smile as the sounds of my busyness echo around the room. The allure of this house needles at me, like a long-lost memory. I'm determined to savour every moment I can spend here and make the most of the normality it offers me for as long as it lasts.

Teddy's fast asleep with his arms around his monkey when I return to the lounge. I watch him for a moment then silently place the drink on the table beside him. Sleep is the best thing. Then I kiss the top of his head, an action which surprises me, before I leave the room to check on my cheese on toast.

After eating, I head upstairs again. It's as though their bedroom has some magnetic force that draws me into it whenever I'm here. And it's not as if I'll be disturbed today. Cassie's miles away in Manchester, and, as she's said herself, Jon's rendered himself unreachable.

I leaf through her wardrobe, running my fingers over the gentle folds of dresses and the colours of soft wools. It's obscene that one woman should have this amount of clothes even after she's got rid of a load. I pull out a dress in the same fabric as one I've got from the charity shop bag.

Standing in front of the glass mirrored doors, I begin peeling off my own clothes like I'm shedding a skin I no longer wish to inhabit. First the leggings, half-price from Primarni. Next, the shapeless tunic that's meant to disguise how skinny I've become. Then I shrug from the bra that was probably white, once upon a time, and finally, I discard my boring and functional knickers, leaving them splayed on the bedroom carpet.

I linger in front of the glass, allowing my gaze to roam from my head to my feet and back again, while imagining what it would be like if Jon were to enter the room, and approach me from behind in a similar stance to the photo I saw of him and Cassie on her social media. Then as quick as this thinking has entered my mind, I shake it away again. It can only ever impair my judgement.

I glance towards the bedside table then go to open the top drawer. I pull out a lace all-in-one and hold it up against the light. Perfect. Lowering it to the floor, I step into it then smooth it up and over my body, enjoying its chill against my naked skin. I preen this way and that before my reflection, before pulling the cashmere dress over my head, a hint of Cassie's scent enveloping me as I let the folds fall around my legs.

These are the clothes I deserve. This is the life I should be living. Fury steals over me as I stomp across the room to the en suite. It's not fair. It really isn't.

I pick up a bottle of perfume and spray it liberally onto the inside of my wrists – tasting its floral undertones at the back of my throat. Then I apply Cassie's lipstick, observing as my chapped lips become a delicate shade of fuchsia. I return to the full-length mirror, swishing the dress this way and that, marvelling at the 'someone' I've now become.

Suddenly, a thud echoes from the stairs, startling me.

NINETEEN

AMY

'That's Mummy's dress.' Teddy stands in the doorway, rubbing his eyes.

'I erm, I'm just borrowing it from her. I spilt some juice on my clothes.' I scrabble to retrieve them from where I discarded them on the carpet. 'You go downstairs and get back under your blanket. I'll be with you in a minute.'

'I want Mummy.' His lower lip protrudes in a pout and the floor creaks beneath his shivering frame. Misery pools in my stomach, like a bottomless well of self-doubt, reflecting every unspoken fear of not being good enough for anyone, not even a child.

'Come on then.' I attempt to inject a cheerfulness I'm not feeling into my voice. 'Let's get you some medicine, shall we? But you'll have to show me where it's kept.' I recall Cassie giving him Calpol yesterday so I'll be fine to do the same.

Teddy consents to being scooped up in my arms and we head out onto the landing, the dress trailing along the carpet behind us. I bet Cassie wears this with heels and beautiful jewellery. I haven't had the opportunity to wear heels since I was a teenager. And I haven't worn beautiful jewellery *ever*.

'Mummy's smell,' he says, wrinkling his button nose. I smile. That's exactly how I want to smell.

He's settled back on the sofa, having had a spoonful of medicine and something to drink.

I scurry back upstairs to get my own clothes back on. I fumble to re-hang the dress and just as I'm about to peel the all-in-one from my skin, something stops me. *She's got a drawer full of things like this*, I think to myself. I'm keeping this one. I tug my tunic back over it, trying not to recoil at the faded, crusty underarms. I step into my paper-thin leggings and slide them back up my legs; the elastic is stretched to breaking point.

I'm filing my nails in the kitchen when the front door slams with a force that reverberates through the house. *I really hope it's Cassie.* But as I jump down from the stool, I can tell by the confident click of the footsteps across the hallway tiles that it's not.

'What are *you* doing here? *Again?*' Jon steps into the kitchen, his solid frame only just fitting beneath the doorway. His expression is difficult to read. One thing I know with every fibre of my being is that I don't want to be in this house with him. Especially when Cassie isn't here. And not only because I don't trust myself.

'I'm taking care of Teddy. He's not very well,' I say, keeping my voice low to avoid revealing my internal unease. 'Cassie couldn't reach you.'

'So where is she? She should be looking after him, not you.' He's not taking his eyes off me.

I want to say, *as if you're asking me where your wife is*, but instead I mumble, 'She's in Manchester. Something to do with her work.' Really I want to shout at him – tell him he should be showing a bit more gratitude to someone who's abandoned their day to look after his son, but what would be the point? Men like him think the whole world exists purely to wait on them, hand and foot.

'Why has she got *you* looking after him? I thought she'd employed a childminder.' He leans against the counter. I don't like the way he's watching me. I don't like it at all. 'You're just supposed to walk the dog, aren't you?'

'She asked *me* because she couldn't get hold of *you*.' The sentence almost comes out like an accusation and once it's out, it's too late to take it back.

Jon gives me a really strange look – half appraisal, half accusation. 'Tell me *Amy*,' he says, putting an uncomfortable emphasis on my name. 'How many references did my wife obtain before employing you? At least two, I hope.'

'You'll have to ask her about that. Anyway, now that you're back, I'd better be getting going. I gave Teddy some Calpol an hour ago.'

'Not so fast.' He smiles as I step towards him but it's a smile that doesn't get anywhere near his eyes. 'Who were your references from?' He's blocking my path and his nose appears to wrinkle up. I hope he can't smell the perfume now we're in closer proximity. His wife's perfume. He's bound to recognise it. Or perhaps he's such a Neanderthal that he won't.

'You seem to be getting very friendly with my wife all of a sudden.' His words form themselves more into a question than a statement as he steps out of the doorway and we're suddenly even closer.

'I'd like to get my coat please.' My voice is a mumble as I look down at his shiny shoes. Shoes that make mine look even more shabby, in comparison. But thank God I changed out of that cashmere dress when I did. 'Since you're here now.'

'And I'd like to know *exactly* who is looking after my son.' Placing his thumb and forefinger gently under my chin, he tilts my face upward in a similar way to how I observed him doing with his wife several nights ago. It's a gentle touch but I've no doubt he'll be able to feel me trembling from head to foot. Trying to avoid direct eye contact with him, my gaze flits around the room, but as he continues to stare into my face, it's almost impossible to look anywhere else. I'm a specimen beneath his microscope and his gaze is piercing me.

'Are you *really* sure we've never met?' He tilts his head slightly to the side. 'I'm absolutely certain I know you.'

My face might be paler and thinner than it used to be, but still... His eyes stray to my lips. He's possibly wondering why I'm wearing lipstick to babysit his son. Either that or he wants to kiss me. I part them, just in case. I'd let him – just once – if only to increase my leverage. Perhaps I'd let him do even more with me – after all, it's been such a long time. I wonder how he'd react if he knew what I was wearing under my tunic.

As the doorbell rings, the tension between us snaps. Jon releases me from his gaze and I quickly grab my coat, desperate to escape from the dangerous game I've unwittingly entered.

I'm almost certain he knows who I am.

PART 3

CASSIE

TWENTY

CASSIE

'Hi, it's Cassie – I've just got back from Manchester.' I run my fingers through Teddy's damp fringe as I speak. He's cuddled up with his toy monkey and is sparked out, which is the best thing for him right now. Though it pains me to see him so lethargic, he just needs to sleep his way through this bug. I reach for the remote and point it at the TV to turn it down.

'You're back early,' Amy replies with surprise in her voice. 'I thought you were there for the whole day.'

'They said I could leave early when I mentioned that Teddy wasn't too well. They were really good about it thankfully.' I glance through the window at our meandering stream, the water reflecting the glow of the setting sun.

I know I'm going to enjoy working there. And living in this house. If only I could shake the sense of foreboding I thought I'd left behind. The sense of being watched. I still haven't actually seen anyone hanging around since moving here, so maybe it *is* me and my silly paranoia, as Jon keeps insisting. I'm trying not to mention it as much to him. The last thing I want is to be irritating him in any way. Hopefully, in time, this feeling will fade away.

'Is he feeling any better?'

Amy's so nice. I'm glad we met. 'He'll be OK with a good night's sleep. It looks like some sort of bug. They pick up all sorts from other kids, don't they?' I regret my words before they've even left me. She hasn't got children, nor does she look like she'll be having them any time soon. And I got the impression this isn't what she's actively chosen for herself.

'I guess so.'

It's time to change the subject. 'Anyway, I was firstly ringing to thank you for saving the day, and secondly...' I wander to the lounge door and peer into the hallway. I can just about hear Jon's voice emanating from his office. It sounds like a business-related conversation.

'Yes?'

I close the door and return to Teddy. 'I wondered if you fancied a drink somewhere. So I can say a proper thank you for everything. I don't know what I'd have done without you this week.'

'Oh right.' She sounds even more surprised.

'It would be my treat, obviously.' She doesn't look like someone with a lot of money – another reason I'm pleased to have employed her for Suki.

'When were you thinking?'

'Right now if you're free? I could murder a glass of wine, to be honest.' I glance at the clock on the mantlepiece which belonged to my mother-in-law. Jon wants to get rid of it but I think this is its rightful place. 'It's after six now so it's definitely wine o'clock, don't you think?'

'What about Teddy? Don't you need to stay with him?'

'He's fast asleep, and Jon's here. He's perfectly capable of taking care of him for a change.' I'm trying to assure myself really but the knot in my stomach remains. My little boy's poorly and all I can think about is meeting Amy for a glass of wine. But sometimes I need to lose the guilt and think about what I need. In any case, he's sleeping and probably won't even realise I've gone.

'OK.' Then she pauses. 'But by the time we get there, I'll probably only have an hour or so.'

'Oh, really? Is that all? That's a shame.'

The line stays silent as though she's thinking of an excuse to get out of it completely. But I can't imagine why – I've already told her I'm buying.

'Why's that then? Do you have to be somewhere?'

'Kind of.' I wait for her to elaborate but she doesn't. She's clearly not going to give anything away. We might as well get on with meeting since time, for whatever reason, is of the essence.

'Well, I suppose that's probably better for me anyway. At least I can get back home sooner. I'll meet you under the guise of taking Suki for a walk – it's easier than facing a barrage of questions from Jon about where I'm going, who I'm meeting and all that.'

'Really? Is that how he is with you?'

'No, it's not that – he just wouldn't approve of me going out while Teddy's under the weather, that's all.' He wouldn't approve of me going full stop but I don't add this. Amy's shown too much interest as it is in whatever flaws may exist between me and Jon. All marriages have them but I'd rather focus on what's going well for us.

'So where are you thinking?' Her voice cuts back into my thoughts. 'It could do with being in the centre of town really.'

'How about the pub on Bridge Street? How long will it take you to get there?'

'Only about fifteen minutes,' she replies. 'Right, I'll get off the phone so I can get sorted and I'll see you soon.'

'Excellent.'

Buoyed by my naughty escape plan, I leave the lounge door ajar and call Suki from her basket.

'I'm taking the dog out,' I mouth at Jon as I curl my head around his office door.

'Hang on a minute,' he says into his phone. 'What – you're taking her out *now?*'

'She needs a walk – I don't know when she last went out.'

'But what about Teddy?'

'He's sleeping at the moment.' I grab a book from the shelf. 'I'll wedge the door open. So you can listen out for him, can't you?'

'Well, yes, of course. But, hang on Cassie. Sorry, hang on a minute.' He speaks into his phone again then presses a button and lays it down. 'I thought that's why we employed a dog walker for Suki? So it would be one less job for us.'

'Well today I've had to pay our *dog walker* to look after our son.' I frown at him. 'But we can speak about that when I get back.'

'What's that supposed to mean?'

'I tried and tried calling but I couldn't get hold of you.'

'I think speaking about the woman you've employed is more important than me not being able to take a call from you.' He narrows his eyes.

'You're only trying to change the subject.' I turn away from him. 'Anyway, I'll let you get back to your call.'

'I want to see her references,' he calls after me as I dismiss our conversation with a wave of my hand.

Though maybe he's right. I'll mention her references when we get to the pub. Normally I prefer to take people at face value but Jon does have a point. Amy has got access to everything that's most important to us. Plus, knowing Jon as I do, he won't leave it alone until I sort it.

TWENTY-ONE

CASSIE

'Hi.' I reach to give Amy a hug. 'Thanks for helping me out today.'

However, she immediately tenses up, her eyes briefly flickering with surprise and discomfort. Jon's always said I can be too demonstrative and maybe I should check before I charge into the personal space of other people. But he's not a hugger either. The two of us don't hug nearly as often as we used to. Though I guess things get like this when people are married for a while.

'It's good to see you,' I tell her. And it's true. I don't like the volume of people at Jon's dinner parties, for instance, but I love one-to-one company and conversation. When we made the time for each other, Jon and I used have some interesting chats, but they've been few and far between lately. What with his job, my job, the house move and Teddy, it's like we've been taken over by outside forces. And feeling as though I must spend so much time on my hair, clothes and make-up every day to always look my best for Jon eats into quality time we might have had too.

The childminder always seems too busy for even the briefest conversation when I drop off and collect Teddy. Nor have I had long enough to get to know any of my new work colleagues yet, though they seem pleasant enough. Before long I'm sure I'll be invited out socially with them which hopefully Jon will be fine about.

'Have you been waiting long?' I ask Amy. 'You should have gone in without me.' I double-check for a *dogs are welcome* sign. 'You didn't need to wait out here. It's turned chillier, hasn't it?' Gosh, I'm sounding like my mother.

'I'm not keen on going into pubs on my own to be honest. Hey Suki.' She bends to make a fuss of her.

'You look nice,' I tell her. She's twisted her hair into a neat bun, and a touch of lipstick brightens up her face.

'Thanks.'

As she unbuttons her coat, I notice she's wearing a top similar to one I once had and is carrying a handbag not unlike something I'd use. I'm pleased she's got some nice things.

'Right, come on then.' I gesture at the bar. 'Since we haven't got long. What are you drinking?'

Amy follows me past the crackling log fire to the bar, her body language a mix of uncertainty and hesitation. 'I'll have whatever you're having.' She looks around as though checking who's in here. It's not too busy apart from a few after-work stragglers.

'There's no need to be nervous.' I nudge her.

'Sorry.' Her face relaxes into a smile. 'I'm out of practice, that's all.'

'Two large white wines please.' I turn back to Amy.

'What do you have to rush off for? You never said on the phone.' What I really mean is that I'm in no rush to hurry back to Jon if he's going to be holed up in his office all night leaving me to take care of Teddy on my own. It will do him good to pick up some of the slack for once. I'll just tell him that Suki needed an extra-long walk.

'Oh it's nothing exciting. I just promised I'd do a favour for someone.'

'You are kind.' I squeeze her arm. 'But I do hope you put yourself first at times.'

She shrugs, though somewhat weakly. Perhaps we came into each other's lives at the right time. Maybe I can help her out as much as she's helping me out. With Mum not living so close now, I could do with someone I can count on.

'Oh, and by the way.' I suddenly remember something I wanted to check with her and feel in my pocket. A sense of unease settles in me as I hold an earring between us. 'I found *this* on the shelf in my en suite before I left the house. It's not yours, is it?' I can't understand how it could have got there.

She glances at it. 'No, it's not mine.' Her almost apologetic face suggests she could be thinking the same thing I was. *What's some woman's earring doing in our en suite?* I've been trying to tell myself that it could have belonged to Jon's mum, but I can definitively say from the few times I've met her that it's not the sort of thing she'd have worn. Besides, Jon boxed up most of her stuff. Most of it ended up in charity shops or in the loft as far as I know.

'I just thought, well you've been upstairs at our house a couple of times, haven't you?'

I hope Jon never finds out she's been up there – he definitely wouldn't like anyone else in our bedroom.

'I've never seen it before.' She peers at it more closely. 'And I haven't been in your en suite. Might it have been there before you moved in?'

'I'm sure I'd have noticed if it had.' I roll it around in my fingers. 'My mother-in-law was a diamond earring sort of lady anyway.' I turn to pay the barman.

'Diamonds eh? Can't be bad.'

'So.' I glance around the pub as I drop the earring back into my pocket. 'Where shall we sit?'

'I don't mind.' She shuffles from foot to foot, looking somewhat uncomfortable again.

'Don't you know this place? After all, you're from around here, aren't you?'

'Like I said, I don't spend much time in pubs.' She points to the window, close to the exit. 'Shall we sit over there?'

I'm surprised she hasn't chosen somewhere closer to the fire but I follow her anyway.

If Jon could see me enjoying a nice glass of wine in the pub window in this comfy leather chair, while I've left him listening out for Teddy, I really don't think he'd be too happy. Yet it was alright for him to be out of range earlier. What's good for the goose, and all that. Still, I won't actually tell him where I've been.

I feed Suki the packet of pork scratchings I bought for her, resisting the urge to pop one into my own mouth. Since I had Teddy, I only have to look at calorific food to put a pound on. Jon occasionally makes quips about my weight so I really need to sort it out. He keeps threatening to take out a gym membership for us both. It would be great for us to have somewhere to go together, but neither of us have got the time. Which is yet another reason why he could be against my new job. Before it, I had all the time in the world.

'Tell me more about yourself Amy.' I pinch the smooth stem of my glass between my fingers, its coolness contrasting with the warmth of the pub. 'I'm starting to feel as if I'm hogging all the limelight. You know lots about me and I hardly know anything about you.' Really, I'm leading up to asking about these references. I don't know how to couch it without offending her.

'There's not too much to know really. Let me see...' She drums her fingers against her chin then reels off her favourite films and music. It's not the information I wanted but it's nice to find we have things in common. Especially thrillers and Coldplay.

'Oh, I'm so jealous you've been to see them.' She drains her drink.

'Another?' I nod towards her glass.

'I'd better have a lemonade this time,' she replies. 'I'm not used to drinking these days.'

'Tell me about how the two of you met.' She's changed the subject back to me and I still haven't broached the references.

'Who – me and Jon?'

'Who else?'

'We both grew up in Yorkshire,' I begin. 'Jon lived around here, as you already know, and I grew up in York; not a million miles away – but we actually met for the first time in Australia.'

'You've been to Australia?'

'I was on a gap year after finishing my degree and Jon was taking one before his final year.'

'Were you backpacking?' Her eyes widen.

'Yes, it was awesome.' I sip at my wine. 'I'd do it all over again if I could. Obviously I wouldn't change Teddy for the world, but—'

'I'd love to have done something like that.' Amy's voice bears more of a trace of resentment than envy which puzzles me. Her eyes narrow then she averts her gaze.

'So why didn't you?'

'I've never even been abroad.' She shakes the ice around in her lemonade and stares into her glass.

'Really? Why ever not?'

'I grew up with my grandparents and their finances didn't run to foreign holidays.' From the pensive look on her face, I'm getting the impression of a not-too-happy childhood. This must be why she avoids talking about herself.

'That's a shame. How come? Are they still around?'

'Honestly, I'd rather not go there if you don't mind.'

Frustration bubbles up inside me. The caution in her voice hints at deeper secrets – I'm going to *have* to mention those references now – if only to keep Jon happy when I get back.

It's now or never. If I offend her, I offend her. 'By the way Amy, Jon's asked me to mention something.'

Her head jerks up. 'Oh? What?'

'Look it's not me, it's him – it's just... he's very set in his ways and...'

'What is it?'

'It's just that... he's not happy that I employed you without getting a couple of references.'

Her face darkens. 'For walking a dog?'

'It's more that you've got access to the house. Look, don't take it personally – it's just the way he is.'

'What sort of references?' Yes she's offended. It's evident in her voice.

'Maybe one from your charity shop and then, you must have someone else you've worked for, or maybe your landlord?'

'Saying what?' Her voice is clipped.

'I don't know. Just to confirm they know you and that you're trustworthy. Look, I know you are but it's for Jon, not me.'

'Do you do *everything* he asks you to?'

Her question takes me aback. 'Of course not but I can see where he's coming from here. If the shoe was on the other foot, and he'd employed someone at our home without checking them out, I'd probably feel the same way.'

'But you allowed me to collect your son this afternoon.'

Oh gosh. She's not happy at all.

'I'm sorry Amy. I didn't mean to upset you.'

'I'll see what I can do.'

'There's honestly no rush for them. As long as Jon knows—'

'I said, I'll see what I can do.'

'Right... thanks, OK. Let's change the subject now, shall we?'

I try to keep the conversation's focus on Amy as we sip our drinks but I only get abrupt answers to every question I ask her. Nothing that really tells me anything. I guess some people don't like talking about themselves but she's on another level with it. My curiosity is certainly piqued. Why is she so guarded?

'Oh my God.' She glances at the clock and jumps up, nearly knocking over what's left of her drink. 'I've got to go.'

'We can't have been an hour already.' I check my watch and realise we've actually been longer. It's twenty past seven. 'Where do you live? I'll book you a taxi and get you another drink while we wait for it. It shouldn't be long.'

'No. It's fine, thanks all the same.' She grabs her coat. 'It'll be far quicker if I make a run for it. Look, I'm sorry. I enjoyed the drinks with you but I've honestly got to go.' She darts around the table to the door. As she rushes off, a twinge of concern tugs at my thoughts. I wonder what could have spooked her to leave so abruptly. It would have been good if she'd answered my 'where do you live?' question. At least I'd know a bit more about her.

Dumbfounded, I stare after her for a moment. Perhaps I should be watching which direction she runs off in; after all, it's dark outside now. Instead, I busy myself in dabbing at the lemonade she's spilt with some tissue I've found in my pocket.

'Well I don't know what the rush was Suki.' I tug her to her feet. 'Come on then. I suppose we'd better be getting home.'

Stepping out into the cold night, I scan the dimly lit street, searching for any sign of Amy. My heart quickens with worry. Why did she leave like that? I've suspected a number of times since we've met that there's far more to her story than she's letting on.

What if she's in some sort of trouble? From the way she dashed off, it was as though she could be living with someone who's controlling what she does and demanding her back at a certain time.

Jon *can* be a little overbearing and set in his ways but he's certainly not controlling.

TWENTY-TWO

CASSIE

'You've been ages,' Jon says as he reaches the bottom of the stairs. His messy dark hair falls just above his forehead, and he's frowning. I wonder if he can tell I've been to the pub.

'Sorry. I'm back now, aren't I?'

'Teddy's been nattering for you.'

'How's he feeling? Is he any better since he's had the chance to sleep it off?'

'I've put him in our bed.' He runs his fingers across his receding hairline. 'He wouldn't settle in his own.'

'I'll nip up and see him in a minute.' I hang my coat on the peg. 'I take it you've finished in your office now?' I gesture towards it.

'It's *you* that's cleared off for the last couple of hours, not me.' He heads to the kitchen. 'Where've you been anyway?' Even though he's got his back to me, I can hear the annoyance in his voice. Damn. That's the last thing I wanted.

'I went for a walk with Suki, like I said I was doing, but then I bumped into Amy.' I'll have to tell him since he asked. There's one thing I can't do and that's lie. My face gives me away every time.

'Amy?' He swings around to face me.

'Yes, you know – our dog walker. I wanted to say thank you to her.'

'And into a pub, by the looks of you.' His tone is even colder now, a hint of something else creeping in which annoys me. After all, it's alright for him to bugger off to the golf course every Saturday.

'I've only had two.' I don't know how he can tell – I guess he knows me too well.

'I'm not trying to be your keeper Cassie.' He slides a glass from the cupboard. 'But speaking of your new *friend* – you never answered my earlier question.'

'If you're going to start up about her references again, don't worry – I've asked her for them.'

'When we first discussed getting a dog walker...' He uses a tone usually reserved for Teddy. 'Do you remember how I asked you to get references *before* you took anybody on.' He plucks a beer from the fridge.

'Can't you just trust *my* judgement for once?'

'When someone we don't know a thing about is letting themselves into our home – the very least we should do is a background check.' He places the glass and bottle in front of himself on the counter.

'Amy's absolutely fine,' I reply. 'I've got to know her. Isn't that good enough for you? Anyway, let's not spoil the evening now we've got Teddy up to bed.' I smile at him. But he doesn't smile back.

'So when this woman robs *everything*, or causes some other kind of damage, I'll remind you of how well you've *got to know her*, shall I?'

'Why do you have such trust issues?' I reach for the half bottle of red wine left over from last night. 'Not everyone's out to fleece you, you know.'

He begins clattering around the kitchen, presumably

looking for the bottle opener for his beer. I'm too irritated with him to help him find it like I normally would.

I stare at the back of his head as he rummages in the drawer. At times, this urge to crack him open and discover what's *really* going on in his mind is overpowering. *Why do I feel like he's always keeping something from me?* It's something that's connected with his inability just to take people at face value; I'm sure of it.

He plonks his bottle next to a box that still needs unpacking. 'I thought you were going to check on Teddy?'

Meaning *subject closed* and *leave me alone.* I walk from the room without saying a word.

I'm surprised at Teddy for wanting to sleep in our bed as we don't have a TV in here. Jon doesn't agree with them in bedrooms normally but since my mum bought the portable as a birthday present for Teddy, Jon couldn't really say no to it.

He's huddled in a little lump at my side of our queen-size bed. My heart melts as I look at him – he's the most perfect thing I've ever done. He stirs as I perch on the edge of the bed and check his forehead. It's less clammy than it was earlier, thank goodness. Nevertheless, I'll keep him at home tomorrow. My new manager knows I've been battling through this first week at work with a child who isn't a hundred per cent. She's already told me to take tomorrow off if I need to. I'll have to remember to let Amy know not to come. It will also give me a chance to check that she's OK after having to rush away earlier.

I swing my legs from the floor to lie beside him. I've hardly seen him today, and I know I shouldn't have gone for a drink with Amy, but at least I'll have the chance to make up for my absence tomorrow if Teddy and I are staying at home together. A mother's guilt is perpetual and I never really feel as though I'm up to the job.

I stare up at the ornate light surround on the ceiling, feeling a surge of gratitude for our new home which is definitely more me than the pretentious rambling thing we've just escaped from. I try to focus on my breathing – I need to slow it down. It's no wonder I'm still frazzled from the inside out after all the change that's taken place in our lives recently.

My boy's growing up far too quickly. I run my hand over the hump of his back down to one of his feet. Only it's not his foot – it's way too small. *What is it?* I reach beneath the duvet. My hand falls on something that could be a large hanky, or... A pair of knickers.

And they're not mine.

I hold them at a distance between two fingers. How has a pair of woman's knickers found their way into my bed, right beside where my son is sleeping?

I bloody knew it. First the earring and now knickers – *no wonder Jon's had less and less patience with me lately. No wonder I couldn't reach him earlier. He's playing away.*

He's taken full advantage of my going upstairs to re-ensconce himself in his office. My heart's hammering as I stand in the doorway for a few moments, watching his face lit up by the light of his computer screen. His brow's furrowed in concentration; is he messaging with *her?* The woman he's had in our bed, whoever she is? Thanking her for the time they've had today. It must have been today for those knickers have only just appeared. They definitely weren't there when I made the bed this morning. A sob chokes in my throat as he glances over the top of his laptop lid.

'Gosh Cassie – you made me jump. Why are you skulking around like that?'

'I'll give you *skulking*.' I stride towards his desk. 'What have you got to say about these?' I dangle the knickers from one finger in front of his face.

'Erm. They're not really my thing.' He clears his throat and pulls a face. 'They don't really look like your sort of thing either, to be honest.'

'Funny.' I drop them on the keyboard of his laptop. 'What I want to know – is why I've just found knickers that I've never seen before in our bed?'

'In our bed?'

'You heard me.'

'What do you mean, *you've never seen them before?*' He pushes them off his computer with a ruler. 'You must have. I've certainly never seen them before either.'

'Well someone's put them there.' I point at them.

'What is it you're accusing me of Cassie?'

'What do you think?'

'I can assure you that they've got bugger all to do with me.'

'So whose are they?' A darkness like I've never known envelops me. I've never seen them before, therefore he *must* have done. 'Is this why I couldn't get hold of you this morning? You were too busy entertaining some woman upstairs – in our bed?'

'Of course I wasn't. As I've already explained to you, I was stuck in a meeting and my phone had died.'

'Your phone never dies.'

'What the hell's got into you?' He slaps his palm against the desk. 'I've been telling you for ages you're over-reacting about things. Maybe that depression's come back. Seriously, Cassie.'

I gesture towards the knickers again. 'I don't know what you want to do with them but you can get them out of my house.' I choke back tears. I can't believe this – I just can't believe it.

'Mummy, why are you shouting at Daddy?'

Jon looks at me with an expression that looks to be bordering on relief at Teddy's sudden intrusion. He'll be thinking he's off the hook.

.   .   .

I wake with a crick in my neck. Teddy's laid out like a starfish with one leg draped over mine, having taken over most of his bed. He's left me with barely a sliver of room at the edge of it. It's the worst night's sleep I've had in ages. My mind's gone around and around like a tumble dryer and the more I've tried to settle it, the faster it's spun. I've longed to get into bed beside Jon but how can I after what he's potentially done? I want to believe he's never seen those knickers before but until I get another explanation, I can't let it go.

Slowly, I open my eyes, taking in the empty wine bottle and the glass I brought to bed with me last night in a last-ditch effort to knock myself out. It clearly didn't work. It certainly wasn't the evening I'd intended. I spent an hour getting Teddy settled again before making myself comfy on his beanbag after he'd drifted off. Drinking wine alone and googling things like *10 ways you know your husband's being unfaithful* certainly hadn't factored into my plans.

Lowering my feet to the floor, I tiptoe across the room back to Teddy's beanbag. Hopefully, he'll sleep for a little bit longer.

Meanwhile, I need to think.

Hopefully Jon's had time to weigh up his defence. There's no other explanation for knickers that aren't mine finding their way into our bed, other than him bringing someone into it. Then there's the earring which I haven't even asked him about yet. Not to mention the fact that we've only had sex once in the past month. If I combine all that with how distant and preoccupied he's been with me lately, I can only draw one conclusion. Another woman is in his life – *and* in our bed.

Thank God I've got the day off work today – I'd be neither use nor ornament with all this rubbish taking up every spare inch of my headspace. At least the cloud of Teddy being under the weather has a silver lining and I can take some time out.

If Jon admits to being unfaithful, I don't know what I'll do. Even if he keeps on denying it all, I don't know how much I'll be able to trust him anymore – I'll always be wondering and on full alert.

This move was supposed to be a brand new start for us. If we end up separating, it's not even as if I could lay any claim to this house either – his mother left it to *him*. It doesn't become Teddy's until Jon's no longer around. What if *I've* got to leave? Where would I go? As my thoughts twist and turn around one another, presenting one awful possibility after another, I hear voices outside. I can't make out what they're saying, only that one of them is very familiar.

TWENTY-THREE

CASSIE

I peer around the edge of the curtain. Jon appears to be having a heated discussion with none other than Becca at the side door to her house. He's dressed in his suit, all ready for work and for some reason, he's waving his arms around wildly one moment, and speaking right into her face the next. She's standing with her hands on her hips, appearing to be giving as good as she's getting, while pointing a finger into his chest.

What the hell is going on between them? Surely it's not Becca he's been sleeping with? We've only been back here for five minutes.

I twist the handle and push at the window. It's the first time I've ever opened it so I pray it opens silently. It doesn't. Instead it jams against its restrictor with a thud. Damn it. Both their eyes flit my way as I dodge to the side, out of sight, with my heart feeling as though it's bashing against my ribcage. Gradually, I dare to peer around it again.

Becca says something else to Jon and if I'm not mistaken she appears to be shushing him. Then with another glance my way, she disappears inside her house, leaving Jon standing there.

· · ·

'Mystery solved then.' I'm ready for Jon as he opens the door and appears in our sun-dappled hallway. I sit on the stairs, hugging my knees to my chest as though comforting myself. I could do with a hug right now but the only person likely to offer me one is Teddy, and he's still fast asleep.

'What are you on about now?' Jon closes the door as though he's just been innocently putting the bins out. Then he has the nerve to look at me as though I'm the one causing problems between us.

He should look tired and rugged after a restless night spent deliberating like I have, but no. As always, he's as groomed as a show horse, with a face as fresh as the daffodils lining our driveway.

'Those knickers. They were *Becca's* weren't they?' I should march round to her door with them right now and ram the things down her throat until they choke her. No wonder she's been so off with me.

Jon laughs. 'You're being ridiculous Cassie.'

'How dare you laugh at me?'

'In answer to your question, of course they aren't.'

'And what about this.' I reach up and rummage in the pocket of my coat hooked over the banister.

Jon strides across the hallway and peers at it. 'What is it?'

'An earring. What does it look like?'

He shrugs. 'What would I know about a woman's earring?'

'That's what I'm trying to find out.'

'I haven't got time for this Cassie. I need to get going.'

'Not so fast. I want to know what all that was about out there?' I point in the direction of next door. 'I saw you both arguing. What is it – does Becca want me to know the truth – and you don't? Is that what it is?'

'What truth? You're talking in riddles.'

'That the two of you are having a bloody affair?'

He reaches to unhook his coat from the pegs. 'I'm off to

work love. I'll leave you with your silly theories. Try not to drive yourself too barmy.'

I can't believe he's being so sarcastic – and so cold about it. If the shoe was on the other foot, I'd be bending over backwards to reassure him and fix things between us.

'You're kidding me.' I jump up from the step. 'You can't just leave things like this between us. I've got a right to know what's going on, surely?' This is such a mess. I can't believe we're even having this conversation.

'If you must know, we were discussing the parking situation out there. One of her home care people was blocking me in. I'd have left by now if it wasn't for that.'

He's really planning to go to work while leaving me to stew in my own juices all day. I really wanted to focus on Teddy, but how can I focus on *anything* apart from the fact that my husband and next door neighbour might be carrying on with each other. Or if not her, someone else. I won't rest until I find out.

'What if I don't believe you.' I stand in front of the door. I'm perfectly capable of blocking him in too. 'We can't leave things like this.'

'I need to get to work Cassie, regardless of what you do or don't believe.' His voice is so passive, anyone would think he was having a business discussion. 'All I can say is that if you don't trust me with other women, you've clearly got some work to do on yourself. I am *not* having an affair with Becca next door, or anyone else for that matter.'

'So who do the knickers belong to?' I'm close to tears now. 'Tell me that.'

He lets a long breath out while giving me an odd look. 'Are you *really* sure they're not yours?'

'No they bloody aren't! I think I'd know my own knickers, don't you?'

'Mummy!'

My old friend, mother-guilt, cloaks itself over me as Teddy's voice echoes from upstairs. He's heard us arguing. Again.

'Look, I can't spend all day rowing over all this. Are you going to let me get past or what? I'm due in a meeting soon.'

I step to the side. *What choice have I got?*

'Just pull yourself together Cassie.' He opens the door. 'We'll talk later when you've calmed down.'

With that, the door bangs behind him, leaving me dabbing my eyes on the sleeve of my dressing gown. He never kisses me goodbye anymore; today he didn't even *say* goodbye. How did we ever get to this?

Teddy's finally breakfasted, dressed and colouring pictures at the kitchen table. He's probably well enough today to have gone to the childminder's but I've definitely got far too much rubbish swirling around my head to have gone into work.

Sitting beside him, I slide my laptop from its case and load up a browser.

'That's lovely.' I point at Teddy's picture. 'Will you colour something in for Mummy?'

He turns pages until he lands on some flowers. 'This one?' He points his chubby finger at the page.

'Oooh, yes please. Now I've just got a bit of work to do then we'll take Suki out for some fresh air.'

Perhaps Becca's social media will turn something up. Not that I really have a clue what I'm searching for. Maybe I'm hoping, well not *really* hoping, but just checking that Jon's not in the background of one of her pictures, checking that he hasn't liked or commented on one of her posts. If he has, that's the proof I don't want to find.

Firstly, I search for *Becca*, then *Rebecca* on Jon's friends list. There's nothing. That's something at least. To find *her* page, I'm going to need her surname.

I suddenly have an idea and type in *Rawdale High. Class of...*

I have to think for a moment. He's already told me he and Becca were in the same school year. He's a year younger than me, so I type in the year after I left school.

Eventually, after much scrolling, and making lots of *I'm listening and interested* noises in Teddy's direction, I come across a *Rebecca Thorpe*. It's the only Rebecca listed in that year group, so it has to be her. It's impossible to tell from the class photograph – faces are too small and everyone looks similar, especially the girls. Shoulder length, highlighted hair straightened to within an inch of its life seemed to be the thing. Exactly as I used to wear mine. The photograph makes me feel almost nostalgic.

I type *Rebecca Thorpe* into the website's search bar but it doesn't return anything. Next, I type *Jon Hemingway*. This time it returns a long list of articles full of phrases such as *man of the match* and *football star*. Just as he's so often told me, he clearly shone in the football scene while at school. He's mentioned how he should have played professionally, if it hadn't been for a knee injury.

In his last year at school, he was year captain, not to mention a mentor to the new, younger cohort, and winner of the Pupil of the Year trophy. As I continue to scroll, images of my husband, aged sixteen, smile out at me time and time again. He was quite the catch. He's told me he had all the girls after him, not that I had any reason to disbelieve him. I'd have been after him myself if we'd been at the same school.

I type *Rawdale High School* into a general search bar and scroll down.

My attention's grabbed by the headline second from the bottom.

Rawdale High Murder – Girl Jailed

I have to look twice at it. *Does it really say 'murder'?* I read on.

The family of eighteen-year-old Jade Calvert have today spoken out at their relief of justice being served after the tragic death of their beloved daughter.

Jade Calvert had just completed her A level exams at Rawdale High School in Yorkshire when what should have been a celebratory party with friends ended in tragedy.

Paramedics were called to Tolbeck Cottage, a property at Cherry Tree Lane in Rawdale at 9.40 p.m. on Friday 19th June to attend to Jade, who was found in a state of collapse.

Tolbeck Cottage! Bloody hell – it's our house!

Extensive resuscitation efforts were made but Jade was pronounced dead at the scene just after 10 p.m.

I don't know what I was expecting to find on here but it wasn't this.

Post-mortem results found a fatal amount of ketamine in Jade's system and a murder investigation was immediately launched.

Ketamine? Murder investigation? I can't believe this. Why the hell has Jon never told me about this?

Today, another eighteen-year-old girl, who cannot be named as she was still seventeen at the time of her arrest and plea, was found guilty at a closed hearing at Leeds Crown Court. She was sentenced to twenty years' imprisonment, for which a minimum of ten years must be served.

'Can I have a drink, Mummy?'

'Just give me another few minutes then I'll put this away.'

Judge Griffen, sentencing, told the court he was passing the highest sentence possible in the circumstances. This was due to the defendant's non-admittance throughout the entire process, coupled with her apparent lack of remorse. He described the now-eighteen-year-old, who spoke only to confirm her name and address, as a threat to society. He added she'd had no thought or consideration before, during or after her reckless actions, which, according to witness testimonies, had been driven by nothing but jealousy of her former classmate.

Blimey. So this all happened ten years ago. The unnamed girl will now be a woman of about twenty-eight, the same age as Jon and a year younger than me. I do a quick calculation. In fact, if she's served the minimum of her sentence, she'll be getting out of prison any time at all. And she'll still have her entire life ahead of her. Unlike poor Jade Calvert.

Jade's mother, Jodie Calvert, spoke to reporters after the hearing. 'Ten years for the life of my daughter is an insult to her memory. I only hope that what's happened serves as a warning for other teenagers about the dangers of spiking one another's drinks.'

A cold feeling creeps over me as I glance around the kitchen. Someone has actually breathed their last in the home I now inhabit. I'd been previously relieved to learn that at least Jon's parents didn't die in here. His dad died in hospital and his mum finished up in a hospice. But where exactly did Jade Calvert die? Was it in here, right in this very room?

The owners of Tolbeck Cottage, Jack and Elsie Hemingway, were also present at today's hearing.

Mr Hemingway said: 'We are devastated with the terrible incident which happened at our home. We had neither sanctioned a party, nor would have permitted this volume of teenagers to convene at our home in our absence. Our sincerest condolences go to the family of Jade Calvert and we hope that today's sentencing brings them some comfort and peace.'

It's strange to read the voice of the man who would have been my father-in-law. His words seem heartfelt and filled with sorrow. But what I really can't understand is why Jon's never told me about any of this. I can't understand it at all.

And while all this is very interesting, it still doesn't help me find out if Jon and Becca *are* having an affair.

TWENTY-FOUR

CASSIE

'It's a period of life my family wanted to get beyond.' Jon rinses his cup and lays it on the draining board, before pulling the blind and closing us in against the darkness outside. I'm feeling like there's enough of it in here at the moment. Somehow, we've got to get beyond this. If only it wasn't for those knickers in the bed. And that earring.

'I'm supposed to be your *family* now. Aren't I?' I take a small sip of the chamomile tea, its subtle floral notes doing little to mask the yearning for a bold glass of wine. But I need to keep a clear head. After making the discovery in our bed last night, I drank enough to sink a small vessel. I'm supposed to be a responsible mother holding down a managerial job, not a lush who is forced to find refuge in the bottle.

'Of course you're my family.' Jon perches on the stool, his shoulders easing slightly as he meets my gaze. A hint of a smile plays on his lips, a sign that the tension between us may be waning. 'But that doesn't mean I have to rake up things from way back in the past to tell you about. Things that, for good reason, are best *left* in the past? Do you tell me about *everything* that's happened in *your* life?'

'I'd have thought you'd want to share something as significant as a murder in our new home. Don't you think I had the right to know?'

'I'm sorry Cassie, I don't know what else I'm supposed to say. You didn't want to live in our old house and I didn't think you'd want to live here if you knew what had happened.'

Sorry. The word, a rare visitor to my husband's vocabulary, feels weightless, offering little consolation for the frustration gnawing away at me.

'I'd have asked you to put *both* houses on the market if I'd known.'

'You said you *wanted* to move to Rawdale.'

'Yeah, but not to a house with such a violent history.'

'Do we really have to keep discussing this?' He settles his arms on the table in front of him. 'Honestly, it was all horrendous enough when it happened without raking back over it.'

'Yes we do. I've waited *all day* to discuss it actually.'

'I don't know why you can't just let it go.'

'Honestly, I feel like I don't know you at all sometimes. And that you don't know me either – of course I can't just *let it go*.' I glance around. 'Whereabouts did it happen anyway?' It's hard to equate a murder happening somewhere like this. When we came here, just after his mother died, I thought the place had a great feel to it. Little did I know that on moving in, our marriage would plummet to the depths it has within a matter of days.

'What difference does it make *where* it happened?'

'I need to know.' I drain my cup of the cold herbal tea, grimacing at the bitter aftertaste it deposits on my tongue.

'Well I really don't need to talk about it.' He's twirling his thumbs around and around one another which is seriously annoying. 'You know all there is to know by the sounds of it from the report.'

'Which is?'

He sighs as his eyes meet mine. 'A girl had her drink spiked by another girl. One of them died and the other went to prison. It was hell for a while and my parents went crazy about it all. End of story.'

'Tell me where she died, Jon.' A shiver envelops me. The worst place possible would be our bedroom. I don't think I could sleep in there again. Though the way things are going in our marriage, who knows how much longer that will be our marital bed for anyway. I have to get him to open up. I'll even go to counselling with him if it'll help us get back on track. He might be a pain at times but deep down, I don't want us to split up – and I certainly don't want to lose him to someone like Becca.

'For God's sake Cassie. Let it go, eh?'

'Why should I? You should have been honest with me in the first place.' My voice bounces around the kitchen walls.

'I'd prefer to get back to discussing these references and background checks.'

'Bloody hell. Talk about deflection.'

'The references and checks you should have carried out *before* entrusting a stranger with our home, our dog and even our son. I'd have thought you'd have had more sense.'

'Like I said, you're deflecting.'

The washer enters its spin cycle, reminding me of the domesticity we're supposed to inhabit together instead of this sudden mire of mistrust and uncertainty. I don't want to live like this.

'I'm doing no such thing. But as well as the parking Becca mentioned this morning...' He tilts his head in the direction of next door. 'She mentioned something about that *woman.*'

He says the word *woman* as if it's something really unpleasant. Why the hell has he got it in so badly for Amy? It's probably a smokescreen. Obviously he doesn't want me to know what he was *really* talking to Becca about.

'What about her?'

'She's been spending hours at a time in here.' He waves his hands in front of himself.

'Well I asked her to, didn't I? When I couldn't get hold of you.' He'll be able to hear the bitter note in my voice. That's still unfinished business as far as I'm concerned. I'm certain it's linked to the knickers and the earring I found too – which if he thinks he's heard the last of, he's very much mistaken.

'Not just yesterday. Every day since she's had a key to the door, she's used it to her full advantage.'

'I didn't just give her a key to look at.' He's not the only one that can do sarcasm.

'I mean *really* used it.' He continues to look at me as if I've done something wrong.

'Why can't you just trust my judgement here?' The strains of music from Teddy's DVD echo from upstairs. I hope he's fallen asleep up there and isn't listening to us again.

'Because the woman you've employed to walk Suki is spending inordinate amounts of time in our home Cassie. Why is that?'

Suki shifts in her basket at the sound of her name. She'll be hoping her walk is imminent. I imagine it will be. The whole situation is starting to close in on me and I'll need to get out of here before long.

'I've no idea why she's spending time in here. But until I have proof other than something *Becca* has conveniently concocted, I don't believe she is.' I spit Becca's name out like a fish bone.

'Why didn't you do background checks on her to start with?' His tone is gentler but still chastising.

'I don't know.' I'm mumbling now. And that's because I *should* have done the checks. He's right. But I've had enough on just lately. It's alright for Jon. He treats everything he decides to do with the home, dog or Teddy as though he's doing me a favour.

'I don't trust her one bit.' His voice hardens.

'Why on earth not?' I stand from my seat. I'm going to pour a glass of wine after all. If we're going to argue all night, I might as well take the edge off it.

'There's something about her, that's all. She's got an agenda – I don't know what it is, but...'

'*An agenda!*' My voice rises so I quickly lower it. Teddy's heard more than enough of his father and I going at one another lately. 'Don't be so dramatic. Look, if you must know, I'm getting a sense that her own home isn't somewhere she really wants to be.' I take a large sip from my glass, a feeling of warmth enveloping me as the liquid slips to my stomach. 'I'm getting a *bad relationship* vibe from her. That she could be in one, I mean. Which might be why she's been taking refuge here.'

'Nope. It's far more than that, and Becca agrees with me.'

'Bloody Becca, we still haven't got to the truth about her, have we?' I slam my palm onto the counter, a sense of foreboding gnawing at me. There's more to her than meets the eye.

'We've got more important things to worry about than some stupid underwear you've found.' His voice remains infuriatingly even. 'Honestly Cassie, for someone who claims to be so concerned about personal safety, I can't believe you've been so careless. I never heard the end of it in the last house.'

'I *am* concerned!' I dump my cup in the sink then glug more wine into my glass.

'Then why would you be so stupid as to trust a complete stranger at face value?'

'I know exactly what you're doing here.' I jab my finger in his direction. 'We were on about something else before and you've managed to completely switch things around. And don't call me stupid – have you got that?' I wait for him to react to what I've just said. He's used to me being more compliant. But for once, I'm standing up for myself and seeing this through until I get to the truth.

'I'm just trying to get you to see what's right under your nose.'

'Look.' I lean onto the breakfast bar. 'I've asked Amy for references now. And in the meantime, I'll do my best to get some more information about her.' What I don't add is that Amy isn't the only person whose circumstances I'm planning to dig into.

'Which is exactly what you should have done in the first place.' He stamps towards the door. 'Anyway, I've got some emails to send.'

'More like you're going to text your *girlfriend*.'

I might sound childish but I'm past caring.

TWENTY-FIVE

CASSIE

It's not good first-week-at-a-new-job behaviour, but there's no way I can face being all happy-nicey at work. No way. I need to sort everything out at home first. There's far more to what's gone on in the past, and *is* going on literally under my nose right now, than I've been told about. And I won't rest until I iron it all out.

Jon and I are barely speaking – he stormed off this morning without saying a word – but at least we slept in the same bed, unlike the night before. I couldn't face a night squished in with Teddy, and the guest bed is still piled high with boxes. We slept back to back for the entire time – I say slept, I spent half the night ruminating about everything as well as worrying whether our bedroom was the room where Jade died.

I'm dressed for work, so at least that's the impression I've given the childminder about my whereabouts today. But instead of driving in that direction, I turn back up Cherry Tree Lane and pull back into our driveway.

But instead of heading up the steps to Tolbeck Cottage, I fumble with the catch on next door's gate. I inhale deeply, trying to steady my nerves as I stand on Becca's doorstep. I'm standing in exactly the same spot as Jon was standing yesterday when I saw them from Teddy's window. Hopefully she won't just slam the door in my face.

'What do you want?' She looks as shocked as she did when she noticed me trying to eavesdrop yesterday.

'Can I come in? I need to talk to you.' I tighten my scarf. The rain's stopped, but the air remains chilly, making it feel more like the dead of winter than the turn into spring.

'No, I'm busy. I take care of my mother, like I've already told you.' As always, she's wearing gym pants and a baggy hoodie. I've never seen her wear anything else.

I take a deep breath. 'I won't take up much of your time.'

'You won't take up *any* of my time. Because I'm not talking to you.'

Her rebuttal hits me like a slap. She reaches for the door to close it, but I instinctively press my foot against it, preventing its closure.

'Come on Becca. I know we haven't got off to the best start, but there's no need to be so bloody hostile with me.' She *must* be sleeping with Jon, or at least be *wanting* to sleep with him. Or else, what's her bloody problem?

'Look, if you don't mind – I've...' She looks down at my foot as though it's a diseased rat invading her kitchen.

'Surely you can spare ten minutes.'

'*No I can't.*' She says the words with such sharpness, it seems she can't think of anything worse.

'I only want to ask you a few questions.' I'm persistent if nothing else. Mum's always said I can't take no for an answer.

'About what?' She folds her arms across her chest and narrows her eyes, reminding me of a cat.

'Not out here. Can I come in?' I move my foot out of her doorway, heartened when she doesn't take the chance to immediately slam the door in my face.

'No, you can't.'

'How about you come into my house instead?' I gesture behind me.

'No thanks.' It could be my imagination but I'm certain that her top lip has just curled as she turned down my invitation. *Who does she thinks she is, looking down her nose at me?*

'Why on earth not?'

'Look, what is it with you?' She throws her arms in the air like I'm the greatest imposition she's ever encountered. I'd love to know what I've done to upset her.

'I only wanted to ask you about our dog walker, Amy,' I say quickly. 'Jon says you've noticed her spending lots of time inside our place.'

'I don't really want to get involved, if you don't mind.' Her ponytail swings like a pendulum as she shakes her head.

'So why were you talking to him about her then? Why can't you tell *me*?' I won't come out and accuse her of having an affair with him just yet. Besides, I'm going slightly off the boil with that theory since my brain's been whirring all night. Something else has started needling at me instead. It's been bubbling away since four o'clock this morning.

'She has been in your house a lot.' Her tone has settled at the mention of Amy, possibly because it's diverting the focus of any accusations she's been fearing I'm going to level at her. 'Yes, I've noticed her in there – like I already told your husband.'

Her words *your husband* have a certain edge to them. I'm confused. *Are they having an affair or not?* Her manner seems to suggest she can't stand him.

'I get the impression you know Amy.'

'Not well – but yes, I used to.' It's the most civil Becca's been so far with me.

'What can you tell me about her?' I'm like a shark with a limb and I'm not letting go.

'What do you mean?'

'Look, I'm going to level with you here. Jon's upset that I didn't get her references before taking her on.'

She shakes her head and juts her chin out. 'I can't tell you anything.'

Judging by her face, I reckon she can. 'Can't, or *won't*?'

She folds her arms and looks the other way.

'What about Jon? You seemed very familiar with each other out here yesterday. How well *do* you know my husband?'

'We were neighbours, that's all. Back in the day, I mean.'

'Come on, I'm not stupid. I know things have gone on around here.' I gesture at my house again. 'Like that murder. You must know about that.'

Her face appears to tighten. 'Who told you?'

'I had to go digging around online. But there wasn't much to find... as you probably already know. So I want to know what exactly happened?'

She narrows her eyes some more. 'I don't want to talk about it.'

'Surely I have the right to know the truth about a death in my home?' I try to meet her eye but she's still not having it.

'Not from me, you don't. Speak to your husband.'

'Why, what do you know that he knows?' We're taking one step forward and two steps back here. *Why is she being like this with me?* It's infuriating. I seem to be taking the brunt of the crap at the moment and I've had enough of it.

'Right, I've tried to be reasonable with you, but...'

'Have you? I'd hate to see you when you're being *unreasonable* then.'

'I'm going to warn you now Cassie.' It's the first time she's used my name. I'm surprised she even remembers it.

'*Warn* me? What are you on about?'

'Just stop digging, will you?' Her voice takes on a new height of exasperation. 'For everyone's sakes, stop it *right now*.'

Her words have the exact opposite effect on me. *Stop it right now*. I'm more intrigued than ever. 'What's that supposed to mean? Stop digging about what? And for *whose* sakes?'

'Any of it, *all of it*. What happened here all those years ago.' She points at my house. 'Stop digging for the dirt with Jon, and *that woman* – it's all in the past.'

'Give me one reason why I should?'

She pauses, as though deliberating how or whether even to reply. 'Because I can promise that you might not like what you find.'

Then she closes the door, leaving me staring open-mouthed at it, more determined than ever to get to the bottom of the past, the present, and now, it seems, the future.

As I try to focus on some more cleaning and unpacking, I'm unable to prevent my mind from doing its wandering. I take in every nook and cranny as I go, while repeatedly asking myself, *was it here? Might this have been the spot where that girl died?*

And then there's Amy – the focus of my 4 a.m. musings. With each passing thought, I find myself questioning what, if any, role she might have to play in everything that's going on right now.

As I slam Teddy's books onto his shelves, I begin to consider the possibility of Amy having some sort of secret agenda in targeting and befriending me like she has. She's repeatedly been evasive about her past, and where she lives. And why did she rush off the other night?

There's something about her – and I'm going to find out what.

TWENTY-SIX

CASSIE

Raindrops tap against the windscreen like a miserable melody as I sit parked in the dimly lit side street, my eyes fixed on the charity shop across the road. It's one of those dreary March days when daylight struggles to pierce the heavy clouds, and the air is thick with moisture. I shiver, pulling my coat closer to ward off the chill and tighten my grip on the steering wheel, yearning for the comfort of home. The shop presents a cosy exterior, with warm light seeping through its windows and reflecting onto the wet pavement.

I've already texted Amy so she knows not to come for Suki when she finishes work. That should give me the perfect opportunity to find out where she'll go and what she'll do instead.

Time stretches endlessly as I wait for her to leave the shop. Finally, she emerges through the main door, her hood shielding her from the rain. I slump lower in my seat, keeping a safe distance. Luckily, she seems oblivious to my presence, her focus fixated on the bus rounding the corner. She runs towards it, all flailing arms and scarf. Clearly, she's never been a runner. She's already told me that she normally walks to the charity shop and back but I don't blame her for jumping on the opportunity of a bus. Not on a day like today.

Also, it makes it so much easier for me to follow her.

She sits on the bottom deck near the front, which might mean she's only travelling for a few stops. I wait at a distance behind each one, and by the time we get to the fourth stop, I ensure there are one or two cars between mine and the bus. I don't know how much notice she's taken of mine and Jon's cars on the driveway, but the last thing I want is for her to spot me following her. Not when I'm so close to finding out more. Once I know where she lives, I'll be able to do some further digging.

Two stops later, Amy descends from the bus and strolls purposefully down the street. At a pelican crossing, she pauses until the signal begins to beep. Once she crosses the road, she turns into a narrow road, disappearing from view.

If I don't get over there sharpish, I might lose her, as it's a maze of terraced houses inside those side streets. Jon's told me it's commonly known as *the wrong side of the river* around here, especially by those who live on *the right side of the river*, which includes me now, which I'm still trying to get used to. When I asked him why, he told me they don't have nearly as much money on this side as we do, and most of the houses are corporation owned as opposed to being private. He said it with a sense of entitlement which I always struggle to understand. But then, he doesn't seem to have known a day's struggle in his life.

I turn just in time, as Amy crosses another road before looking back behind her. I shrink into my seat. *Has she noticed me?* No – she's heading into a driveway. It leads to a huge Victorian building. Maybe she's not going home after all. Perhaps this is going to be a longer afternoon than I anticipated. But it's fine – I don't have to pick Teddy up for ages. And what else do I have to do? Both Becca and Jon have shut me down. Amy grew up around here too and I've had the sense since I met her that she and Becca have some kind of history. I feel certain that doing this will lead me towards some answers.

I pull forwards slightly. She's speaking into an intercom at the main door. She's going inside. *What is this place?*

Pulling forward some more, I spot a sign above the door – *Juniper Lodge.* That doesn't tell me much. And another sign directing deliveries to go around the back. It looks like some kind of business, or it could be an institution. Perhaps she's got an appointment here.

As quickly as Amy's entered the place, the same door opens again and spits a different woman out. She's one of the most dubious-looking characters I've ever seen with her mostly shaved head, leaving just a ponytail at the top. At her approach, I press the central locking button for the car doors. As she gets nearer, I notice the tattoos all up her neck. She gives me a look as she passes my car, as if to say *who the hell are you?* I certainly wouldn't like to get on the wrong side of her.

As she carries on walking, I feel the vibrations of a car going around me, before parking up in Juniper Lodge's car park. This time a more respectable-looking man gets out. He looks as though he's on official business of some description and also heads for the intercom.

The anticipation gnaws at me, and I reach for my phone in search of answers. My fingers fumble across the screen as I type *Juniper Lodge* into the search bar.

Oh my God. It's an approved premises for people being released on licence – from *prison*! Why would Amy be here? Hang on a minute. An awful realisation creeps over me. This could be why Becca seemed to be warning me off when we spoke earlier.

Amy must have done something. Why else would she be living in a prison-release institution? Could this be why she needed to suddenly rush off from the pub like she did last night? Could she be under some sort of curfew?

Oh. My. God. Could *Amy* have been the woman who committed the murder at our house? I stare at the imposing stone building. *No, surely not*; she looks *nothing like* a *murderer*. But then, what *does* a murderer look like?

I watch the door she disappeared into. I'm struggling to get my head around all this. And all it takes is one glance from a window for her to notice me watching her. After all, the shiny new Mini Jon bought me for Christmas doesn't exactly fit in around here. I'd better get moving.

With my thoughts tumbling over one another, I make the ten-minute drive home. How's Jon going to react? As if things aren't rocky enough between us right now. Not only did I not check Amy out in the first place, which is crime enough in his eyes, it seems as though I've employed the worst person possible to a position of trust. Thank God I've realised who she might be before she's been able to try anything.

If Amy *is* the same woman who was responsible for Jade Calvert's death, how has Jon not recognised her? He's met her twice now, and I don't care what anyone says, people don't change *that* much in ten years. I haven't altered too drastically, and judging by the pictures I've seen of Jon, neither has he. He must have *known* Amy if she was at that party. Becca must have known her too – if it's the same person, that is. I'm still telling myself there's a chance it might not be. I really, really hope it isn't and that she's latched onto me for some other reason than wanting to return to the scene of her crime.

As I pull away from the street, I know I have to give the situation the benefit of the doubt and not jump to conclusions yet. Jon *hasn't* recognised her as the person from his party. All hell would have broken loose if he had, I'm sure of it. And Amy could be going into that place for any number of reasons. She could just be visiting someone.

But one thing I do know is that he's going to go mad when I tell him she might be a released prisoner. If she really is, I need to be able to give him more than *the woman I hired is on licence from prison.* I need to dig a bit deeper first.

One thing is for certain, until I know the full story, I can't have Amy in the house. I thought she was a normal, run-of-the-mill, albeit lonely woman who just wanted to be my friend and earn some extra money helping me out with Suki.

Now I find out there's a possibility she could be a killer. Pulling over to the side of the road, I switch off the engine and rummage for my phone. I need to sort this right now. *Straight away.* To think I even asked her to look after Teddy. Someone who's possibly an ex-convict. I couldn't feel any worse than I do at this moment.

'Hi Cassie. How are you? And how's Teddy? I got your message earlier.' Her voice is sing-song. Friendly. There's no reason for it not to be. Yet. At least she didn't notice me watching her journey from the charity shop.

'He's back with the childminder today.' I pause, steeling myself to go on.

'I'm glad he's better.'

Right, out with it. 'What can you tell me about Juniper Lodge Amy?'

There's a pause as the realisation seemingly sweeps over her. 'What do you mean?'

'I think you know what I mean.' My voice is shaking. 'Do *you* live there?'

'Have you been following me?' Her voice rises. As if she's questioning my audacity.

'Just answer the question. I need to know.'

She falls silent which can be nothing other than an admission that she does.

'What did you do Amy? Why are you living in a place like that?'

The line goes dead.

I prod at my phone screen to call her back. It goes straight to voicemail. Shit. I didn't even get around to telling her I don't want her walking Suki anymore. Perhaps I should go to the door of Juniper Lodge. But if she's hung up the phone on me, surely she's even less likely to come to the door? So for now, I'll go home. I'll make a coffee and work out what I'm going to do next.

Becca's looking through our letterbox as I turn the final corner to our house. Without even pulling onto the driveway, I bring the car to a stop at the side of the kerb.

'What the hell are you doing?' I demand as I slam the car door. I'm sick to death of being friendly and nice with people – it's time to start fighting back. Starting right now.

'I was just—' She bolts down the steps. I dart to the gate, blocking her exit.

'Just *what*? Looking for my husband?' I glance at his car on the drive. Clearly she doesn't know that he travels in by train. They must have been *her* knickers and *her* earring after all.

'I thought I saw someone hanging around,' she says.

'I don't believe you. I want to know what's going on between you and Jon?'

'I've no idea what you're talking about.'

It must have been *her* hanging around out here that first night when Suki was growling. Maybe it was *her* when Amy heard those noises upstairs as well. No wonder Jon's been telling me I'm imagining things.

'Oh I think you have. Come on Becca – you've been hostile since I moved in. I want the truth – are you and my husband having an affair?'

She snorts. 'You must be joking.'

'And what about Amy?' I continue. 'I've just found out she's living in some sort of prison-release hostel. Was it her who killed the girl in our house? Is that why you were telling me to stop digging?'

There's a wail from within Becca's house. 'I need to go to my mother,' she says.

'Not until you've given me some answers.'

'Let me past.' She tries to barge past me but I stand firm. 'I mean it – she might have fallen – I need to get back in there.'

There's another wail, louder this time.

'You haven't heard the last of this.' I've no choice other than to step to the side. And she hasn't. Though the situation with Amy is probably more pressing right now. Not only could she turn up at any moment, she's also still got a key.

TWENTY-SEVEN

CASSIE

I can't risk Amy having access to my home any longer. Without hesitation, I call three locksmith companies and the third one assures me they can arrive within the hour.

She only has the key for the front door but I make a request for the side door and the conservatory door to be changed as well. After all, if she *is* intending to do some kind of damage to my home or my family, she could have made copies.

I rifle through the kitchen drawer where we keep instructions for everything. Well, more to the point, where *Jon* keeps instructions for everything. I don't think I've ever looked at an instruction manual in my life. Eventually, I pull out the booklet for the house alarm and set about trying to steady my breathing as I try to decipher the tiny and complicated-looking print. Before I go any further with all this, I should let Jon know that I'm changing the alarm code and the locks. There again, if he *is* having an affair, maybe I should let him return home and not be able to get in. The prospect is both tempting and fearful in equal measure.

A thought suddenly blindsides me. What if *Becca's* the person who's been hanging around our old house after dark as well – maybe watching Jon. If there *is* something between them, that would make sense. The memory of Suki growling and that sense of being watched makes the back of my neck tingle. And not in a good way. I've had enough of it all. I really have had enough.

'Excellent work Cassie. So you've managed to employ *a convicted criminal* to enter our home, walk our dog *and* look after our son.' Jon sounds almost smug with what I've just told him about Juniper Lodge. He'll be thinking he's off the hook about Becca – that's what it will be.

'I'm not taking responsibility for this. *You* must have recognised her.'

'Why must I?'

'She grew up around here.'

'So what?'

'Presumably she was at the party you had? That's if it *was* the same girl who killed Jade Calvert.'

'I was eighteen for God's sake. Besides, there were lots of people at that party. Plus I'd been drinking.'

'Surely you'd remember a girl who bumped off another one. You're hardly likely to forget her.'

'There was lots of finger pointing at the time, but to be fair' – at least his voice has lost its sarcastic edge – 'I didn't really know the girl who was eventually arrested.'

I suppose what he's saying *could* be plausible. It's not as if photos of her were ever splashed across the press.

'As you already know from reading the articles,' he goes on, 'they wouldn't name her because she was still under eighteen.' I wonder if any of his colleagues are listening in to his conversation. They'll be wondering what he's talking about. Though on second thoughts, because he's got his own swanky office, he's probably alone.

'You must have at least remembered her name. Amy's not *that* common a name, is it?'

'Well, that's the thing. As far as I can recall, the girl everyone was blaming was called Amelia.'

'Amy. Amelia. They're not a million miles apart, are they? I still don't buy that you wouldn't be able to remember what she looks like?'

'Come on Cassie, it was years ago. Besides, if they gave her anonymity when she was sentenced, perhaps they've given her a new identity on being released. It happens, doesn't it?'

'Surely they'd have let you know when the girl was due for release from prison? After all it happened *here.*' I glance around the hallway. How can such a beautiful house harbour such an awful secret? How could Jon's parents have continued to live here after it all happened? I would have moved like a shot. However, they probably had a similar amount of empathy and sensitivity as Jon's got. After all, it was them who brought him up.

Perhaps I should get a vicar round here, or some kind of spiritual healer. All of a sudden the house in which I'd have gladly seen out my own days is wrapping me in a suffocating negative energy. I drag Jon's caddy of golf clubs from his office and stand it next to the front door. Just in case Amy turns up.

'The police *did* let me know. Well, they let Mum know and she told me. It was just before she died.'

'What? And you *still* didn't think to talk to me about any of it?'

'I had more important stuff going on then didn't I? Like my mother needing hospice care and having to sort this place out. Besides, it's all ancient history. At least I thought it was.'

'Why do you think she's come back here?'

Jon is silent for a moment, as though he's pondering my question. 'OK, if I'm honest—'

'It would make a nice change,' I cut in.

'I thought there was something familiar about her. I even asked her if we knew each other.'

'But you never acted on it, did you?' I walk into the lounge and check the outside from the window. 'Which makes you as bad as I am for not doing the checks. No – worse, in fact. You've probably put Teddy in danger just as much as I have.' The street is quiet apart from one of the neighbours getting their groceries delivered. Everyone's at work. I should be at work. 'The difference is that I didn't have a clue about Amy's possible background. What you've done is far worse – you had at least an inkling.'

'I wouldn't go that far,' Jon replies. 'I only thought she was *possibly* someone I might have gone to school with. Never would I have connected her to that same girl.'

'A girl,' I continue, 'capable of giving a lethal dose of keta-mine to another. It's a bit extreme for an seventeen-year-old, don't you think?' I glance towards next door where I stood trying to pummel Becca for information earlier this morning. 'How well does Becca know Amy anyway?'

Jon's pause tells me all I need to know.

'I caught her looking through the letterbox when I got back.'

'Got back from *where*?'

'Spying on Amy.'

'Shouldn't you have been at work? It's supposed to be your first week.'

'Says the man who didn't want me to take a job in the first place. How am I supposed to concentrate at work? I need answers Jon. In the last few days, I've discovered there was a murder in our new home, I've employed a dog walker who might or might not be responsible for it, I've got a husband who might be having an affair with the woman next door, who also seems to know more about the whole thing than she's prepared to tell.' I stop to catch my breath.

The truth is that I'm going back and forth in my head about

who those knickers and that earring might belong to. Jon may *not* be having an affair at all. Amy could even have planted them there to drive a wedge between Jon and me. She could be hatching some kind of plan – some vendetta back at the scene of her crime. I just wish I could find out the extent of it. And I haven't a clue how or where to begin to find out either. Before I can get any further with this, I need to get confirmation that Amy and the murderer of Jade are definitely one and the same person.

And no matter how much I go around in circles in my own mind, none of it explains why neither Jon nor Becca believed I had the right to know the truth.

'Becca only *thought* she'd recognised Amy,' Jon replies. 'That's what we were *really* discussing yesterday morning – whether it *could* be her or not. That was when you must have seen us talking.'

'You weren't talking. You were arguing.'

There's something in his tone which still doesn't add up. It's so frustrating.

'We were wondering what we were going to do about it,' he carries on. 'And I *was* going to tell you what we suspected but it's hardly the kind of revelation that can be blurted out over breakfast in front of Teddy, is it?'

'The question is what *are* we going to do about it?'

'Well, she can't continue walking Suki, that's for sure.'

'I know. That's why I'm getting the locks changed.'

'That's a little extreme, isn't it Cassie? Why don't you just take her key back from her?'

'Because I don't want to see her again. If part of her agenda was getting back into our house, she probably shouldn't even be out of prison. I'd love to know what she felt she could gain by it.'

'It might just be a game she's playing. Who knows what warped stuff goes on in the mind of someone who's killed someone.'

'Well whatever she's doing, this was the *crime scene.*' I glance at the blown-up photograph of my son on the wall. 'I'm going to let the police know she's been here – maybe they'll confirm whether Amy really *is* Amelia.'

'Hang on just a minute Cassie. Perhaps we—'

I cut him off before he can try talking me out of it. All he'll care about is what the other neighbours will think when they see the police out here. But all that matters is keeping me and my boy safe. Jon doesn't seem to give a shit about that – not really. I feel as though I've got to know him more in the short time we've lived in Tolbeck Cottage than in all the years we've been together.

And I'm done with dancing to his tune.

PART 4

AMY

TWENTY-EIGHT

AMY

Cassie wasn't supposed to discover who I am. Who I *was*. Not yet anyway. I can hardly believe that my cover has been blown so quickly. If it gets out, I'm not going to be safe around here. I'll be lynched, hounded out – maybe worse. I already have to look over my shoulder coming and going from the hostel. Like we all do.

I have to be extra vigilant as Jade's family still live in the same house. In their shoes I'd want to move away – make a new start, but I guess we all handle things differently. There was a time I thought I'd *never* return here but as the years passed by, I knew I would have to. Everyone who was part of my release process tried to talk me out of it but in the end, it was my decision.

I caught a glimpse of Jade's mother in the supermarket a few weeks ago. Our eyes met and there was a flicker of recognition in hers but she quickly returned to studying the wine shelves. If she'd remembered me, she'd have definitely scratched my eyes out. I longed to tell her she was blaming the wrong person but she wouldn't have believed me.

There's the other matter of my probation officer, who might

soon find out I've broken my licence conditions set around Tolbeck Cottage. I'll be recalled for sure. So I've got to do whatever is in my power to sort this mess out before she gets to me. It could be hours, or it could be days but one thing that's obvious is that things are coming to a head far more quickly than I'd planned for. I feel almost as desperate as I did all those years ago when there was only me and those responsible for me taking the blame who knew I was innocent of killing Jade Calvert.

Everything was looking up for me a few days ago, but it's all gone to shit again. It's been horrendous enough having to live in this grotty hostel – *and* under a curfew. Yes, I might have been released from my sentence early but I might as well still be under lock and key for the amount of freedom I've been afforded since I got out of prison.

Sometimes I fear I'll never be able to move forward with my life, even with this new identity. The events of ten years ago will always drag me back in time. Maybe I should have died in Jade's place. Everyone would have been satisfied then.

My phone's shrill ringtone slices into my miserable thoughts. The shit's hitting the fan sooner than I envisaged. It's Judy, my bloody probation officer. I'm not due to speak to her until the end of the week since I only saw her on Friday. She was about to move me to fortnightly contact as well. I've blown everything.

It's too much of a coincidence that Cassie's found out where I live and, within a couple of hours, Judy's trying to get hold of me. Until today, she's only ever arranged to meet me or speak to me on the phone at pre-appointed times.

I let her call ring off, then stare at my screen for a moment waiting for a red circle to appear next to voicemail. I'm relieved when nothing happens. If Judy knew something, *really* knew something, she would have at the very least left a message telling me to call her back.

Within a few minutes, however, the sound of the office phone reverberates along the corridor. I hold my breath but thankfully, it sounds as if it's rung off. I've only just managed to catch my breath when my mobile bursts back into life.

This time when it stops, the dreaded red bubble *does* appear next to the voicemail icon. I gaze at the screen, knowing as soon as I play the message, everything gets even more serious than it is already.

'*Amy, you need to contact me urgently. I've just tried calling you at the charity shop as well as Juniper Lodge. I'm coming to the hostel to see you shortly. If you're not already there, please get back straight away.*'

Then a text.

We need to speak asap. As soon as I've finished up my current meeting, I'll be setting off to Juniper Lodge.

In a surge of frustration, I hurl the handset to the floor before stamping on it. Enough. I have had enough.

As if I'm going to hang around here for the ticking time bomb that is my probation officer. Her next port of call will probably be to call the police – if she hasn't already. I need to get out of here.

I'm going to be recalled to prison as soon as she's done the paperwork. I don't need *Judy* to tell me how spectacularly I've breached my licence conditions. I can't take on work, any work, without her approval, even walking a dog. But even more important than that, I shouldn't have been *anywhere near* Tolbeck Cottage or Jon's family, and I especially shouldn't have been in charge of a four-year-old.

So yes, there's only one place I'm going when they catch me. Then a feeling washes over me – one of power and determination. *If* they catch me. I can't allow it to happen.

Before it gets to that point I'm going to confront the one

person who can help me turn this all around. If only I can get her to listen.

This might be my final chance to walk up Cherry Tree Lane unchallenged. My final chance to walk up *any* lane until I've served out the remainder of my sentence. *Another ten years!* I can't let that happen. No way. I'll go insane. I would rather die than go back to prison.

A sharp jolt stops me in my tracks as I notice the van parked in front of Cassie's Mini. *LS Joinery and Locksmiths.* Misery pools in my chest as I realise that she couldn't even bring herself to ask me for the key back. She'd rather shell out what could be hundreds of pounds, instead of having to face me again. I'm not putting up with this. I've been punished over and over again in the last decade and it feels like I'll be punished forever. I'll make her listen if it's the last thing I do. I am not a killer. I am *not* guilty. I never was.

I'd even thought Cassie and me could have been friends – albeit in different circumstances. She's the only person in a long time who's shown me any trust. Maybe *ever*. It's been a struggle at times not to allow a *real* friendship to develop between us – I've really had to hold myself in check. I'm never going to give up on saving myself, no matter what it takes – perhaps there *is* something I can still do to prevent the inevitable. I must fight, with every ounce of strength left in me, to change my fate.

I bend as I pretend to adjust my shoe, while sneaking a glance towards Becca's house to make sure she isn't watching from a window or her garden. Miraculously, there's no sign of her.

The workman's busy messing around with the lock on Cassie's front door so while he's got his back to me, I sneak along the driveway past Jon's SUV.

I reach over the top of the side gate for the bolt and gently slide it across. Even if it had been locked, I'd have wheeled the bin to it and climbed over. The locksmith's cheerful whistle grates on my nerves, but one good thing about his noise is the reassurance that at least he's busy and out of my way.

'He's sorting it now,' I hear Cassie saying. I freeze as I realise she's in the conservatory. My heart pounds in my chest as I crouch out of sight, straining my ears for every word she utters. I'll wait until she's finished speaking before I make my presence known.

'Yeah, they said they'd be here in the next hour or so. Look, I'm sorting it – like *you* should have done years ago.'

She must be on the phone to *him*. The door's propped open with the box of photos. Why is she having the conservatory lock changed as well? I've only got the key to the front door. Then it dawns on me. She truly does mistrust and fear me. She clearly has no idea of what I might or might not be capable of. She's exactly the same as everyone else. Which is all I've ever known. Yet she seemed so *different*. I'm gutted that she's automatically assumed the worst of me.

'Yes, I suppose so,' she continues. 'All I want is to go forward as well.'

It's alright for you, I want to bellow at the top of my lungs. *You've stopped me from going anywhere other than back to a locked cell.* Though I guess she's as hoodwinked by Jon as everyone else always has been.

'Alright – just get back here, will you? Alright – I'll see you then.'

A mix of anger and envy churns within me as I witness their façade of normality. He doesn't deserve to keep going as he has. Jon Hemingway deserves nothing less than what's coming to him.

TWENTY-NINE

AMY

'Cassie.' I stand in the space where the door's ajar. 'Can we talk for a minute?'

She leaps to her feet and lunges at the door but I beat her to it.

'You shouldn't be here. Didn't you do enough damage in this house ten years ago?'

She's heard the so-called truth. She knows what I was found guilty of. 'Look, whatever you've heard about me, none of it's true. I'm just trying to find a way to prove it, if only you'll help me.'

She steps back and grabs her phone, still lit up, from the chair arm. 'So you haven't just spent ten years in prison for murder then?' She looks from her phone into my face. I hate what I can see in her eyes. I'm sick of people looking at me as though I'm something they stepped in.

I jab a trembling finger at the phone in her hand. 'Don't call the police Cassie. It wasn't me. Please. I swear to you that it wasn't *me* who killed Jade Calvert. I can prove it, I promise. I just need your help to find something.'

She laughs – a sound like shards of glass as it echoes around the conservatory. 'Isn't that the classic prison line? We can chat all day if you like, but the police are already en route – they'll arrive any second now.'

The reality of what I'm facing sweeps over me. I'm done for here. I'm going back to prison again. Twenty years for someone else's crime. 'The police? What have you called them for?'

'To give them a statement. How the hell could I have been so stupid? I thought I could trust you, Amy.'

She's just as bad as everyone else. A surge of anger courses through me, swiftly followed by an overwhelming tide of sorrow. Of course she doesn't believe me. Nobody ever has.

I've got a choice here. I either hang around until I inevitably get bundled into the back of a van, or I get the hell away from here. Right now. Somehow, I'll come up with a way to save myself.

As I dash back to the gate and check over it, a police car swiftly pulls up at the end of their drive. I lock eyes with one of the officers, who gives me a half smile – she must think I'm Cassie.

I jump back and glance into the conservatory. Cassie's no longer there; presumably she's on her way to the front door to get help from the locksmith. Because I'm obviously a dangerous killer who should be back in prison. Tears blind me as I stumble away.

I hurtle to the end of the garden, panic rising in my chest as my leg grazes a nail, tearing my jeans. I clamber over the top of the gate into the park. My heart pounds in my ears, drowning out the distant sounds of dog walkers and young mums with prams as I weave in and out of them all. Several of them titter with disapproval but they let me through. They'll have something to titter about later when it comes out that they've allowed a convicted killer to get past them. Convicted, yes. Guilty, no.

The ground beneath my trainers alternates between soft grass and hard pavement as an energy I've never felt before takes over. I don't dare to look back, focusing only on putting as much distance between me and that house as possible. What the hell am I going to do now? I can't go back to the hostel. I can't go anywhere. My life, if it can even be called that, is well and truly over. I'm going to have to do something drastic.

With my chest threatening to explode, I eventually seek refuge beneath the bridge, a place that used to be frequented by smoking and drinking teenagers. It probably still is. Here, in temporary safety, I gather my thoughts and ponder my next move.

It's all Cassie's fault that my probation officer has found out about the breach of my licence conditions. It's all her fault that the police are soon to be searching for me. Why couldn't she have come to me? Talked to me first? She'd rather believe anything but the truth. They'll all be saying things to her like, *Don't worry. We'll have her back in custody soon. You've done the right thing, calling us.*

She and Jon will go back to living their perfect little life while pretending I never existed, in their perfect neighbourhood with their perfect son.

Teddy.

He's the one way I *can* gain some leverage although it hinges, at least to start with, on him being back with his child-minder today. There was no sign of him at the house before so he could be. A plan begins to formulate inside my mind. It's a long shot but it's one I've got to try.

'Hi again.' My voice is as bright as a saleswoman's, and my smile is probably brighter. 'Cassie's asked me to collect Teddy for her.'

'Really?' She twists her watch towards her face, the skin on her upper arm wobbling with the movement. '*At this time?*'

He *is* here. Hurdle number one is cleared. The familiar panic returns to my chest. It feels so tight I can barely breathe.

'Yeah. He's got a birthday party to get to.' I fight to keep my voice on an even keel. 'She'd apparently forgotten all about it until she was reminded by the other mum an hour ago.'

'Right.' The woman doesn't look convinced.

'It's at one of their neighbours', but Cassie's stuck in meetings all afternoon. That's why she rang me to pick Teddy up for her again.'

'I see.' She frowns. 'I've not heard anything from her though.'

'She's going to give you a call when her current meeting's over. When she rang me, she only had a moment, then she had to get back in there.'

'And when will that be?'

'In about an hour, she said.' Hopefully she can't sense the fact that I'm a jangling wreck with what I'm doing here. Hopefully she can't hear the dryness of my mouth as I speak. I look at her, silently pleading with her for her to just let me take him. Then if I take him to somewhere only I know where he is, I'll call Cassie to see me there. She'll have to listen to me then.

'Well, I—'

'To be honest,' I continue, 'Cassie's lucky really I just worked the morning today. And it's fortunate I just happened to be out with their dog when she called to ask. I came straight here for her.'

Teddy beams at me from behind her legs then creeps nearer to the door. 'Where's Mummy?'

'She's still at work.' I reach forward and ruffle his hair. If only to demonstrate how familiar we are with one another.

'Why are *you* here?'

'Because we've got somewhere *very* exciting to go. A party.' I pull a face to convey my supposed excitement. If only I really were picking him up to take him to a party. If only my life was anything else than what it's become.

'Wow.'

'Do you want to go to it?'

'For jelly and ice cream?'

'Of course. You'll have to get your coat on though.'

He dashes off – it looks as though I'm home and dry here. There's just Hazel to convince. She still looks very unsure.

As my heart races, the childminder beckons me inside. 'Can you just come in a moment – Amy, is it?' Her voice trembles with uncertainty, adding to my own tension. Maybe I'm not as home and dry as I'd hoped.

'Erm yes. But why?' I tap at my wrist. 'We could do with getting going to be honest. We don't want to miss the start of the party, do we Teddy?'

I smile down at him as he returns to the hallway trying to thread his arms into his inside-out coat.

He shakes his head and beams at me.

'I need to double-check with his mum before you take him. To be on the safe side.'

'It's fine. It's not as if I haven't collected him before.' My voice must be too firm, as she looks at me through narrowed eyes.

'It's not fine. I take safeguarding children in my care *very* seriously.'

Safeguarding. This woman has clearly got the same low opinion of me as everyone else. The only people who know I'm incapable of hurting a fly are the ones who forced me into this predicament in the first place.

'But as I said – Cassie's in a meeting. She probably won't answer.' Nevertheless, I follow them inside, wondering how on earth I'm going to swing this. I can't let her make the phone call. *How the hell am I going to stop her?* 'And we'll be late if we don't get going.'

'I want jelly and ice cream.' Teddy's managed to put his coat on.

'I'll try his father then.'

'He's unlikely to know anything.' I laugh. 'You know what men are like.' Shit. Shit. Shit.

'If you could just wait there please.' She points to the door-mat, fixing her gaze on me like I'm a speck of dirt on her carpet. I'm not even good enough for her to ask through to her lounge. 'I'll only keep you waiting for a few minutes.'

She disappears into the room, battling her way through toys and children playing on the carpet before closing another door behind her. Presumably she doesn't want me overhearing whoever she ends up getting through to. There's nothing I can do to stop her. There's only one thing I can do.

I beckon to Teddy. 'Are these yours?' I point at the frog wellies he was wearing at the park.

He nods.

'We don't want to miss the start of the games, do we? Are you a very fast runner?'

He nods again, grins and reaches for the hand I extend to him. Then silently, I twist the latch on the door and away we go.

THIRTY

AMY

I loathe the musty smell of old clothes, many from house clearances of the recently deceased. Who wants to walk in a dead person's shoes? Not me. I've been walking in shoes not meant for me for long enough.

Teddy hovers in the doorway, his face falling as we get our breath back. 'Is it the party?' His cheeks are pink from running for the last fifteen minutes. I can hardly believe what I've done – taking Teddy was never part of my plan but what else could I have done? I'm running out of options.

'It's going to be.' I lock the door behind us. I always knew this key would come in handy at some point. Sandra, the shop manager, assumed it had been swept up amongst the mountain of donations we sift through. Instead of bothering to look for it, she just got another one cut. I once asked if I could have one for the mornings I'm early and forced to wait in the rain. Her reply was not until I'm no longer on licence. However, my plan has always been to be long gone by then. One way or another.

Teddy scans the room and I follow his gaze over all the bags and boxes. 'Will it be the party *soon?*' His voice is heavy with disappointment.

'It'll be starting real soon.' I tug the velvet curtain across the steamed-up window and flick the light on. 'We'll move all this stuff out of the way when the party starts.'

'I want Mummy.' He heads back to the door. I rush back there too, removing the key from the lock and dropping it into my pocket. I feel dreadful for what I'm doing here, effectively imprisoning him in this stockroom with me. This is how desperate the situation has become.

'I know – she'll be here soon. I tell you what, why don't we play our own game while we're waiting for everyone?'

'OK.' He brightens.

One thing we're not short of in this place is board games. However, I can't risk going through to the shop to get one. Anyone could be walking past and the window remains lit up all the time, even when we're closed. We'll have to make do with whatever we can find in here. I slide a Connect Four box from beneath a pile donated yesterday. 'Do you know how to play this one?'

He shakes his head.

I look into his blue eyes, earnestly trusting that I'm going to look after him here. And of course I will. I'm not the monster they think I am. Teddy's a good kid. Jon doesn't deserve him.

'I'll teach you how to play it.'

I show him how to set up the frame, and how to separate the colours, then I watch absently as he takes a few minutes sorting out the pieces. *Red, yellow, one for me, one for you.*

It's such an ordinary thing for us to be doing in such an out-of-the-ordinary set of circumstances. And the seriousness of what I've done is threatening to swallow me whole.

He drops another counter in. 'Is it the party soon?'

I check my watch. We've only killed ten minutes. 'Just a bit longer.'

His shoulders slump as he looks up at me, suddenly looking younger than his four years. I realise even more the responsibility that I've heaped on myself here. 'I'm hungry and I want my mummy.'

'We'll see her very soon,' I say, loading as much enthusiasm into my voice as I can. 'While we wait for her, I know where there's some biscuits.' I rummage through one of the bags until my fingers brush against a small packet. I tear it open and the sweet aroma of chocolate chip cookie fills the air.

He perks up slightly. I imagine most children would at the mention of cookies. Not that I've ever had the chance to have anything much to do with children. How could I have done when I've spent the last ten years locked up for something I didn't do?

I find him some Lego which he seems momentarily content with. I lean against the steaming machine, watching him. *What on earth am I doing here?*

As impulsive as I've always been, I've taken a child from his minder without even having a serious plan or anything proper for him to eat. I never thought beyond the actual taking of him; I guess I didn't really believe I'd be able to pull it off. I wonder if Cassie has tried to collect him yet? Or if Hazel managed to get through to her or Jon to raise the alarm. Whatever the situation, I've little doubt they'll have involved the police by now. I'm going to be in even deeper shit than I already was – I've got to turn this around. Somehow, I've got to use the fact that I'm the only one who knows where Teddy is to force the truth out of Jon.

I peer at the clock. News is always read on the half hour by the station I usually listen to when I'm sorting and steaming in here. I hit the power button on the radio, silently praying nothing's been reported yet. I need time – I desperately need more time.

'Mummy sings this song.' Teddy looks sad as he looks from me to the door. 'Is she coming now?'

'Have another biscuit.' I thrust the packet at him, hoping for distraction. 'Eat them all if you're hungry.' There's only so long I can keep this up. *What am I going to do?*

'*This is your drive-time news at five-thirty on Friday, twenty-fourth March. The top story this evening is that a nationwide alert has been issued for the disappearance of four-year-old Theodore Hemingway, who is known to his family as Teddy.*'

Oh my God. It's out there already. *A nationwide search.* I suppose it would be. I am, after all, on the face of it, a convicted killer. I turn the radio right down and press my ear up against it. Although he's only four, Teddy seems bright and I don't want him suspecting that anything's more wrong than he possibly already suspects. He seems engrossed in the Lego and doesn't appear to have heard his name being mentioned.

'*Teddy Hemingway was abducted from his childminder's home on the west side of Rawdale in Yorkshire approximately an hour ago. He was taken by Amy Jarvis, a woman known to the police and already wanted in connection with another matter.*

'*We would appeal to Amy, if she's listening to this bulletin, to contact West Yorkshire Police immediately, in order that we can get this little boy safely back to his parents.*

'*Teddy has blonde hair, blue eyes and is wearing a* Thomas the Tank Engine *hooded top, blue jeans and green frog wellies. He is wearing a navy blue three-quarter length coat.*'

I look at his feet. I should have considered this before. If we end up back on the move from here, I'll have to find some less attention-grabbing footwear in the children's donations we've had to the shop. That's if I dare to move him from here. I don't know what to do – I really don't know what I'm going to do.

'*Amy is twenty-eight years old, with long light brown hair and blue eyes. She is around five feet, six inches, of very slim build and is wearing dark coloured jeans, and an oversized grey woollen coat.*

'As the pair are believed to be on foot, the search is currently being concentrated around the local area. Public transport and private hire operators have been informed of the missing pair and the public are urged to be on the lookout for them. Please report any sightings immediately by calling 999. We will keep you updated on this story.'

The weight of guilt and the possible consequences suddenly hang around my neck like a noose, tightening with each passing moment. *What have I done?* I'm not going to hurt him – I could never hurt anybody, yet that's what everyone will be thinking. I'm surprised they haven't mentioned my conviction yet. It's probably only a matter of time.

'Need a drink.' Teddy looks up from the Lego, his mouth full of crumbs.

I really hadn't prepared for all this – for the fact that he'd be hungry and thirsty. I open the mini fridge, just about big enough to store a milk carton and a sandwich. There's the dregs of some milk, and that's it – there's barely enough to make a cup of tea.

'There's only water, I'm afraid,' I tell him, while searching for something he can drink it from. I'm feeling guiltier by the minute. If only Teddy didn't have to be caught up in all this. But it's not as if I had many other options to choose from. The minute Cassie involved the police, she ruined everything.

'Don't like it.'

'I'm sorry. It's all there is.' I haven't felt this level of stress and anxiety since the day I was sentenced ten years ago. It's reached fever pitch today, probably because I'm only too aware of the likelihood I now have of returning to where I've only just been released from. It feels more as though I'm punishing myself with what I've done so far. And I don't know what to do next.

Teddy's bottom lip wobbles. 'I want my mummy.'

If I'm not careful, he's going to start screaming the place down and this is a well-walked route through the day – though I'm not so sure about night-time. I fiddle about with the radio until I find something that passes for music, then check around for something else to distract him.

'How about some cars?' My eyes fall on a box that the manager wants to sort through for her grandson before she puts them in the shop. All kids like cars, surely?

'Need a wee-wee.'

I lean against the wall as he stands at the staff toilet. It's looking as though we'll have to stay in this stockroom all night. But someone will open up in the morning and find us, so we need to be out by then, at the very latest. At least I can keep him safe and warm overnight but past that, I haven't a clue.

I need to get my act together, and quickly. I could use the landline and perhaps pose some kind of monetary condition in exchange for their son's safe return. They're not to know I wouldn't harm a hair on his head. Enough money to get out of the country. No, that's a stupid idea – the call would be traced here immediately. Plus, every port and airport would be on alert. Besides, I haven't even got a passport – it's not like I've needed one in the last ten years.

I tuck the phone out of sight. I'm not sure why it suddenly comes to me but a vision of the insulin in Cassie and Jon's en suite bathroom cabinet emerges in my mind. There's every chance they could have taught Teddy how to call for help if it was ever needed. I don't think I've got much longer before he starts to really get upset.

Since I've got the leverage of being the only person who knows her son's whereabouts, I'd possibly be better confronting Cassie directly, one on one. All I know is that somehow, I've got to get her on side and make her believe my version of everything that happened. Or at least get her to consider it – for her own sake as much as mine. As for Jon, I won't be happy until he's exactly where he should be. And then, there's the other person who's a factor in all this. Becca.

I slide the curtain back a fraction. Part of me expects swirling blue lights, raised voices and mayhem out there. But now all the shops are closed for the night, everything is dark and still. I fill the chipped mug with more water and I watch Teddy for a moment. He seems reasonably happy with the cars for now and is lining them up across the floor. His clothes are dirty from it and he stares up at me with sorrowful eyes. Fresh guilt tugs at me.

'Is Mummy here?'

'Not yet.' I can't just wait here, doing nothing. Sooner or later we're going to be found in here. I've got to act while I've still got the chance. 'I tell you what. I'll go and find out where she is and I'll bring her back. She might be lost.'

'Out there?' He points at the door.

'Yes. I just need to tell her where you are.'

'Can I come?' Teddy's eyes widen as he drops the cars he's been playing with.

'No, you wait here. I promise I won't be very long. I'll be back before you know it.' I'm trying to convince myself of this more than him.

'I'm scared.' Tears fill his eyes.

I waver. Can I really leave this little boy all on his own in here? I haven't really got any choice.

'There's nothing to be scared of.' I step towards him and ruffle his hair. 'You play with the cars for a few more minutes, and I'll be back with your mummy before you know it.' I can hardly believe I'm doing what I'm about to do.

I lurch to the door before I can change my mind, sliding the key from my pocket as I go. The bottom line is that Teddy's perfectly safe in here and most importantly, only I know where he is. This gives me something to barter with and right now, it's all I've got. As I unlock and open the door, he springs from his position on the floor. But I've closed it and I'm locking him in before he can reach me, feeling like the cruellest person on the planet.

The cold air stabs at the back of my throat as I struggle to get my breath again. I stride away from the door with the echo of him shouting *Mummy* in my ears. Oh my God. What am I doing? I've left that poor little four-year-old all on his own. I couldn't hate myself any more than I do in this moment. But it's either this, or I go back to prison.

THIRTY-ONE

AMY

As I turn the corner into Cherry Tree Lane, my heart pounds in my chest, matching the rhythm of my frantic footsteps. I flip my hood over my head, trying to conceal my identity, but it can't shield me from the guilt gnawing at my conscience at how I've left Teddy. How I'm going to scramble from the hole I've dug, I really don't know. This is my last chance at saving myself from being sent back to prison, and the weight of that reality bears down on me. Doubts and regrets swarm my mind, but I've come too far to turn back now.

It certainly won't be as dignified as merely being 'recalled' now. Instead I'll be held face-down to the floor, snapped into handcuffs and slung into one of those dreadful cubicles in the back of a van. I can't let it happen. Once I've been locked up again, I've no chance of ever being able to clear my name.

There are three police cars and a news van outside Tolbeck Cottage. Clearly the consensus is that Teddy's at terrible risk. That was never part of my plan. They all think I'm a terrible monster and they couldn't be further from the truth. I was as much a victim as Jade was. I was jealous of her, yes. Really jealous. But never in a million years would I have spiked her drink.

Somehow, I've got to prove it. I shouldn't have gone anywhere near that party. I couldn't have done anything to save Jade but I could have saved myself. But now that the police are involved, my original plan of finding what I needed to in that house and getting between Cassie and Jon so I can expose the truth and clear my name has gone to shit.

But it's not as though I can just waltz in there and demand that I'm listened to and taken seriously. I need leverage, and Teddy is the only person who can offer me that. It's extremely risky, using him as a bargaining tool like this and my success relies on a balance between persuasive threats and desperate measures. I'll do whatever it takes to put everything right. This is my last chance.

It's not as if I can hang around out here either; the longer I linger, the greater the likelihood that someone will see me and I won't get the opportunity to change *anything*. So I backtrack and dart into the snicket that leads to the darkness of the park, my heart as heavy as the day I was first locked up. I've come full circle in more ways than one. I can't go back there. I'd rather die than go back to prison.

I've been dicing with danger ever since returning to this house, to where it all began. But I set my sights on doing this while I was still in prison – I could often think of little else than clearing my name. Tonight is my final stab at revealing the truth. And as I've now proven with what I've done with Teddy, I'm prepared to do whatever it takes.

I crouch behind a bush before entering the main part of the park, expecting barking dogs, probing torches and expectant voices. But there's none of that. I'd have thought the police would be combing every inch of the park behind Teddy's house by now. I expect they soon will be.

I end up in exactly the same spot I hid in when they'd first moved in – when Teddy was safely tucked up in his bed watching TV, rather than being locked on his own in a charity shop storeroom. A pang of remorse needles at me as the look on his face as I left him floods my mind. He's perfectly innocent in all this yet has ended up caught in the crossfire of my desperate bid for the truth to be heard. But I've only done what I had to do and I'll get him out of there as quickly as I possibly can.

The air is heavy with mist and the rustle of trees echoes my own terrified breath. Every snap of a twig and distant hoot of an owl seems to echo louder than it normally would. The darkness of the park surrounds me like a cloak as I crouch behind the bush. It's the calm before the storm.

It's not clear what, if anything, is going on inside the house. Shadows move behind the new kitchen blinds, blinds that probably cost as much money as I'm entitled to in a year in my current situation. Because of my conviction, I can't even get a proper job to alleviate things. As if anyone would want to employ me anyway. As soon as I get to the box about criminal convictions and having to disclose what I've supposedly done and where I've been for the last ten years, it's over and out for me. Which is why the stakes are so high and why what I'm doing here *has* to work out, no matter how slim the chance.

I imagine Cassie and Jon pacing the kitchen floor in anguish. She'll be clutching a glass of wine, while he'll be hollering at the police to get out there and find his son. He's probably blaming her – that's the sort of man he really is. I was concerned when I got out and discovered Jon had married. There was no way he'd have become any less of a threat with age – he was only going to get worse. That's why I had to find their old house – make sure it was safe. All the time she and Suki sensed the presence of someone, it was me. But I didn't wish any harm. Not to her, anyway. There was many a time I heard Jon shouting at her when they were still in their old house. Just as I am now, I'd be crouched in the shadows, dying to intervene, knowing that sooner or later I'd have to step up but being totally powerless to do anything. I'm sorry I scared her now. Hopefully I'll get the chance to tell her that I was part keeping an eye on her, part working out how I was going to find a way into her life.

Jon's face floods my mind; it's contorted with impatience and anger over the fact that Teddy's missing and he can't do anything about it. He's always got everything he's ever wanted, either through manipulation or through commanding his desired outcome with money. He therefore won't be accustomed to things being so out of his control.

Unless someone discovers Teddy at the charity shop, there's only one way their son will be returned this evening. And soon I'll have the chance to spell it out.

Becca's in her kitchen window. I wonder if she knows what's going on yet. She must do. No doubt, she'll have been one of the first people to be asked whether she saw anything out of the ordinary earlier today or if she's noticed me hanging around. However, I'm certain she won't want to be dragged into this mess. Not for a second time.

Which is tough.

I crawl through a gap in her hedge and emerge behind the shed. So far, so good. Then remaining on my hands and feet, I pick my way through the shadows at the edge of her garden until I reach the rear of the house.

I need to move on this – it's now or never. I rise to my feet and softly tap at the back door, praying Becca answers straight away.

She does.

The moment the door parts ways with the frame, I burst forward, sending her catapulting into the cooker with my sudden force. Then simultaneously, I kick the door shut with my foot while wrenching a knife from the block.

I've got her exactly where I want her.

THIRTY-TWO

AMY

'What the hell are you doing?' Becca presses herself against the cooker, not taking her eyes away from the glint of the knife.

'I need you to tell the truth.' I step closer to her. I want her to be in no doubt that I'll use it in order to get her to do what I need her to. I grip it tighter, my hands trembling with adrenaline and fear. I can't ignore the fact that the consequences of failure here are unimaginable.

'Mu—' The word begins to form itself at her lips.

'Be quiet, I mean it.' I place my hand across her mouth. The knife wobbles in the grip of my other hand but I doubt she'll notice that. 'I don't want to hurt you, or your mother, but I will if you force me to.'

'What do you want?' Her words are muffled beneath my hand.

She probably thinks I'm here for money to get away with. Though even I know I'd be lucky to get to the edge of Rawdale. All I want is the resolution I should have had years ago.

'You're going to get Cassie over here right now, then we're all going to have a nice little chat.' I lower my hand from her mouth.

'What do you mean?' Her eyes momentarily flit from mine to the blade. I feel dreadful threatening another person with a knife like this but I'd have got nowhere without it.

'You're going to explain to Cassie why you told all those lies ten years ago. And why you've been continuing to do so ever since.'

'I... I can't do that.' She inches herself to my left as she speaks, seemingly trying to edge herself towards the door into the hallway.

'Keep still, do you hear me?' My voice is a hiss but I don't raise it. I don't need to with this knife in my hand.

'After you've told Cassie the truth,' I continue, 'you're going to tell the police. You're going to make a full statement.'

'Where's their son?' Her face darkens. 'What have you done with him?' So she *does* know.

'He's safe.'

'But where is he?'

I'm gripping the knife so tightly, my hand's beginning to ache. This could go badly wrong for me at any moment. Catastrophically wrong, in fact. However, before I face Cassie, Jon *or* the police, I need to hear Becca's explanation for why she did what she did to me.

'What was ever in it for you? That's what I've never been able to understand.'

'It's all a long time ago now. I can't think. I don't—'

'I'll repeat my question shall I?' I hold the knife higher. She doesn't know I've no intention of using it. 'Why *did* you do what you did to me? Why did you ruin my life?'

'My mum's upstairs, you know. She'll have heard what's going on down here. She'll have called the police. If you run for it now, you'll—'

'Your mother's too far gone to do that. I've seen the carers coming and going. I've heard them talking. She doesn't even know what day of the week it is.' I poke the tip of the knife right up to her chin, feeling powerful, yet as though I've been taken over. This is what it's all come to. I've locked a little boy in the charity shop and I'm holding a knife against someone's throat. I can hardly believe it.

'You're going to end up back in prison for all this, *Amelia*, you know that, don't you?' She stares straight into my eyes, her gaze unwavering. She obviously suspects I won't use the knife on her. That's because, really, she *knows* me. Yet all I see in her eyes is unadulterated hatred. It's all I ever see from *anyone*.

Her calling me Amelia evokes a melancholy so deep it almost winds me. Part of me isn't Amelia anymore, yet another part of me longs to return to the person I was meant to be.

'My name's *Amy* now.' My voice is a snarl. 'And as we both know, *Becca*, you're one of the only people in a position to prevent me from being sent back there.'

'You'll be going back there anyway. It doesn't matter what I say to the police. Not just for taking Teddy and threatening me like this. But stalking's a crime too, you know.'

I don't respond which she seems to take as an invitation to continue.

'I've watched you, hanging around outside here every evening. And I've noticed you spending hours on end inside their house.' She rolls her eyes in its direction. 'What were you hoping to achieve in there? That's what I want to know.'

At least we've got a dialogue of sorts going on. But within the next few moments, things have to move to the next stage.

'To get to *him*, that's what. To find something in there that proves I'm innocent. As *you* very well know I am.' I pull the knife back as I jab my finger at her. 'Which is where you're going to come in.'

What I don't add is I haven't known *exactly* what I'm looking for in their house. Any shred of evidence that might have helped me to clear my name would have been a start. One thing I've been looking for all along is revenge. At least I've been able to upend Jon's smug and privileged life. And from what I've seen of how he treats Cassie, she might eventually thank me for unmasking him and setting her free.

Ever since I was released, I've been biding my time, knowing I've got to get in and amongst the Hemingways, always knowing it would be easier from the inside. It was almost too easy to get Cassie to trust me. But I expected it to last longer than it did.

'Perhaps this is what I should have done in the first place.' I snarl the words into Becca's face. '*Forced* you to tell the truth – the moment I found out you still lived here.' It's true. I've been messing about, wondering how to go about proving my innocence to make sure things are watertight, and look where that's got me.

I'd got the shock of my life when Cassie initially introduced me to Becca. So did she, judging by the expression on her face. I thought she'd be long gone from around here. She must have suspected there was every chance she'd eventually have to face up to the lies she'd told back then, as well as the testimony she swore to.

'There's no way you can prove *anything*. You never could, Amelia, which is why *you* got sentenced. *Everyone* said *you'd* killed Jade.'

'But it was you, wasn't it, who provided the *killer* statement? You know as well as I do who should have rightfully been serving my time. How could you have said you'd actually watched me spike her drink like that, when it was a complete lie?'

I notice her eyes flit to the side as she says, 'Alexa, call 999.'

THIRTY-THREE

AMY

As her phone lights up at the other side of the counter, it takes a moment for me to react. I lunge at it and hit the end call button, praying it hasn't connected. Becca takes the opportunity to rush to the door. Dropping the phone, I get there at the same time as her.

'No! Please!' I grab her arm with my free hand and push her up against the door. 'Please, Becca – I need you to help me, that's the only reason I'm doing this.'

'You wouldn't use that knife. You wouldn't have the guts.' Though she still surrenders herself against the door. After all, she's probably aware of how panicked I am now. And desperate people do desperate things.

'That's because I'm not a killer, am I?'

The room feels suffocating, our heavy breaths echoing around the walls as we lock eyes and breathe into one another's faces. 'Am I?' I raise my voice slightly.

'What is it you're trying to do here?' Becca sounds almost exasperated that I'm taking up her precious time.

'You're going to help me clear my name.'

'You're out of prison now, for God's sake. It's all ancient history.' Becca shuffles to the left and so do I. 'Everyone's getting on with their lives. You should just get on with yours.'

'I haven't got a life.' These words sound so hopeless. But I'm not giving up yet. Until those handcuffs are snapped on my wrists, I've got to keep fighting to get one again. 'I'll ask you again Becca. All I need is for you to tell the truth. You don't know how desperate I am. How do you even sleep at night, after what you've done?'

'Why are you dragging it all up again? The past should be left to rest now.'

'It's so easy for you, isn't it? You're not having to live under a curfew in a grotty probation hostel, are you? You're not having to go by a different name, not able to tell anyone who you really are in case you get beaten up. Or hounded out of town. So no, I don't have much of a life to be getting on with as it happens.'

Lights move against the wall of the kitchen as though a vehicle is turning in the street. With my hand containing the knife still outstretched towards Becca, I use the other one to inch the curtain in the window of the door to the side. There's only one car and the news van out there now. It could be an unmarked police car, or it could be *anyone*. It's time for me to stop messing around in here – it's time to act. If I don't, it's going to be too late.

'Tell me what you want me to do, Amelia.' She still isn't taking her eyes off the knife.

'Stop calling me that.'

I can't be Amelia anymore – and do I even want to go back to being the lonely teenager who scrabbled for scraps from so-called friends and potential boyfriends? The memory settles heavily in the centre of my being. But at least Amelia had the chance of a future. She could have gone to college or university. She could have travelled, she could even have had a great career. Ugly ducklings *do* become swans. She could have even been a wife and mother by now. But all that was snatched away. And it's time to make those responsible pay for what they've done to me.

I fish in my pocket for the scrap of paper with Cassie's number scribbled on it – it's been there since the day we met at the park. 'I want you to send Cassie a text.'

'Why?' Becca looks baffled.

'You're going to tell her to get round here. Straight away. *On her own.*'

'She's not going to listen to me.'

'She will. You're going to let Cassie know that coming around here and *on her own* is her only chance of getting Teddy back safely.'

'OK.' Her voice lifts. She's probably relieved that things are moving forward. 'Let me get to my phone then.'

Still pointing the knife at her, I reach down to the floor to retrieve her phone. 'I'll tell you what to write.' I pass it to her. 'Right. Do as I say. Unlock it.'

Her fingers hesitate over the screen, uncertainty flashing in her eyes as she seems to contemplate her next move.

'Just do it.'

'What do you want me to write?'

She'd better not do anything unexpected. My freedom is dangling by a thread here. She could quite easily do that 'Alexa' thing again. The technology is another reminder of all I missed while I've been inside. Looking at how quickly her phone lit up before, it seems that all it would take is a connection to the emergency services for them to be able to trace it straight back here.

'Write, *It's Becca. I need to speak to you urgently about your son. Come straight here now – on your own and not with Jon. Teddy's at serious risk if you say a word to anyone, especially the police.*'

She types the words in. 'Show it to me.'

I check what she's written then I read her the number. 'Send it.'

She presses send. 'This won't work, you know. Whatever ridiculous plan you've concocted, there's no way this is going to work.'

'I'll decide what's ridiculous.'

She's right, of course. My plan couldn't be any flimsier. It consists of Cassie hearing the truth – with a kitchen knife and a child hostage as my persuasion. Even then, I'm only too aware that Becca coming clean in front of her still might not be enough, especially when I've gone to such desperate measures to obtain it. But I have to do *something*. Surviving in that hostel and living my life as an ex-convict is not a path I can stay on.

What I'm really counting on is that once Cassie has a seed of doubt planted in her mind, she continues searching until she uncovers *everything*. She definitely seems like that kind of person. Even if I'm locked up for a short time again while she gets to it. She already seems mistrustful of Jon; all I can hope now is that she'll be the one who'll prove my innocence. I just want this to be over.

'You've already gone too far with all this Amelia.'

A wave of sadness washes over me. 'I'll decide what's too far. You should try swapping places with me.'

'You might as well go out there and give yourself up now. The police will be all over this house in a few minutes.'

'It's a good thing I've got you to bargain with then, isn't it?' My trembling arm lifts the knife, its blade reflecting against her skin as she flattens herself against the door. Something in her eyes says she knows I won't use it. Only, she doesn't know for sure. 'I don't know how you live with yourself after the lies you've told.'

'I had no choice. None whatsoever,' she whispers. 'If it's any consolation, I've had to live with myself all these years too.'

It's the first time she's offered a hint of remorse.

'Don't you want to do the right thing now?' There's a soft tapping at the kitchen door. Police don't softly tap at doors. I reach back again, this time for the handle. It can only be Cassie. I just pray she's on her own.

THIRTY-FOUR

AMY

For a split second, Cassie lingers in the doorway, her eyes flitting from me to Becca, then to the knife.

Then, Jon appears behind her. I should have known she wouldn't come on her own. There's a moment when I think he's going to say something, but no – I'm in real trouble here. As though the knife doesn't exist, he charges at me, his fingers like a vice around my throat, squeezing for all he's worth as he frog-marches me backwards through the kitchen and into the hall-way. I panic as he slams me against the wall – I've got no chance against him – he's pinning me here with just one hand.

'What have you done with my son?' I get a whiff of the acid bitterness of his spittle as it lands on my cheek.

'You tell the truth and then I'll tell you.'

'What truth? You're deranged! You come here – you worm your way in. Give me one reason why I shouldn't just squeeze the life out of you here and now.'

'Just tell us where he is Amy!' Cassie is shrieking from behind him.

'Not until your husband tells you what he's really capable of. Get the hell off me.' I whimper, squirming in his grasp.

'Why the fuck did you come back?' His voice is laced with fury as he moves his face closer into mine. 'No one wanted you here before and no one wants you here now.'

'I'm going to clear my name.'

'You killed a girl. In *my* house,' Cassie cries as she tries to get between me and Jon. 'Then you pretend to be my friend – you trick me into trusting you then you take my son. What the hell is wrong with you?'

'I need you to believe me Cassie! Your husband set me up.' My voice is a gurgle with his hand pressed onto my neck.

Jon laughs but relaxes his hold slightly. I take the chance to force a breath in. 'As if she's going to listen to your crap.' His lip curls in hatred as he looks at me before turning to Cassie. 'I'll deal with this. Go back to the house in case they bring Teddy back.'

'I'm staying right here,' she shouts in reply, trying to pull Jon away from me by the shoulder. 'I need to know. Amy, where's Teddy?!'

'I said go home,' Jon shouts as he shrugs her off and points to the door with his free hand. 'Now.'

'And you, you idiot.' He jerks his head towards Becca, who seems to be frozen to the spot at the right of us. 'Why didn't you just call for help when she turned up, why trick us into coming here?' I close my eyes for a moment. *How the hell am I going to get out of this?* How am I going to get one of them to admit to what they've done to me?

'That.' She points towards the knife I'm still clutching. 'When someone's got a knife to your throat, you tend to do as you're told.'

A wail from upstairs echoes around us, momentarily averting Jon's attention. I take the chance to lash at the back of his shoulder with the blade but miss completely.

'I don't think so.' His arm swings round and he seizes my wrist, crushing the bones so tightly I lose my grip on the knife as

I cry out in pain. It clatters to the floor. This is it – I'm done for. How the hell did I ever think I could beat these people?

'Stop! No!' Cassie lunges behind Jon, tugging at the arm that's gripping my neck. 'She's the only one who knows where Teddy is.'

Her words must strike a chord within him for, momentarily, he relaxes his hold on me again, giving me the chance to choke out the reason I got them here. His fingers continue to graze against my windpipe.

'Cassie, please. You've got to believe me. It was *him* who spiked Jade's drink. Then he pinned it on me. And *she* knew all along.' I point at Becca. 'If I end up back in prison, you know the truth. I served *his* time.'

'There's only one place you're going. And it's not back to prison.' He really *is* going to kill me. And he'll get away with it. He'll cook it all up so he gets away with it. *Diminished responsibility.* My name will be even darker in death than it's been in life.

'What's she talking about, Jon?' Cassie hasn't moved from behind him.

I wriggle around in his grip. There's hope here. She's doubting him.

'As if you'd even *think* of believing a deluded ex-con over your own husband.' He twists to look at her. 'That's you all over, isn't it Cassie? Gullible and downright thick.'

'Listen to how he talks to you,' I croak. 'And I've seen how he treats you. I've heard him shouting at you and leaving you on your own all the time.'

Something in what I'm saying or how he's just snarled at her must strike a chord for her expression softens. If only she'd come around here on her own, I might have had a chance of getting her to listen. Perhaps I should have tried convincing her earlier but I had little proof of anything.

'Do you really think I'm going to let you damage my reputation, you silly little bitch.' He literally spits the word *bitch* into my face. 'Who the fuck do you think you are, believing that you can spread this crap about me? You need locking back up.'

'You seem more bothered about your *reputation* than you do about your own son!' Cassie pulls again at the arm which still pins me to the wall. 'Let her go. *Now!* I need to know where Teddy is.'

'I told *you* to go home, didn't I?'

'It was *me* outside your old house, Cassie. After I was released. I wanted to tell you the truth. And I wanted to make sure you were alright. He had you right where he wanted you. Cut off and alone. And then you moved before I could speak to you.'

'It was *you*?' Cassie's mouth forms itself into a similar O shape that Jon's did on first re-encountering me in his kitchen.

'I knew you wouldn't believe what I had to tell you straight away. I had to bide my time. That's why I tried to make friends with you here. And I wanted to get into your house. I wanted to find the evidence to prove what he did to me.'

'Like what?'

I open my mouth to reply but Jon squeezes my neck. I can see the rage in his eyes.

'Let her go Jon, I mean it,' Cassie demands as she tries again to wedge herself in between us. 'We need to get to Teddy.'

'No chance.' He pushes her back. If he ever *does* let me go, I'm going to have some right bruising around my neck.

'Tell me where my son is.' Jon's eyes lock with mine. 'Now.' His hold loosens again.

'You deserve so much better Cassie. Just like I do. But first I need to clear my name.'

'Tell me now.' His breath is pungent in my face.

'What – so you can finish strangling me?' I continue to wriggle in his grasp. 'Until you admit it was *you* who spiked Jade's drink, I'm not telling you a thing.'

Becca grabs the knife from the floor and comes up behind Jon, pointing it at me. 'Just tell them where he is.'

I try to laugh but it comes out as a splutter. 'You're no more capable of using that thing than I am.'

'Do you want to bet on that?'

For a split second Jon turns his eyes to Becca and I take the opportunity to bring my knee up in between his legs. I haven't got him square on but it's enough to make him let me go as he leans forward, his eyes bulging out of his face.

'Just tell her the truth, Becca.' I lunge towards her, stopping short of the knife. How the tables have turned. 'You lied to the police. You lied to the court. Why did you do it? How do you live with yourself?'

Our attention's again diverted as another loud cry from upstairs rips through the air. 'I need to get to my mother,' she says, still gripping the knife.

'What the hell is wrong with you? Why are you covering for him?'

'Is any of this true?' As Cassie rounds on Becca, Jon rises back up and springs at me again, this time taking me straight to the ground with the force of his weight.

'You're nothing but an evil bastard,' I gasp. 'You can do what you want with me but the truth's going to come out and there's nothing you can do about it.' My chest feels as though it might implode as I struggle to get some air in. 'Unless you kill your wife as well to shut her up.'

'This is your final chance. Where's my fucking son?'

'Alright! I believe you Amy!' Cassie cries as she tries again to pull Jon off me. 'Just tell me where Teddy is.' His grip on me eases, just for a second, as he elbows her away again shouting the words *deluded bitch*, a term that could be aimed at any of us.

But that's the least of my worries. The seconds stretch into eternity as his hands grasp my throat once more. I gasp for air, clawing at his grip, the sound of my own gurgling filling my ears.

Panic surges through me. I attempt to get free again, but his weight is bearing down on me. Cassie's voice echoes in the background, pleading with him to stop. His face is contorted – not just with his efforts to silence me once and for all, but with the loathing he has towards me.

'No, Jon. Stop! Please!'

Cassie's words fading into oblivion are the last thing I hear as my world blacks out. The chill in Jon's eyes is the final thing I see.

PART 5

CASSIE

THIRTY-FIVE

CASSIE

She's turned from a nauseating shade of red to purple. If I don't do something drastic, she's really going to die. We won't find out where Teddy is and Jon will go to prison for Amy's murder. Whether there's any truth in what Amy said still remains to be seen. God, I hope not but a nasty feeling is unravelling in my gut. And it's to do with more than what's happening here.

'Stop it! Let go of her. She knows where Teddy is. Please!'

I force my way between the side of him and the wall and manage to hook my fingers under his. It takes all my might to wrench them backward, the effort burning in my own fingers, but somehow, I'm able to break his stranglehold on her neck and push him to the side.

Her head rolls to one side. She could just be unconscious. But she looks more like she's dead.

'Look what you've done!' I scream. 'How could you? What about our son?'

Becca's frozen to the spot, gripping the rail of the banister as we all stare at the lifeless form on the floor. Meanwhile, the whine of the old woman echoes from upstairs.

'I'm going to find my son.' Jon staggers to his feet, his mouth grim and set hard as he wipes the spittle from it with the back of his hand.

'What have you done?' I rise to my feet and swing my arm out to grab his. I can't let him get away. If there's even a grain of truth in what Amy was saying...

He shakes me loose. 'I'll leave you both to weep over that deranged bitch.'

'Was she telling the truth, Jon? Get back here!'

I rush out into the street after him, shouting at him to come back. *He can't just leave me to deal with all this.* Plus, I need answers. But he disappears around the corner and into the night.

'Someone call an ambulance,' I shriek to anyone who might be listening. My heart wrenches with conflicting emotions – am I prioritising saving Amy's life over searching for my missing son?

Teddy could be trapped, hurt, or much, much worse. He's probably all alone and the only person who knows his where-abouts is unconscious on that hallway floor. Or worse.

Linda, the family liaison officer, dashes down the steps of our house. 'You said you were going to the toilet,' she cries, throwing her hands in the air. 'What's going on? What's happened in there?'

'She's, she's in there.' I point at Becca's house, barely trusting myself to say anything else about it. I can't fall apart. Not now. Not yet. I need to stay strong. I need to find Teddy. 'She's unconscious.'

'Who?'

'Amy.'

'Right.' With an expression I can't decipher, she reaches for her radio.

'We, we need an ambulance.' My words are pumping out in gasps.

'Sierra Oscar one zero seven.'

All the neighbours are out gawping at us. I suppose I would want to know what's going on if I were in their shoes.

'Someone call an ambulance,' I shriek into the darkness. Someone must have a phone in their hand. I can't wait for this woman to get her act together with her *Sierra Oscars*.

'What's actually happened in there?' Linda's voice is calm. Perhaps I should calm down and let her take control. After all, she's trained for this. I haven't a clue what to do.

'My husband's tried to strangle her.' There, I've said it. What else can I say? How can I protect him after what he's just done to her? And who knows what else he's done?

I sink to the garden wall of what should have been our dream home. Instead, it's become the centre of an absolute nightmare. We should have remained living where we were.

'Request urgent backup.' She's still on her radio. 'Tolbeck Cottage. Cherry Tree Lane, Rawdale.' She lets go of her radio and turns back to me. 'Where is your husband now, Cassie?'

'He said he was looking for Teddy. I don't know where. But he went that way.' I point after him then wrap my arms around myself as I stare back at the house. Amy's probably dead in there and Teddy's been missing for hours. He could be dead too for all I know. She reckons she's not capable of murder. But my husband is? I don't know what to make of what she's said at the moment.

I rise from the wall and break into a run back to Becca's door. I have to find out if Amy was telling the truth. And *she* knows.

'Cassie!' Linda calls after me.

'Becca,' I shout as I land back in her kitchen. I half expect her to still be rooted in shock by the banister but she's nowhere to be seen. 'BECCA!'

Amy's in exactly the same position as before – still motion-less on the floor and as floppy as a rag doll. I drop beside her and feel the soft skin of her wrist for a pulse. I can't find anything. I don't want her to die; especially now there's a chance she might have been wrongly imprisoned for all these years. And most importantly, I need to find my boy. Her skin isn't quite as purple as it was a few minutes ago, but her chest doesn't look to be rising and falling. I should do something.

Just I as position my hands to start chest compressions like I've seen on the TV, the swirling blue lights outside cast an eerie glow onto the walls, matching the turmoil inside me. I startle at the sudden hammering at the door.

Rising from my crouch at Amy's side, I slide the bolt across and twist the top latch. 'Thank God.' I'm aware my concern is probably misplaced here. I should be out *there*, helping the search for my son, not *here*, taking part in a lifesaving attempt for the woman who took him in the first place.

But as the first police officer to arrive told me, it's best if I don't move from here. There's every chance Teddy could find his way back home or he could be returned to me at any time. Amy might not have been acting alone. Or maybe Jon will find him. *Jon*. A man I thought I knew, who I've just seen strangle someone, possibly to death. And what about everything Amy was saying? As soon as Teddy's safely home, I need to find out if it really was him who spiked Jade's drink all those years ago like Amy said.

Two ambulance crew burst in and land at either side of her. One turns his ear to her chest and then feels around on her neck. His fingers probe her wrist.

'She's still alive but she's not going to make it to hospital,' he tells his colleague, shaking his head. 'She needs a tracheotomy.'

His colleague unclips her bag, pulling out an antiseptic wipe and sliding a scalpel from a sleeve. Presumably it's the implement they're going to cut her open with – right here on Becca's floor. I can't watch this. No way.

'What's her name please?' The man's tone is urgent.

'Amy,' I reply in dull shock, looking away.

'Right, Amy,' he says, feeling around on her lower neck with gloved hands. 'I'm Tom, one of the crew. I'm going to help you to breathe again.'

I don't know why he's bothering to talk to her; it's not as if she can hear him. She looks totally out of it and is going to be lucky to come back from this. Or maybe, given where she's probably destined for if he does save her life, she'd be luckier not to come back.

'If you could wait outside, please,' the other one tells me.

As if I need telling. No one in their right mind would want to watch someone's throat being sliced into with a scalpel. I return to the kitchen and attempt to distract myself from the gruesome procedure happening only feet away by watching what's happening in the street from the side window.

When I first reported him missing, things were reasonably quiet. There was one police car and everything was fairly low key until the report went out on the news. Strangely I feel calmer now than I did earlier. Then, I believed Amy to be, without a doubt, Jade's killer. Now, I don't know what to think, but one thing I do have now is a deep sense that wherever Teddy is, he's probably OK.

The news is obviously spreading for the crowd out there seems to be swelling by the minute. Until Teddy is found, I suppose it will continue to do so.

My gaze, without meaning to, returns to the hallway but my view of Amy is obscured by the paramedic leaning over her. I catch words such as *suction*, *pressure*, and *incision*, which is quite enough for me to ascertain what's going on.

Amy's still alive, but for how much longer?

THIRTY-SIX

CASSIE

A wave of nausea washes over me. My trembling hands grab a glass from the draining board, which I fill with water and gulp down, trying not only to distract myself from the sickness in my belly but also from the gnawing guilt about my son's whereabouts.

A gut-wrenching gurgle escapes from Amy's throat, and I struggle to hold back the bile rising in my mouth. My heart races as the male responder breaks the tense silence, his voice blending with the rhythmic beeping of medical equipment. 'Hurry – hook her up to the air – we can't waste another second.'

'Will she make it?' I can't help but peek around the door, my eyes falling on the tube protruding from a hole in her neck. My stomach churns at the sight as I battle to maintain some composure.

Ignoring me completely, they remain focused on Amy. Evidently, updating me is the last thing on their minds.

Linda is still out in the street, helping two uniformed officers to hold back the still-gathering crowd.

'Is there any news on my son?' I race towards her and she shepherds me back to the footpath.

'Not yet, but the search has been stepped up.' She nods towards the park. Between the gap in mine and Becca's houses, I notice torches progressing forward in a line.

'Surely they don't think he might be...' I can't say the word. I just can't say it. Teddy showed Amy his room. She drank coffee with me in my kitchen. Besides, she gave us no reason before to suggest she could have hurt him. She said he was safe – that's how she got me to go round there.

'Not at all.' She rests a reassuring hand on my arm. Her eyes are kind and I'm grateful for her. I'd be completely on my own if she wasn't here. I haven't even had a chance to let Mum know what's going on.

'So what *are* they thinking?'

'They'll be keeping an open mind, but clearly we're all extremely hopeful he's safe and warm somewhere.'

'I'm certain they're looking in the wrong place there.' I nod towards the void of darkness that is the park. 'If she'd left him somewhere, surely it'll be inside.'

'They've got to comb every nook and cranny of the neighbourhood and that's just one team – there are others out looking as well.'

'Have they checked the place where she's been living? Juniper Lodge?' Then I think of the charity shop. 'And working?' I add.

'We've checked her place of residence, yes. We did that as soon as you reported him missing. And we're just waiting for the key holder to arrive at her workplace.' Linda's reassuring touch on my shoulder provides a brief moment of comfort. 'Stay positive, Cassie,' she urges. 'The entire force is searching for him, and we've even brought in units from North Yorkshire to help. One thing I will say, though, is that you've managed to complicate things much further with going around there like you did.' She nods towards Becca's house.

'I'll show you the text Becca sent,' I reply. 'It said that going around without telling anyone was the only way I'd get Teddy back safely. What was I supposed to do?'

'You should have told me. We've got specially trained officers to handle that sort of thing.'

'I was only thinking of my son.'

'We'll be asking Becca why she didn't call us the moment Amy turned up.'

'She had her at knifepoint when we arrived. That'd be why.'

She pauses, as though searching for another argument as to why we shouldn't have gone in like we did.

'What about my husband?' Muddled in with all this anguish is the disbelief that he's just left a woman for dead in there and disappeared into the night. I know what she's done with Teddy but I never suspected, not in a million years, that Jon would be capable of such violence towards another person. It's looking as though I might not have known him at all. A cold dread steals over me as I briefly contemplate how the hell we can go forward from here but this isn't the time for that.

I should definitely be telling Linda what Amy accused him of in there but something's stopping me. I need to hear his side first. And Becca's. Amy could easily have been making it all up and I don't want to make things worse than they already are. If Amy was telling the truth then clearly my marriage is over. But if she *was* making it all up and I tell the police exactly what she's accused him of then my marriage is over anyway.

'The officers searching for Teddy have been made aware of the situation. It goes without saying we'll need to question him when we find him – after what's happened, I mean.'

It's on the tip of my tongue to say, *what's happened in there might only be part of it all*. But once I say it, I start a storm I won't be able to stop. Right now, the important thing is for Teddy to be found safely. Then I'll deal with the rest of it.

I glance at my watch. It's been almost four hours since Amy took him from Hazel's. *Four hours.* I know Linda's tried to reassure me but in that time, anything could have happened to him. He's four years old for God's sake. He hasn't had any dinner. He's scared of the dark. My mind starts to unravel as panic suddenly hits me. Wherever Amy's left him, at least an hour must have passed by since she did. And Jon's robbed any chance of her telling us where he is.

'Why haven't they found him yet?' I'm getting to the verge of hysteria. I slump against the wall and tears I didn't realise I was crying are streaming down my cheeks. Finding a young boy shouldn't be this difficult. Everything has happened so fast that I've only just allowed the enormity of it all to hit me. My whole world is falling apart. 'I just want him back here.'

'I'll be back in a moment,' Linda tells me. 'I just need a word with my colleague.'

I drop my head into my hands. If Teddy's found safely, I'll read to him each and every night. I'll take him to the *Thomas the Tank Engine* museum, I'll do something special with him every weekend – I'll—

My attention's averted to Amy being wheeled out of next door's gate. A second paramedic car has arrived and her stretcher is being flanked by police. Maybe it's in case Jon suddenly appears out of nowhere and tries to have a second go at her. If there's a grain of truth in what she's been saying, I just wish she'd spoken up before. Though whether I'd have listened is another matter.

Paramedics hold wires and tubes as they ease her out of the gate and towards the open doors of the ambulance. At least she's still alive. I honestly thought they'd be carrying a body bag out of that house.

Becca appears in her doorway. I rush at her, only just

making it, before she realises what's happening. She steps back and goes to slam the door in my face. But I'm quicker than she is. I bolt into her hallway and kick the door shut behind both of us, while doing my best to ignore the discarded tubing and streaks of blood across the wooden floor.

'I've had more than enough for one day,' she cries. 'And so has my mother.'

'What do you know about Amy?' My voice trembles as I confront Becca. 'And about Jon? She claimed to have served his time for him. She said you know something.' I study her closely, hoping to find my answers in her expression. 'And you must, or else why would she have even come here?'

'I don't know a thing.' She backs towards the stairs, presumably intending to return to wherever she's been hiding for the last twenty minutes. Clearly, there *must* be something between her and Jon for her to be keeping quiet like this.

'Hey, not so fast.' I grab her arm as she gets her foot onto the first step.

'I need to get back to my mother.' She wrenches it away.

'And I need to know the truth – can't you see that? Which according to Amy, *you* seem to have been hiding. You either tell me or those officers out there will force it from you. They'll be asking me to make a statement soon.'

She takes another step away from me, just as Linda appears at the door to the kitchen.

'Come in, why don't you?' Becca's voice is the most sarcastic I've heard since first encountering her. And to think we'd pulled up here on moving in day and I'd thought we might become friends. That day feels like a lifetime ago.

'*She* knows something.' I point at Becca. 'Not just about what's happened in here today, but she also knows the so-called *truth* about what put Amy in prison in the first place. You need to be interviewing her.'

'We'll be speaking to everyone concerned soon enough.'

Linda gently takes my arm. 'Come on Cassie. Let's get you back to your own house.'

'I wouldn't go far if I was you,' I snap at Becca. 'You're going to tell the truth even if I have to force it out of you.'

THIRTY-SEVEN

CASSIE

As we reach the pavement, a car door slams, followed by another one. Two officers march towards us.

'Shit. Shit. Shit.' My heart pounds like a drum in my chest. I stare at the approaching officers, trying to read their expressions. Each of their steps could be a step nearer to my life changing forever. If anything's happened to my baby, I don't know how I'll go on.

The female officer introduces herself, 'I'm DC Reynolds, and this is my colleague DS Thorpe.' Her words hang in the air, leaving me in unbearable suspense. I don't care what their names are. With a smile that could mean anything, she adds, 'It's good news, don't worry. We've found him.'

'Who?' For a moment I wonder if they mean Jon. Then I realise. 'Teddy?!'

'Yes.'

He must be OK, or she would hardly be smiling. She's about my age; maybe she's got kids herself and will be able to identify with the agony I've been in.

'Thank God.' I could fall at her feet. 'Where did you find him?'

'He was locked inside the storeroom of the charity shop Amy works at,' she replies. 'One of our colleagues heard him crying in there while they were waiting to be let in. They ended up having to break the door down.'

'He was in there on his own?'

She nods. 'For quite some time, it appears. He was distraught when they finally got in to him, the poor little mite.'

'But other than that, he's really OK?' I've never felt so relieved in my life. I know only too well of the situations like this where parents *don't* get a happy ending. Yes I'm heartbroken at the thought of him crying on his own for all this time but he's safe. Really, that's all that matters.

'He's very shaken, but physically, he seems fine. He's on his way to the Yorkshire Infirmary.'

'But why?' Fear clutches at my chest. *She's just said he's OK.* Amy's on her way there too. She might be out of it *now* but who knows what miracles they might perform with her. I've no idea how soon she could be on her feet and I can't risk her coming anywhere near him again.

'It's just so he can be checked over – it's a standard precaution,' she adds, probably noticing my expression. 'It's procedure, that's all. But he's been asking for his mummy, in fact I don't think he's stopped asking for you since we found him.'

'Could you take me to him? I don't think I could trust myself to drive right now.' But I need to have my son back in my arms more than I ever have before.

'Of course we will.'

'I'll wait here Cassie,' Linda says. 'In case there's any news of Jon.'

'I'll radio for another officer to wait with you.' DC Reynolds reaches for her radio.

I swallow hard, torn between the realisation that she's scared to be alone after what Jon's shown himself to be capable of and worrying about my child. 'I know what he's done tonight, but something must have made him act like that.' My voice quivers as I speak, just as DC Reynolds starts to request the presence of a second officer. 'Until tonight I'd never have suspected my husband could be a danger to anyone.'

'That's what we'll be getting to the bottom of,' DC Reynolds replies.

'Mummy!' Teddy's joyful voice echoes through the playroom, and he darts towards me the moment he spots me. I should be honoured. I've distracted him from the train set he's been given to play with. 'Where were you? I was crying.' He raises his still-swollen eyes to meet mine. It's horrible to see his face so tear-stained but I have never been so delighted to see him in my life. For now I'll celebrate the fact that he's alright. Worrying about the effect all this has had on him can come later.

'Everything's OK.' I swing him into the air and kiss the top of his blonde head. 'I'm here now.'

'I was scared.' His voice is muffled against my shoulder. 'On my own.'

'I know sweetheart. But you're safe now. Nothing like that will ever happen again.' I hold him tighter as the tears that have become frequent companions today release themselves once again.

'Don't cry Mummy.' His arms wrap tighter around my neck. I want to ask how Amy treated him, and make sure she didn't hurt him in any way, but there'll be plenty of time for all that soon. Teddy lifts his head from my shoulder and looks towards the door. 'Where's Daddy?'

Good question. I exchange glances with the two police officers who brought me here. Teddy might be safe but who knows what's going to happen from this. 'He's gone looking for you sweetie pie. We've both been very worried about you.'

A woman appears in the doorway of the playroom. 'I'm

Doctor Louise Fuller. Hey, Teddy.' She steps towards us. 'I just want to check you over. Make sure everything's OK.'

He clings tightly to me, burying himself into my neck. 'Don't want to,' he whimpers. A surge of protectiveness fills me, and part of me wants to whisk him away to the safety of his warm bed with his bears and trains.

'Do we have to do this now? You can see he's had enough for one day.'

She nods slowly. 'I'm afraid so. Listen Teddy.' She bends slightly and tries to meet his eye. 'We need to have a little listen to your tummy and just one or two other things – then you can go home, I promise.'

'I'm hungry,' he replies as he continues to cling to me.

'Can we at least get him something to eat? He won't have had anything since lunchtime.'

'I had biscuits.' He lifts his head again. Relief washes over me. If Amy was giving him biscuits, she was hopefully being kind to him in every other respect.

'We'll talk to you about that soon,' the doctor replies. 'But first, we'll get you some toast. While you're eating that, there is a very nice police lady waiting for you. She's going to ask you a few quick questions and after that, when we've checked you over, you can go home with your mummy.'

'OK.' His voice is small.

I'm not sure I even want to be at home anymore. I don't even know if I'm safe there. Not after everything that's happened. Just as we were beginning to settle in, it's all being wrenched away. I was so scared of the 'stalker' that's been hanging around. At least now I know I wasn't going mad. Jon was wrong the whole time, even insinuating at times that I should see a doctor. Yet it was Amy all along, although I'm struggling to understand why. Hopefully, she'll get the chance to explain what she was doing. But now, being scared of my own husband has taken over. I hope they find him – I hope they keep him tonight. The more I think about it, the less safe I'll feel, alone in the house with him. I used to think my biggest danger was outside the home but now there's a chance it could be within it. In my own bed.

As the doctor proceeds with Teddy's examination, I can't shake off the urgency of the situation with Jon, Amy and Becca. The time is ticking, and I want to get Teddy out of the hospital as soon as possible so I can find out what the hell is going on. Have they found him yet? Is Amy still alive? Has Becca told them what she knows? I might have Teddy back but this situation is far from over.

THIRTY-EIGHT

CASSIE

Linda and a male officer are at the house when I return. I'm relieved that they've waited; it's better than returning to an empty house and still not having a clue what's going on with Jon or Amy.

I've managed to pick up bits and pieces on the journey back. I caught the words *adult male on foot*, and *fitting the description*, over the police radio, but DS Thorpe quickly turned the sound down, maybe because of Teddy being in the car.

'What's the latest?' I ask as I step into the hallway and Suki rushes to greet me. It still smells like home even if it doesn't feel like home anymore. 'We just heard something about it on the radio.'

'It's lovely to see you, Teddy.' Without replying to me, Linda smiles down at him. 'You get him settled in,' she says. 'Then I'll fill you in on everything we know.' She gestures to her colleague. 'Cassie, this is Sergeant Walsh.'

'I'll get going back to the station.' He nods at me before rising to his feet. 'We've caught up with your husband and he's waiting at the station to be interviewed.'

A weird combination of relief merged with dread surges through me. At least I know where he is. 'What does that mean? What's happening?'

'We're going to need to get a full statement from you.' DC Reynolds checks her watch. 'But we can call back in an hour – will that give you enough time to see to your son?'

'It should do.'

'In the meantime, we'll get a statement from your neighbour.' He jerks his head in the direction of Becca's house.

'Will you be staying with me?' I turn to Linda. 'There were still several reporters hanging around when we came from the car – the last thing I can cope with is any of them coming to the door.'

'Don't worry. I'll be right here. You get Teddy settled, then I'll fill you in with as much detail as I can.'

'OK.'

'How's he doing?'

'He's been given a clean bill of health. He's just exhausted.'

'I'm hungry, Mummy.'

Linda laughs. 'If he's thinking of his tummy, he's definitely alright.'

'I'd better feed Suki as well, hadn't I?' Her ears prick up at the mention of her name. 'But first, let's get you a sandwich and some fruit Teddy, then you can have a shower.'

'Don't want a shower Mummy.'

'Just a quick one.'

I know he's probably too tired but really, I just want to wash his awful experience clean away from him.

As I help him into his pyjamas, I feel like the luckiest mum in the world. Just a couple of hours ago, I had no idea where he was. Thank God I got him back safely. As for what's left of my marriage, who knows? And how much can I trust of what Amy was spouting? I'm veering between wanting to disregard everything she said to knowing in my gut that there *has* to be some truth in her accusations.

Teddy's asleep before I get to the third page of his story. I smooth my hand over his damp hair and tuck the duvet around him. Tears fill my eyes as I gaze at his little arm wrapped around his bear. All I want to do right now is snuggle down beside him.

Yet this update from Linda awaits me, along with the necessity to make a statement about everything that's happened tonight. I wish it could all wait until tomorrow but I do understand why it can't, especially now they've got Jon in custody.

As I return downstairs, I'm at a total loss of how much to tell them. Do I wait until I've spoken to Jon before I give a full account of everything Amy was accusing him of? Do I wait to see what Becca says to the police first? The moment I can, I'm going round to speak to her myself. Amy called her a liar, over and over again, so I need to find out if there's something in that.

I badly want to believe it was Amy who killed Jade and that she's a deluded stalker getting her kicks on returning to the scene of her crime. Perhaps Amy had a thing about Jon when they were young – maybe he was more interested in Jade than her and her jealousy made her do what she did. Maybe I was earmarked to be next.

I don't want to make things worse than they already are – if that's even possible. No matter what, I still love my husband and just want to get back to the way things once were between us. Yes, he can be controlling and unpredictable at times but I'm almost certain he's not some sort of monster. At least, this is what I'm trying to tell myself.

I know I'm clinging to what is probably false hope here but I can't help it. If my marriage falls apart now, I don't know what I'll do or where I'll go. Maybe, there's some way we can still get through all this and carry on. Jon was my first proper boyfriend and I can't imagine there ever being anyone else. He knows me. And I thought I knew him.

Linda follows me into the kitchen. She looks tired too. It's been a rough few hours, and with Jon at the police station, it still shows no sign of abating. At least Teddy's back where he belongs.

'Have a seat.' I gesture to the breakfast bar. 'Would you like one?' I pluck a wine glass from the cupboard and hold it aloft.

'No, thanks. I'm on duty. But I wouldn't say no to a cup of tea.'

I flick the switch on the kettle, then slop some wine into a glass. I'll just have the one. I've no idea what I might still have to face so I need to keep my wits about me this evening. Jon may or may not be let out of the police station tonight, Amy may or may not die tonight. One thing is for certain – I'm highly unlikely to get any sleep.

We make small talk about Teddy as I brew Linda's tea. That he likes drawing and playing with anything that has wheels. That he's starting preschool in September. How he's thankfully gone out like a light.

But we need to get to the main topic of conversation.

'So what's happening?' I swing around and face her, unable to put it off any longer.

'Your husband will be interviewed under caution,' she says as I place the cup in front of her. 'They caught up with him in the Mason's Arms pub.'

'He told me he was looking for Teddy,' I say, my voice tinged with shock and disappointment. 'Not hiding in a pub! Has he actually been arrested?'

'Yes.' Linda sips her tea. 'Given the state that Amy's in, they *had* to arrest him.'

I sit facing her. 'Did he go with them willingly?' After the mood he was in earlier, I can imagine them having to pin him to the ground to get handcuffs on him.

'Yes, he did.' A shadow of what looks like an apology crosses her face. 'You should be prepared Cassie – there's every chance

Jon will be charged with attempted murder for what he did to her.'

Attempted murder. As if our life has turned into this nightmare. 'Even after she snatched Teddy like she did?'

Linda nods solemnly. 'The mitigating circumstances would be taken into consideration in court, but yes, I think he'll be charged, regardless of what led up to his actions. It all comes down to the force that's deemed reasonable in the moment.'

'Will he be allowed to come home?' I'm scared, but I think I need to see him; I need to hear his explanation for why he lost control to the extent he did. And I need to know for certain if there's any truth in everything Amy said. At least then, I'm not left wondering and can make some decisions about what I do next.

'I'm not entirely sure. Whether he'd get police bail would depend on the Crown Prosecution Service, if and when he's charged. I'm not saying this will happen but I'm saying, prepare yourself.'

'And what if he doesn't?'

'He'd have to appear before the court to decide what happens next. Then the court might bail him or he might get remanded.'

I close my eyes. We've had our ups and downs, Jon and me. But fundamentally I thought we'd get through whatever life could possibly throw at us. However, I truly don't know how we'll make it through this. My brain is spinning with conflicting emotions. This house move has got to be the worst decision I've ever made.

'Is there any news on Amy?' I raise my eyes to meet Linda's. I'm not even sure that I want to know the answer, nor am I sure she'll be allowed to tell me, given my husband is responsible for the state she's in.

'As far as I know, she's stable. The emergency tracheotomy appears to have saved her life.' She pauses, as though gauging my reaction before deciding to continue. 'However, if she *does* recover, her quality of life will depend on if and how long her brain was starved of oxygen.'

'Right.' I fall silent as I try to take the enormity of it all in. Even if she lives, Amy might not be able to tell me her side of the story properly. This shouldn't be all I'm bothered about, but right now, it is. I've been in the dark about things for long enough. I need to know if she was telling the truth or whether she's just a deranged maniac with an axe to grind.

'If she's been lucky and there's no brain damage, it's still entirely possible she won't be able to speak again after everything she underwent.'

I stare out into the darkness of the night. Who'd have thought that in less than a fortnight of living here, everything would come to this?

Becca is possibly the only person who I've got a chance of hearing the truth from any time soon. As soon as the police have left her house, I'm going to do whatever it takes to prise it out of her. But in the meantime, I'm going to have to tell Linda about Amy's accusation.

'There's something else you need to know,' I begin.

Making my statement to DC Reynolds and DS Thorpe takes well over an hour. I tell them about Amy being the stalker that's been hanging around, not only at this house, but at the old house too.

I move on to how I secretly followed her to the hostel, which is when I suspected who she really was.

I recount the shock I felt when Jon attacked her in Becca's house, and how out of character this level of violence is, or so I thought. I repeat the accusation she made about having *served Jon's time for him.*

Earlier, I felt drained. Now, as I see the police out, I'm

wired. There seems to be no in between at the moment. And they couldn't tell me anything more about what's going on with Jon at the police station, other than he's unlikely to be let back out tonight, especially after what I've told them.

I climb the stairs and head into Teddy's room. I check his window is locked before kissing his head again. I'd love to crawl in beside him but he needs a good night's sleep after today's ordeal. And I need answers from Becca.

I dart back down the stairs, slide my feet into boots and shoo an expectant Suki back into the kitchen.

'Sorry girl. I'll take you for a good walk in the morning.' I click the door behind me and head down the steps towards the gate.

THIRTY-NINE

CASSIE

Becca's house is in darkness. But I don't care. I knock on the front door first and look up, expecting to see a light appear in one of the upstairs windows. But there's nothing. I head to the back door and knock a bit harder. Still – nothing. I glance at my watch. It's going on for midnight so I can't exactly make a scene out here, even if the reporters *have* finally given up and gone home. I knock again, try the handle and then go around into the back garden. It crosses my mind to throw stones at the windows but the last thing I want to be doing is frightening Becca's mother. After all, I don't know which is her window. There's nothing I can do here – I'm going to have to leave this until the morning.

After taking a shower in the en suite, I tug some pyjamas from the drawer. My gaze rests on our bed. As comfortable and inviting as it looks, no way can I face sleeping in a bed where the pillows smell of Jon. Not that I can imagine getting much sleep. But if I'm to have any chance, it'll be in the guest room.

DC Reynolds said it's likely that Jon won't be finished at the police station until the morning at the very earliest. And then it's fifty-fifty whether he'll be charged and fifty-fifty again whether he'd be bailed after that.

Part of me wants him to come back tonight – I want him to reassure me that he's not the monster Amy's provoked him to be. Yet there's also a voice in the back of my head warning me to be careful. Very careful. There's a very good chance that the more negative parts of his personality could be far, far worse than I ever imagined. But surely he'd never hurt *me*?

As I lie in the guest room bed, my mind races with questions, each one more perplexing than the last. Who am I really married to? What really happened when Jade was killed? And the biggest question, was Amy wrongly imprisoned? Although I keep trying to talk myself out of it, I don't feel safe anymore around my own husband. The longer I lie here, the more terrified I am about his return. And I don't know what to do about it.

I sit bolt upright with a sharp inhale. My chest is pulsing like a freight train. At first I think I'm seeing things. Jon's standing at the side of the bed, looming over me like the Grim Reaper.

'Bloody hell.' I try to catch my breath in the shadowy room. I can't believe he's here. Not after what I told them.

I tap my phone lying on the other pillow. It's 2 a.m. It feels like I've only been asleep for about ten minutes.

'What the hell are you doing, standing there like that?' My voice is raspy and worn. I accepted a cigarette from one of the neighbours when the stress was at its height earlier this evening. I haven't smoked since I was a teenager, and I'm not really sure how I thought it might help me.

'Why are you sleeping in here?'

'I was wiped out,' I whisper in the darkness, hoping he'll lower his voice too, so as not to wake Teddy. 'I thought I'd sleep better in here. Without you being at home, I mean.'

'Well, I'm back now, aren't I?' He's acting like nothing's happened. Which could either be a good thing, or a bad thing.

Surely they wouldn't have said *do you know what your wife has said about you...*

'I, I was told you might not be released tonight. They said they'd arrested you.'

'I answered their questions, and they've let me go.' His voice is as confident and assured as it usually is. '"Pending further investigation," they said.'

'But they haven't charged you?'

'Nope – it's true what they say about paying for the best,' he says.

'You mean a solicitor?' He'll be getting irritated at any moment with all the questions I'm firing at him. I need to balance my need to know with mine and Teddy's safety though.

'Why do you think I've been so long?' His tone rises. 'I had to wait for him. But it was worth it.'

'Ssshh, you'll wake Teddy.'

'They said they'd found him. How is he?'

Teddy should have been the first thing Jon asked about when he woke me. He's only said something because I mentioned him first. 'He's worn out, but he's alright now he's home.'

'No thanks to that psychopathic bitch.' Jon sits beside me on the bed. 'Has there been any news?'

'She's not dead, if that's what you mean.' I should point out that his earlier behaviour can't be described as anything other than psychopathic either but I don't want to go there now.

'Clearly I didn't squeeze hard enough.'

I sit up straighter, and pull the covers up under my arms as though creating a barrier of protection between us. 'We need to talk about what she said Jon.'

'She's a maniac,' he replies. 'Nothing she said is worth a minute of your consideration. I can't believe you're even bringing it up.'

His voice is still reasonably even so I'm going to continue. 'Did you spike that girl's drink?'

'I'm not even going to answer that.'

'I need to know, Jon.'

'Do *you* think I did?' He peers at me in the darkness. A fresh fear sweeps over me. If I say the wrong thing now he could easily do to me what he did to Amy earlier.

'I don't know. That's why I'm asking.' My voice is shaking.

'Well if you'd rather listen to some deluded bitch than your own husband' – his voice rises some more – 'then you're even more stupid than I ever gave you credit for.'

Oh God. I've done it now. 'Look Jon. Why don't we just talk about this in the morning?'

'What if I want to talk about it *now*?' He slams his palm at the side of me, narrowly missing my leg. I shrink back. I've got to get him out of here.

'I'm sorry Jon. I'm not saying I believe her. I just wanted to hear it from you. But the last thing I want is Teddy being woken by us.'

'You wanted to hear *what* from me?'

'Just the truth about what *really* happened.'

'I have already told you.' His voice has calmed again. Thank God.

'Look Jon. My head's pounding. Let's get some sleep and leave this until the morning. There's nothing we can say to each other now that can't wait a few hours.'

Nor is there much he can say that can change anything. As soon as the coast is clear, I'm getting some stuff together and taking Teddy to Mum's. I can't stay somewhere I don't feel safe.

'I'm off to get a drink.' He rises from the bed and slams the door after himself. *Bastard.* He knows Teddy's sleeping through there and that he needs his sleep tonight, more than ever. He doesn't give a shit about anyone other than himself. I wait for a few moments, either for Teddy to wake up or for Jon to burst back in, unable to accept that I might believe what Amy told me. I listen as he bangs about in the kitchen. Several moments later I hear the squeak and click of his office door. Only after ten minutes or so does my breathing begin to return to normal. He's hopefully too busy drowning his sorrows to bother me again.

It's that time of day between dark and light, when the world teeters on the edge of uncertainty, much like my mind. The momentary relief of not remembering yesterday evaporates quickly, leaving me with a gnawing sense of dread.

I'm not sure if Amy is alive or dead. The truth she might have paid for with her life is haunting me. My husband is a potential murderer, and the fate of our marriage is hanging by a thread.

Yet amidst this chaos, I find solace in knowing that Teddy is safely tucked up in bed, and today, after I've spoken to Becca, I'll take him to Mum's, away from all this.

The rays of dawn paint the room in a gentle blue hue, casting elongated shadows of the still unpacked boxes on the walls. It must be really early; even the birds haven't started yet. I lie back against my pillows, willing the respite of sleep to rescue me from our reality for a little longer. But it doesn't come. Jon's soft snores echo across the landing. At least he went to bed without returning to carry on where we left off a few hours ago. Sighing, I sit up, and reach for my phone.

The local news from last night is full of reports about Teddy having been found safely; there's nothing specifically reported as yet about what's happened to Amy or anything about Jon.

The press probably can't report certain details with it being an ongoing investigation. However, I'm certain it will be all over the news soon enough and those damn reporters from last night will be hot-footing it back here and camping outside my house again.

I find the online articles from ten years ago again, looking for something I might have missed. The only link between Jade Calvert and my husband so far is that she died *here*, in this house. I shiver, and not just because the heating hasn't come on yet.

As Jade's image smiles back at me from my screen, I'm struck by how similar we were at sixteen. She wore her blonde, shoulder length hair exactly as I did and she's got the rail track braces on her teeth, just like I had. They were the cool thing to have back then. We're similar in terms of our features and eye colour too. As well as our high cheekbones, blue eyes and dimples. I place the phone face down on the bed and shiver again, more violently this time. The fact that he pursued me when I looked so much like her worries me. Could I be next?

I swing my legs around the edge of the bed and open the bedroom door an inch at a time. Tiptoeing to the top of the stairs, I wrap my dressing gown around myself as I go. There's no point just lying in that bed with my brain spinning like a child on a playground roundabout – I might as well make some coffee. There's no telling what fresh hell the coming day could bring so I need some time to myself to prepare for it.

Every creak I cause on the stairs makes me cringe. After a particularly loud one, I wait for a moment for any stirrings from one of the bedrooms. I don't know the house well enough yet to avoid the spots where the stairs creak – not like I did with our last house. Whether I'll get to know every nook and cranny of this place too remains to be seen. It's certainly not looking promising.

As I reach the bottom step, the house is thankfully still swathed in silence. Suki opens one eye at me from her basket and wags her tail. She'll be expecting a run out after barely being walked yesterday but she'll have to wait a bit longer. I'll take her when Teddy wakes. I want to spend every waking moment with him after what he's been through. Hopefully the police won't need to speak to me again today – if they do, they'll have to come to Mum's house. Though I'll be seeing Becca as soon as I possibly can before I set off.

As I wait for the coffee machine, I fire off a text to my manager with a brief explanation of what happened yesterday though no doubt she'll have already seen something on the news. Surely she'll understand me taking another day off?

Although she might query the fact that Teddy was abducted from his *childminder's* house when I was supposed to be keeping him at home because he was poorly. However, I'll cross that bridge when I reach it – work is the least of my worries right now. Potentially protecting myself and my son from my husband is much more important.

Until I know whether Amy's going to be able to tell her side of the story, and what Jon might or might not be charged with, I can't put my mind to anything other than what's going on around here.

Linda confirmed that Amy will definitely be charged with child abduction when she comes round, if she comes round, and she'll also be recalled to prison for breaching the terms of her licence. She shouldn't have been anywhere near this house, according to Linda. *But there's every chance she shouldn't have been in prison in the first place.* I still don't have a clue whether they've even quizzed Jon about that yet. He never mentioned it when he came back and I didn't dare to ask.

Looking at the state of her last night, I can't imagine she'll be anywhere near a fit state to be sent back to prison. Despite what she did to Teddy yesterday, something inside me feels desperately sorry for her. And though I'm struggling to accept it, my instincts are screaming at me that there's more than a degree of truth in everything she's said.

The fire Jon laid in the wood burner the night before last looks too inviting not to set alight while I let Teddy sleep for a bit longer. I sit back on my heels and wait for it to truly take hold. Wrapping my fingers around the warmth of my cup, I sigh so deeply it's painful. If only things could have been different here.

The flames lick up higher, dancing with an energy I wish I possessed as well. I feel about a hundred years old today and am not sure how much more stress I can cope with. The depression I suffered after Teddy's birth seems to be tugging at my edges again but above all, I just feel sick. I don't know what to do for the best. Stay? Leave? Talk to Jon? Or get away from him as quickly as I can?

Then the lounge door crashes against the wall, making me slop what's left of my coffee into my lap.

FORTY

CASSIE

Jon's entrance is so without warning it's as though he's trying to catch me out with something. What that could be is anyone's guess. After all, he's the one who's been keeping massive secrets by the looks of it. He's wearing his running gear so at least he's planning on leaving the house. I'm torn between not being able to bear being around him and being desperate for him to tell me the real story. But the last thing I want to do is antagonise him.

'What are you doing?'

'I could ask you the same question.'

'I couldn't sleep.'

'One minute you're leaving our room so you *can* sleep, then you're telling me you're up at the crack of dawn because you can't.' He comes further into the room. 'Which is it?'

'Will you keep your voice down.' Rage pools in my belly but I have to keep a lid on it. 'Teddy needs to rest after everything he's been through.' I begin folding items from the pile of laundry that's needed to go upstairs for the last two days. As if I'm putting my focus onto laundry but if I keep myself occupied, at least I don't have to look at him.

'Who was it who invited the deluded weirdo into our life?'

He drums his fingers against his chin as he leans against the wall. 'Hmmm, let me think. That'd be you.'

'But you knew her before me.' I keep my voice small and non-confrontational as I fold a towel into quarters and drape it over the chair.

'She was talking utter bullshit last night.' He straightens up and stares straight back at me as though proving that looking me in the eye means he's being honest. I used to think it did.

As I pick up one of Teddy's jumpers, I'm reminded for the zillionth time how lucky we are to have him home safely. The rows of policemen with their torches in the park is a sight I shall never forget.

'You do believe me, don't you?' His jaw tightens, and he looks away from me, though at least his voice lowers. 'I should've known you'd be taken in by her. She's trying to mess with your head. Which isn't so difficult these days, is it?'

'How come you didn't recognise her before Jon? That's what I want to know.'

He perches on the arm of the sofa. 'To be fair' – his voice takes on an even gentler tone, which in the circumstances, is unnerving – 'if I were able to show you a picture of her then, alongside one now, you'd think it was two different people.' He clasps his hands in his lap.

'Why would she say it was *you* who killed Jade all those years ago?'

'Because that's the sort of nutter she is. Bloody hell Cassie, if even *you* don't believe me, what chance have I got against the police?'

I throw another towel onto the chair. 'For as long as I live, I'll never fathom what was inside you last night to make you nearly kill her.'

'Like I said, I should have squeezed harder.' He rises back to his feet.

'But why?'

'In that moment, as far as I was concerned, she could have killed our son.'

'She hadn't hurt a hair on his head.' I drop the laundry basket to the ground. I don't know why I'm bothering to do housework.

'We didn't know that. He'd been missing for hours. Anyway, why do you seem more bothered about *her* than your own son? It's all you seem to want to go on about.'

'Teddy's safe; I don't think she'd have ever hurt him.'

'That's easy to say now he's back here, isn't it?' He strides to the window and peers out onto the early morning street where the sun's starting to rise behind the houses. Normally I'd love to watch it. But Amy may never watch a sunrise again. And Jon may end up charged with her murder. No matter how I try to slice it all, this is our new reality.

'No thanks to you Jon. You nearly killed the only person who was able to tell us where he was.'

'They found him without her, didn't they? *Didn't they?*'

I nod and close my eyes. We're getting nowhere here. Perhaps I just need to accept that whatever comes next is totally out of my control and get to Mum's. I'm all over the place and don't seem to know what to do for the best at the moment.

'I would have hoped my own wife would take my word against the word of a convicted murderer,' Jon continues as he turns away from the window and back towards me.

'I want to believe you, of course I do. But there's more to all this than you're telling me.' Really, I want to say, *she might not be a murderer* but judging by the stony look on his face, I'd better not.

'We'll talk when I get back.' He fiddles about with the buttons on his fitness tracker. 'I'm going for a run.'

'OK.' Thank God he's going out for a bit. I need to decide what I'm doing next.

'I need to clear my head before work.'

'You're *working* today? With all that's going on.'

'Well, aren't you?'

'I've already messaged to say I'm not going in.'

'I'm working from home. But if you think that means you can be on my case all day, think again.'

'If you're wanting to work today, you'd be better going into the office. I'm planning to spend some time with Teddy – I don't want to be having to keep him quiet to keep *you* happy.' Really, I need him to go to work so me and Teddy can leave. Unless we get out of here while he's going for his run...

'I haven't got it in me to face all the questions everyone will have after what's been in the news. It's bad enough being around all *your* bloody questions.'

'But—'

He grabs his headphones and slams out of the room. I hear Suki's lead rattle in the hallway. He's taking her with him which means me and Teddy can't leave yet. I can't leave my dog behind. Then he slams out of the house.

The pillock. I've asked him to keep the noise down so as not to wake Teddy. I need time to myself, before I have to feign cheer and normality. I need to get my head straight too.

I creep upstairs and peer from the landing window just as he and Suki disappear around the corner. Then I look into Teddy's room again. It was around half past ten when I finally got him to bed last night. Thankfully, he's still sleeping soundly.

I wander up and down the landing for a few moments, wondering what's going to become of us, of this house, of the family and the life that was supposed to be happy-ever-after for us.

A light suddenly illuminates the kitchen window next door. This might be my only chance today. *I'll make that woman tell me what she knows if it's the last thing I do.*

I can't just stand back and let things happen all around me. I've put up with enough crap from Jon as it is, always dancing to his tune and pacifying him to keep the peace and I've had enough. The only thing that matters to me now is Teddy and keeping him safe and happy.

I rush back down the stairs, grab joggers and a hoodie from the laundry pile, quickly change out of my pyjamas and then race towards the door. Jon can be more than an hour when he runs, especially when he's got things on his mind. I've got time.

I drop the latch on the door and slip the keys into my pocket, pausing to steady my breath. I shouldn't be leaving Teddy alone in the house but I reckon he'll sleep for at least another couple of hours. And I need to know what *she* knows.

FORTY-ONE

CASSIE

Becca's more likely to answer the side door, I tell myself as I lift the handle on her gate. Hopefully, she'll think it's her mother's carers, arriving early. They never use the front door from what I've seen when I've been looking out.

I knock on the glass panel and stand to the side, out of sight of the window. Footsteps tap along the floor at the other side. There's a pause. She's probably trying to see who it is.

Becca's shoulders sag as she opens the door. 'What the hell are you doing, standing where I can't even see you?' Her eyelids droop with fatigue, mirroring the exhaustion I feel.

'I wanted to make sure you'd answer.' I infuse my voice with as much civility as I can muster towards this woman. After how she's been with me, I don't like her any more than she appears to like me. Especially now. 'I've been kept in the dark for long enough.'

'I've got nothing to say to you Cassie.' Her hand moves to the side of the door, seemingly preparing to close it in my face. 'And I'm busy with my mother if you don't mind. She's still distressed after last night.'

'Just five minutes.' I push the door back at her. 'You saw

what Jon did last night – he nearly killed someone for God's sake. I'm not going anywhere until you speak to me.'

She looks at me as though considering my motives. It's the first time she's ever looked me directly in the eye and I notice how clear and green her eyes are. Until now, for reasons I have yet to fathom, it's been as if she can't bring herself to look at me. 'I've actually tried ringing the hospital, but they won't tell me anything,' she says.

'Really?' Why would cold and aloof Becca care whether Amy lives or dies?

'I can't stop thinking about it. *How can I?* It happened right here, in my hallway.' She sweeps her arm back behind her. Suddenly, she's giving me an *in*. A moment ago, I was convinced she was about to slam the door in my face.

'You heard what Amy came out with to Jon last night: "*I served your time*".' I say the words slowly, allowing the chance for them to sink in with her. 'You were at school with them and knew them both. You must have some idea what she meant by it?'

She folds her arms and leans against the doorframe. She's going to crack. She's going to tell me what she knows – I'm certain of it.

'Come on, you lived next door to him,' I continue. 'What did she mean? I'm not going to let up until I get to the truth. How can I?'

Still, she says nothing but her thoughtful expression conveys she seem to be at least considering what, or how much to tell me. After a moment of waiting, I decide to change tack.

'I need to know whether I should be getting myself and my son away from here – away from Jon.' I gesture up to Teddy's bedroom window behind where I'm standing, praying he stays asleep a bit longer. 'You're the only person who can help us here – you do know that, don't you? Don't you think I've got the right to know?'

'Where is he?'

'He's gone for a run.'

'Alright.' Becca lowers her gaze to the floor and then back to me. It appears as though admitting fears for our safety has managed to get through her frosty exterior.

'Alright... what?'

'Look. I've been terrified to tell the truth in case he comes for *me* next.' She drums her fingers against the doorframe.

Oh no. *Who the hell am I married to?* Becca's hostility towards me is rooted in her fearing my husband. It's looking more and more like Amy *was* telling the truth.

'Whatever you say, we'll stand together afterwards, I promise you.'

Her expression doesn't change, nor is there any acknowledgement of what I've just said. She doesn't appear particularly moved by my promise of an allegiance.

She hesitates again. *Come on, come on.* I actually feel like shaking her.

'That party, the one after our exams,' she eventually begins. 'I was there.'

'I suspected as much, though Jon said the two of you didn't get along?'

'He was OK when we were much younger, but he turned into an egomaniac as a teenager. The girls used to fight over him. I mean *literally* fight over him.'

'But you weren't one of them, I take it?'

'Not at all.' She shakes her head. 'He was just *Jon from next door* to me.'

'Right.' She's finally talking; I can barely breathe as I wait for her to continue.

'Anyway, towards the time of us all leaving school, he had two or three girls on the go, all off and on – that's what he was like.'

'Right.' Even in spite of all that's going on, I can't help but feel a tug of jealousy. I slap it back down – I've let my unhealthy dependence on the man cloud my judgement of him for long enough. It's fightback time.

'There was Jade, the one that all the girls trailed after in envy – she was pretty, talented at sport, nice through and through, maybe too nice. Anyway she excelled at everything she ever touched.'

'I get the picture.' I wish I could speed her up – I need to get back to Teddy soon.

'Then there was Amelia.' A strange look enters her eyes. 'She was nothing special, but she had a colossal crush on Jon right through the final year of school.'

'*Amelia?* Do you mean Amy?'

She nods. 'Jade wouldn't sleep with Jon – but Amelia would. He could have told her to bark like a dog and she would. Anyway, Jade became really bitter about it. Not enough to sleep with him though.'

'What did she do?'

'Because she was so popular, she managed to turn just about everyone against Amelia,' she says. 'Her life at school became hell.'

'Were you against her too?' I think back again to when I introduced them recently; it was clear enough then that it probably wasn't their first meeting and there was definitely the echo of bad blood between them.

She nods. 'We all called Amelia *the Rawdale bike*, although to my knowledge, Jon was the only boy she'd been to bed with.'

A vision of those knickers re-emerges in my mind. *What the hell has been going on?*

'He ricocheted between the two of them for weeks.' Becca moves her finger from side to side then back again. 'Months even. All his friends made fun of him but secretly, I guess, they looked up to him.'

'He'd have liked that then.' My words are laced with sarcasm. It's hard not to feel this way at the moment.

'Anyway, by the night of the party, he seemed to have his sights firmly set on Jade and was ignoring Amelia.'

'What I don't understand, is how can he have actually *slept* with Amy over and over again, but then claim not to recognise her? I know it's been ten years, but still.'

'He really *didn't* recognise her. When we spoke the other morning, he didn't believe me when I said it was *definitely* her.'

My mind races back to the moment I caught sight of Becca talking to Jon from Teddy's window and began leaping to all kinds of conclusions.

'He said he thought she looked familiar, but that was as far as it went.'

'That's what he told me as well. Maybe he *is* being honest about that part of things then.'

'She's completely changed, you know. She doesn't look *anything* like she used to.'

'But *you* recognised her? Why didn't you say something straight away? Sorry, I'm interrupting.' I need to let her speak.

'It's OK, and no, I'd never forget *her* face. Anyway, *everyone* was invited to that party.' She gestures towards my house. 'His parents were away and had apparently said he could have a few friends round to celebrate after the final exam. Obviously, it grew from there and was the talk of the school.'

'Was Amy invited?'

Becca pulls a face. 'She was the only person who wasn't.' She pauses, as though recollecting. 'But she came anyway. I didn't see her arrive but I noticed her in the corner.'

'On her own?'

'Yep. Scowling at everyone, especially Jade. Everyone was talking *about* Amelia, but nobody was talking *to* her.'

'You seem to have a good memory of that night.'

'I've plenty of reason.' She backs into the kitchen in

response to a noise from within the house. 'Hang on Mum. I won't be long,' she calls, before returning to me.

I need to step this up. I have to know the full story while we're here like this and Teddy could wake at any moment. 'So Amy's there in the corner, giving off an atmosphere. Didn't Jon ask her to leave?'

'He was probably enjoying the tug of war over him, to be honest – he always did.' A hint of a smile crosses her lips for the first time since she answered the door.

'That figures. He's still got that same ego – it's been the size of Brazil ever since I met him.' What I don't add is how his ego has been fattened by *my* insecurities and how he's made me feel. It's a relief to be finally seeing him for who and what he really is.

'I went over to talk to her; I thought I'd try to cheer her up.'

'Really?' She's shocked me again. Becca doesn't strike me as the sort of person who'd go out of her way to be friendly to *anyone*. But then, I hardly know her. 'What happened next?'

'At first she seemed grateful that I'd taken the trouble,' she replies. 'But she soon started quizzing me on how often I'd seen Jade coming and going from Jon's in recent weeks. That's all she wanted to talk about.'

'*Had* you seen Jade coming and going? Did you tell her?' It's an effort to reconcile my current home with the same place my husband used to have his girlfriends coming and going from. It's little wonder he's found it strange to move me and Teddy in there.

'Yes, I was totally honest about it. I figured it was best to be cruel to be kind. I'd hoped she'd say, *well stuff him then*. But she didn't.'

'What *did* she say?'

The look on Becca's face suggests this is *it* – the crux of our conversation, perhaps.

FORTY-TWO

CASSIE

Her expression darkens. 'She told me that she was prepared to do *anything* to get Jade out of the picture. And she sounded as though she meant it.'

'Which presumably would include lacing her drink with ketamine,' I say.

She swallows and folds her arms across her chest. 'Right.' She glances at our house as though checking she can't be overheard. 'I left Amy to it and went to get myself a drink. They were all stacked in the utility room.'

'OK?'

'Jon was already in there.'

'And?'

She takes a deep breath. 'He was tipping white powder from a polythene bag into a glass.'

Bloody hell. Amy *was* telling the truth last night. 'Did you ask him what he was doing?'

'I didn't need to – when he noticed me, he just grinned and said, *this should make the evening more interesting*. He didn't even try to hide the stuff, so I assumed he was adding something recreational to his *own* drink – there was no reason to think anything else. But a short time later...' Her voice cracks. 'Jade collapsed in the middle of the lounge.'

'She died in our lounge?' A knot forms in my stomach.

'Yes.'

The early morning sun casts long shadows over the street, and the distant birdsong creates an eerie contrast to the gravity of Becca's revelation.

'I couldn't believe it.' Her voice is almost a whisper.

'*Ketamine*. That's a horse tranquilliser, isn't it?'

'It's also a date rape drug.' She brings her eyes back to meet mine.

So there I have it. My husband *is* capable of rendering someone senseless to get what he wants out of her; at least, he *was* capable. As well as that, he's allowed an innocent girl with her whole life ahead of her to take what should have been *his* punishment. I can't wait to get away from him.

'Jade had a terrible reaction. She never regained consciousness after she collapsed,' Becca goes on, a tremble in her words. I get a sense this is the first time she's opened up about it since it happened.

'To be honest, what happened with Amelia last night has brought everything flooding back. Not that it ever went away. I didn't get a wink of sleep last night.'

'Me neither.' Thank God she's finally talking to me. She's going to have to tell the police all this too, though judging by her silence for all these years, I can't imagine she will. After all, she's probably going to be in trouble herself. There must be more to this. Why would she have kept someone else's guilt a secret for all these years? What did she stand to gain – or lose?

I can't get my head around any of it. I should have thought to have my phone in my pocket, recording this conversation, for proof, should I need it.

'If you're saying it *was* Jon, how could Amy have been locked up for it?'

'The police took a statement from us all at the party and everyone was giving the same name to them. *Amelia.* Over and over.'

'But *you* knew he had done it?'

'I still thought he was adding something to his *own* drink – I didn't connect that with what had happened to Jade to begin with.'

'Were these statements the only proof they had on Amy?'

'As far as I know. The glass she'd drunk from had been cleaned; there'd be no prizes for guessing who might have done that.' Becca jerks her head towards our house again. 'That they pressed charges seemed to boil down to Amelia being the only person at the party with a motive. Her jealousy. She'd also been standing over Jade as she died.'

'Why?' My mouth is dry, as if the weight of Becca's words has drained all the moisture from my body.

'She said she'd been trying to help her. But everyone told the police it was to make sure no one else could help.'

'Then Amy was arrested?'

Becca nods. 'To be fair, in that moment, I genuinely thought they'd got the right person. But then something else happened.'

'What?'

I look around. I've got a sudden sense of being watched. The street is still relatively silent, apart from occasional foot-steps when someone walks by or the momentary hum of a passing car.

Becca follows my gaze. 'What's up?'

'Nothing.' I turn my attention back to her. 'I'm just being paranoid.'

'A day or so after it all happened, Jon's dad collared me in the street and asked me to go into the house for a word.'

'Did you go?'

'Jack was someone you didn't really argue with.'

'That's the impression I've been given.'

'Jon had apparently confided in him that I'd seen him adding powder to a drink. If he hadn't used the word "drink", I'd probably have never added it all up.'

'Jon admitted *to his father* that he'd spiked Jade?'

She nods. 'According to Jack, Jon was terrified the police were going to think it was *him*, not Amelia, who'd done it. And I was the only other person who'd seen him with the powder.'

'So why didn't you report what you knew?' My mind races, imagining myself in her situation at eighteen. Next door neighbour, friend, or whatever – I'd have gone to the police. No way would I have let an innocent girl take the blame for something so devastating, no matter how unpopular she was.

But how weird life is. If Becca had done the right thing, I'd have never met or married Jon – therefore Teddy wouldn't even exist. My life could have turned out entirely different to how it's been. Jon could be the one getting out of prison on licence, with his life in ruins, under a new identity, forced to live in a probation hostel – instead of Amy.

'I... I couldn't, could I?' Becca's eyes glisten with tears, her voice trembling as she speaks. 'I was threatened.'

'By Jack?'

'I should *never* have gone into the house to speak to him.' She points at it. 'But we'd lived next door to them for years. Our mums went shopping together. Our dads, before mine died, had got together for beers over the fence all the time.'

'How did he threaten you?' To think this man was my father-in-law. I'm just glad he never had the chance to meet Teddy and exert his influence over him.

'He didn't threaten anything to begin with. He just offered money to keep me quiet. Lots of it.'

I stare at her.

'I know what you're thinking of me,' she says. 'I can tell by your face. But it wasn't as simple as all that. He told me that I either accepted the money, or he'd use it to employ the best legal team it could buy.'

'But how would that have affected *you*?'

'Jack warned he'd make sure *anything* I said about Jon was completely discredited.' Her face darkens. 'But then came his biggest threat.'

I can't imagine what threat could have been so great it would have coerced her to tell such a horrendous lie.

'He warned me he'd ensure I'd be seen as an *accomplice* rather than as a *witness*: in league with Amelia to get rid of Jade.'

'*An accomplice?* How?'

'Lots of people had seen me talking to Amelia at the party, like I just told you. I was only eighteen at the time, obviously no match for a bloke like him.' She lets a long breath out. 'When he died, he was described as a "stalwart of the community" at his funeral. No one would have taken my word over his.'

'No wonder Jon cut all ties with him in the end.'

'It was the other way actually. Jack saw Jon right financially, but that was it. There was no way Jack was going to allow his family's name to be dragged through the mud – he wanted him as far away from here as possible.'

'Why didn't you tell anyone? Being threatened like that by some man, whether you knew him or not, is a lot for an eigh-teen-year-old to handle.' I picture myself at that age. I might not have been particularly close to my parents when growing up but I'd have asked for help.

'My mum was grieving my dad's death at the time,' Becca replies. 'I had no one I could trust. Maybe I could have done something but at the time I didn't think I'd be believed.'

'You can't have *known* that.'

'Jack Hemingway was a powerful man in this town – you ask anyone who remembers him. He made donations to charities, spoke publicly at events – people respected him.'

'That wouldn't have made any difference.'

'It would have been my word against his – and Jon's. Besides,' she continues, 'once the initial opportunity to speak up had passed, I thought I'd be in too much trouble.'

'Did you have to go to Amy's trial? I read about it.'

She nods again. 'I told the jury I'd seen Amelia adding the powder to Jade's glass. I was in the witness box for all of ten minutes. That's all it took.'

It's weird talking about Amy, and Amelia, so interchangeably. It must have been horrendous for her, being forced to serve time, then live under a new identity for someone else's crime.

'But that ten minutes was long enough to cost Amy ten years of her life.'

'In the end...' Becca continues, 'it all came down to whether the jury believed the opinion of *everyone* at the party, or Amelia. It was nearly a majority verdict. Her mother had been a drunk, I don't think she ever knew her father, her grandparents had taken her in after her mother had died, and she was a loner at school.' She counts this list of Amy's misfortune on her fingers.

'In those days,' she adds, 'the jury were always going to believe a well-to-do family, over an unpopular and underprivileged girl, whose grandparents didn't even come to court to support her – I heard they'd washed their hands of her.'

'That shouldn't have mattered to the jury.' Though I know, even these days, that it does. Money and status talk.

'Amelia had a huge crush on Jon and had almost stalked him in the final school year. She was portrayed in court to be jealous of anyone that came near him, and, ultimately, a vindictive person, capable of murder. The amount of ketamine found in Jade's body afterwards proved that it couldn't have been an accident – there was enough of it in her to kill a horse, let alone tranquillise one.'

I try to swallow. My husband *is* a cold-blooded murderer. *Enough to kill a horse.* Poor Amy. I think of her, clinging to life in that hospital, that's if she still is.

'How have you lived with this for all these years?' Guilt like she must have had to carry would have destroyed me.

'With great difficulty,' she replies, her voice lowering with her gaze. 'It's been a miserable existence, here with my mother, but it's no less than I deserve.'

It's hard to feel sorry for her. I'm certain the police would have believed her if she'd been honest at the time. No matter how much of a big shot my father-in-law might have been.

'The judge handed down the longest sentence he could impose,' she continues. 'I was allowed back into the courtroom to watch as he summed it all up. He talked about her lack of remorse and the fact that she'd continued to lie about what she'd done – to protest her innocence. I'll never forget the sound of her sobbing when they took her down.'

'What then? Everyone just went back to life as usual?'

'Jack forced Jon to move away for college, even though he was supposed to be staying in Yorkshire.'

'It sounds like he wanted him completely out of the way.'

'Jon's mum told my mum there'd been a huge family falling-out. Jack had told Jon *never to darken his doorstep again.* His mum was heartbroken, but Jack ruled the roost in that house.'

'Did you see Jon after that?'

She shakes her head. 'I was relieved when he moved away to college; at least I didn't have to face him anymore and be reminded of it all. I heard he went travelling after that.'

'That's when he met me.' If I'd only known I was falling for someone who'd done something so terrible as an eighteen-year-old. I don't know what I'm more shocked at, that he's capable of date-rape or that he's allowed Amy to serve his prison sentence like she's been forced to.

She's missed the best years of her life for something *he's* done. It sounds like her only crime was having an enormous crush on someone who was too busy playing the field to offer her more than a few crumbs of his affection. I should know what this feels like; at times, it's all I ever got from my husband.

'Jack died of a heart attack about five years later. Well you'll know that, won't you? I think I saw you at the funeral.'

I want to say *serves him right*, but I'm not coming down to the man's level. 'I wondered about that when Jon told me his father had died. I knew *something* must have happened between them; I mean, how many sons would need so much persuasion to attend their own father's funeral, no matter how difficult the relationship?'

I think back to how hard I'd had to persuade him, insisting that not going might be something he'd live to regret, while at the same time having the ulterior motive of being curious to see who his family were and where he'd come from. In the end, it was his mother who'd persuaded him to attend and as far as I can remember, they'd all kept up appearances unashamedly.

I *was* reassured when I saw where he came from – a solid community, a stable home and a life of privilege. However, because of this, I ended up marrying a construct of Jon. The man he'd reinvented himself to be. And I never believed I was good enough for him.

'I was forced to attend,' Becca says. 'My mum was in a wheelchair by then.' She rolls her eyes to the upstairs of her house. 'And asked me to take her. I hated having to sit through it, listening to what a *pillar* of the town he was, what a *committed* family man.'

I recall a woman who kept staring at Jon. It must have been Becca. I'd even asked him if she was an old girlfriend. Even though we were engaged by then, I was often insecure. As though someone could take him away from me.

'Anyway,' I say, 'I need to be getting back to Teddy.' My words are tinged with guilt. 'I've left him on his own for long enough.'

'Is he OK on his own?' Her eyes widen as if to suggest I'm a bad mother, especially after what happened last night.

'He's still fast asleep. It's that quiet out here that I'm sure I'd have heard him if he'd woken.'

'What are you going to do Cassie?' It's the first time she's used my name.

'Well, you know what he's capable of. And when he finds out I know what really happened...' My voice trails away. 'Or you, if he finds out you've told me the full story.'

Becca grips the rail next to the door, her knuckles whitening, uncertainty written across her face. 'Are you going to tell the police?'

'I'm going take Teddy to my mum's and then, yes, I'm going to have to. I don't know what else I can do.'

FORTY-FOUR

CASSIE

The door's off the latch. This isn't how I left it. To keep Teddy safe, I made a point of dropping the latch as I went next door.

I dash up the stairs and heave a sigh of relief as I look into his room. He's still fast asleep. Clearly, he needs the extra rest after yesterday's ordeal. At least, while he's sleeping, he's safe from his memories of being terrified and alone – locked in that storeroom for all that time. Eventually he'll get over it. And so will I. I know only too well that it could have been worse. Far worse. I just wish I could get these thoughts from my head.

His *Thomas the Tank Engine* curtains billow in the breeze. That's odd. I stare at them. Very odd. I locked that window last night and recall double-checking it too. I tiptoe across his room and peer through a crack between the curtains as they bulge towards me. Then I remember. This is exactly where I was standing as I observed the conversation between Jon and Becca.

It seems it's not only me who's used it as a vantage point. Oh. My. God.

Jon must have returned from his run while I've been out there, talking to Becca. Were we so engrossed that neither of us noticed him? But, and far more importantly, how much of what we were saying has he overheard?

I can barely breathe as I creep back towards the landing, the floor creaking beneath my feet as I click Teddy's door behind me. Checking in our room, I notice the bed that's only been slept in on one side and the still-closed blinds. I poke my head into the en suite, expecting steam and the scent of shower gel. He always takes a shower the minute he's returned from a run. *So why not today?*

The main bathroom is still littered with Teddy's clothes from last night, his trains strewn across the bath. The guest room is just as I left it, and the spare bedrooms are still piled up with yet-to-be-unpacked stuff, and there's barely room for a human in either of them. So where is he? My heart's beating so fast, it feels like it's going to jump out of my chest. I was so desperate to hear what Becca had to say. Yet, the moment he left for his run, I should have taken Teddy and gone. I could have come back for Suki later.

I descend the stairs, first checking the lounge, then his office. There's no sign of him. He must be hiding somewhere. Panic rises in me like bile. *How much has he heard?*

'Are you looking for me?' Jon's voice makes me jump as he appears in the kitchen doorway – arms folded. Normally after a run, his hair's matted with sweat and his skin has a sheen. Yet, with the broad smile across his face, he's as cool as an ice-pop. It would appear that he hasn't even run to the end of the street. I could be *really* in the shit here.

Act normal. Act normal. 'Ah, there you are.' I force a smile back at him though I'm shaking from head to foot. 'Yes I was, actually.'

'Well look no further.'

'I'm thinking of doing us a cooked breakfast, you know, Teddy's favourite, and wondered if you'd nip to the supermarket.' I keep my voice as light and breezy as I can but he must be able to pick up the tremor in it. Surely he wouldn't be smiling if he *had* overheard us. 'We need eggs.'

'What – to go with the two dozen we've already got?' He strides back into the kitchen. I follow and watch as he pulls two egg boxes from the bottom of the fridge and places them on the counter. Suki emerges from her basket and arches her back.

'Sorry, I'm being daft; I meant hash browns.' I force a laugh as I slap my palm into my forehead, while pointing at the connecting door from the utility room towards the garage. I can't imagine he'll have the volition to venture into the garage to check the chest freezer.

I need to get him out of here. I feel even less safe around him now Becca's confirmed everything. If I can just get him out of the way for ten minutes, I can bundle Teddy and Suki into the car then drive to Mum's while I work out what to do next.

He opens the small freezer box above the fridge. 'Haven't we got enough already?' He tugs out an unopened bag and holds it aloft. 'Try again Cassie.'

'Oh, I didn't realise. Don't mind me, my head is all over the place after everything that's gone on.' I attempt to load a false airiness into my voice but he knows me too well.

Jon's smile fades into a cold stare. 'I watched you put the shopping delivery away the other day – remember?'

He's right. I was inwardly seething that he barely looked up from his laptop where he was sitting at the counter while I was unloading it all. The notion of helping me didn't seem to enter his head. But that's the least of my worries now.

'We've got eggs. We've got hash browns.' His voice is even, bordering on almost normal but there's an edge to it I haven't heard before. 'Are you trying to get rid of me Cassie?' He cocks his head to one side as though whatever answer I'm going to give him is the most important answer in the world. The room feels suffocating, the air thick with unspoken accusations. Suki, probably sensing that I'm *not* about to take her for a walk, slinks back to her basket. Either that or she can sense the tension in here.

'Of course I'm not.' I laugh again, wondering if he can hear the nerves within it. Something in how he's behaving tells me he's heard every word that passed between me and Becca. But I must stay calm. If I can't get him to go anywhere then I need to try something else.

'I'm just off to wake that boy of ours.' I turn on my heel, back towards the door. 'You know what he's like – he won't settle tonight if I let him sleep much longer.'

'What are you up to Cassie?' Jon darts in front of me, blocking my path back to the door.

'What do you mean – *what am I up to?* I'm just going to get Teddy up and then I think I'll take him and Suki to the park.' Suki's ears prick up from her basket at the mention of the word *park*.

'I thought you were making breakfast.'

'I am. I'll sort it when we get back.' I smile. He doesn't.

'Suki – in you go.' He flings open the door of the utility room, points to it as she trots inside, then slams it shut, trapping her inside. Immediately, she starts to whimper.

'What have you done that for?' I start towards her but he moves to the side again, his hand brushing against mine as he obstructs me. This brief contact sends a chill through my veins. I could be in real trouble here.

'Because I don't believe you, Cassie.'

'Why wouldn't you? Suki needs a walk and going to the park will do Teddy good. He needs a normal day today. And so do I.' I'm wittering here. I always do when I'm nervous.

And right at this moment, I've got a lot to be nervous about.

FORTY-FIVE

CASSIE

'Let me past Jon.' I still don't know for certain how much he overheard of my conversation with Becca – if any of it. He could be acting like this for any number of reasons. At least, that's what I'm trying to tell myself.

He doesn't move. 'I want to know why you're betraying me like this.'

'Like what?' I take a step to my right. And so does he. Suki's whimpering is becoming louder. She'll know something's going on out here.

'You're trying to set me up, aren't you?'

'Set you up for what?'

'I heard you out there.' The line of his jaw hardens. 'Every. Single. Word. What's going on?'

'You tell me.' I try to square up to him even though my legs have gone to jelly.

'You and *her*.' He jerks his head in the direction of Becca's house. 'I heard what you said – word for word.' He elongates each word he speaks. 'You've been had hook, line and sinker, haven't you?'

'I'm willing to hear you out Jon.' Though I'm standing firm,

I'm shaking inside. 'I promise.' He *did* hear us. 'But I need to see to Teddy first.' The tremor in my voice is difficult to suppress as I meet Jon's cold eyes. My mind is racing with thoughts of how to escape. I struggle to hold his gaze but I need to convince him I'm not scared. He'll despise that and it might just make him angrier than he already is. There's a darkness in his eyes I haven't seen before. Somehow, we really need to get out of here.

Not that it's ever been put to the test but I'm certain Suki would defend me against Jon if push came to shove. Her allegiance has always been with me. Which is why he'll have shut her in the utility room. No one wants thirty kilograms of German Shepherd flying at them. *But what's he planning to do to me?*

'Surely you don't want to tear our family apart?'

'A girl *died* because of what you did to her Jon. And another one might still die.'

He's often laughed about my so-called 'moral compass'. All the times I've insisted on conforming to rules, speed limits and other expectations. He once managed to talk me into taking a speeding ticket for him, but he certainly won't be talking me into standing by him after everything I've discovered.

'Were you really going to squeal to the police without talking to me first? Even more than you have already?' We haven't held each other's gazes so intently since we stood facing each other at the altar. I blink the memory away. Tears burn at the back of my eyes. It's all gone to shit.

'I saw what you're capable of.' Suki's whimpering seems to have died down slightly. She'll be wondering why on earth I haven't let her out of there.

His entire face hardens. 'That bitch was trying to ruin my life. When she didn't manage it, my parents did. Everything I knew, everything that was familiar – it was snatched away like I'd never mattered.'

His fists are bunched at his sides. He's never hit me before. He's grabbed my arm and once held me against a wall but he's never hit me. My eyes flit around for something I might be able to defend myself with. I've got to keep myself safe – I've got Teddy up there.

'Mummy!'

He's awake! Jon might allow me to get past him now. My phone's up there – I'll be able to get help.

'I was *forced* to move away from here when I was eighteen. Do you know what that did to me?'

'Just let me see to Teddy. Then we'll talk properly.' I step to my left. And so does he.

'You really think I trust you to leave this room. Remember, I heard what you said out there.' His voice lifts as he throws his head back and laughs. To think that until a couple of days ago, I thought I was married to a 'normal' man.

'I was shocked, that's all. After what you did to Amy.'

'Extenuating circumstances.' For someone so good looking, it's hard to believe there's something inside him which is so clearly warped. There's no remorse whatsoever. 'The woman had snatched my son. My solicitor's already told me the worst I'll get is a suspended sentence. The very worst.'

'Mummy, I've wet the bed.'

That'll be why he hasn't come bounding downstairs like he normally would. The poor thing – after what he went through yesterday, it's no wonder. Plus, he's slept much later than he usually would.

'I'm coming sweetheart. Just give me a second. I really need to get to him Jon.' This is a nightmare. He really isn't going to let me out of his sight. How the hell are we going to escape? Why didn't I do it earlier?

'Then what?' He folds his arms but doesn't budge.

'Like I said, I'll take Teddy and Suki for some fresh air; I'll clear my head, and then we'll talk when I get back.'

I step closer but the only movement he makes is to grasp my

shoulders in each hand. To an onlooker, we might look like a happily married couple about to kiss. Yet I won't ever be kissing him again.

'I can't let you leave the house Cassie.' His voice is soft, yet sinister. 'Surely you must realise that? I can't let you and her from next door spread more lies about me, can I?'

My shoulders are shaking within his grasp. 'You can't keep me in here Jon.' I attempt to load a strength I'm not feeling into my words.

'You'd really do this to our family, wouldn't you? Everything should have been left well alone.' He looks down at me as though he's chastising Teddy. 'It's all in the past.'

'I didn't go looking for this.' I try to shake my shoulders free as Suki steps up her whining to a new level, probably because she's heard Teddy's voice. 'Until a couple of days ago, I thought I was a normal wife and mother, starting again with a new home and a new job. *You've* done this to us Jon, not me!' My elevated voice echoes around the kitchen.

Something in my tone must have changed for the expression in Jon's face hardens some more.

'You couldn't stop sniffing around, could you?' His voice cracks with anger. 'You couldn't just leave it alone.'

'Mummy! Why's Daddy shouting?'

'Let me get to my son.' Right now, that's all that matters.

'He's my son as well.'

'Then act like his bloody father.' I shout the words into his face. I couldn't feel any worse about the effect of all this on Teddy than I do at this moment. He'd already had enough upheaval. God knows what's going on inside his mind.

'Don't you fucking shout at me. Who the hell do you think you are?' He rams me against the door frame.

'Please, Jon, stop. Think about Teddy.'

I can't just roll over and die here. The only option I've got is to fight. What did my mother always used to tell me to do if I needed to escape from someone?

Go for the balls Cassandra.

Jon yowls and bends double to the floor.

Stepping over him. I hurtle up the stairs to where Teddy is curled into a ball at the top of the stairs. I've no time to feel guilty. We just need to get out of here and somehow I need to get to Suki as well. I'm not leaving her behind. I don't trust Jon not to hurt her.

I wrench Teddy's dressing gown from the back of his door and rush into the guest bedroom where I left my phone. He's waiting for me on the landing.

'Come on.' I reach for his hand.

'Where Mummy?'

Jon's on his way up the stairs. No-no-no. He comes closer.

'Get into there.' I push Teddy towards the bathroom and race to where my phone is. 'Lock the door.'

I only manage to press two nines into my phone before Jon wrenches it from me and hurls it against the wall. I scream as he lunges at me. I dodge. His arms swing out but he misses me, giving me the chance to get to our bedroom. I'll yell for help from the window. Becca will hear me – she'll guess what's going on.

As I grapple with the lock to the en suite, he's pushing what feels like his full body weight against the other side. Even as I throw all my weight behind it, crying out with the exertion, it's no match for his strength. In less than thirty seconds, he's crashing in.

'Please Jon, no! Don't hurt me! Please!'

'I told you, didn't I?' He stands in front of me, breathing heavily, his face contorted with hatred. My gaze flits from his face, to the window, and then to the cabinet. I can either shout for help, or...

The cabinet door's open. I grabble for his box of insulin

pens. I'm well versed in how much he can have. Each pen contains three doses. Possibly enough to at least disarm him – though I've no idea how long it'll take to have an effect. I don't see what else I can do.

I don't even get as far as removing the lid before everything from the cabinet scatters around us. Jon wrestles me to the ground, grunting with anger, while trying to prise the pen from my fingers. I stretch across the tiles for another of them with my free hand but just as I reach it, he's stabbing at the exposed flesh above my waistband.

'No! Stop!'

He yanks the needle back out of me, before plunging it once again. I screech with the pain. My stomach freezes as the liquid permeates my skin.

'Please. No. Jon – what about Teddy?' I writhe on the floor beneath him as he plunges the needle into me a third time, this time into my hip.

'Help me – somebody,' I scream out, my words reverberating around the walls.

Jon rises from his crouch. I yelp as he boots me in the stomach and crunch double with the pain when he does it again. I cry out as he boots me in the back. By his second kick to my head, I know I'm done for. I've no longer got the energy to scream. The metallic tang of blood fills my nostrils as I try to get back up.

As the door opens and light from the bedroom filters across my face, I vomit onto the floor beside me. The door closes with a click.

I attempt to get up but dizziness forces me back to the ground. Him sticking the boot in shouldn't kill me.

But three hundred milligrams of insulin might.

PART 6

FORTY-SIX

BECCA

I crouch next to the wall, listening as the yelling, screaming, and crying from next door pierce this normally tranquil street.

Since they moved in, the Hemingways have been quiet on the whole. *Perfect neighbours*, some might say, except there's no one I'd want as neighbours less.

'Help me – somebody!' Cassie's cry echoes around my brain, shredding at my nerves. Then a silence so palpable I can almost touch it.

Dread chases through my veins. Something's happened in there. Something awful. She must have confronted Jon. There's no way he'd risk her reporting him after all this time. He's got away with it for far too long already.

Which means, if I don't call for some help sharpish, he'll most likely come for me next, the only other person who can nail him.

If Cassie manages to get out of there unhurt, what she knows is going to cause insurmountable levels of trouble for me – after all, she told me she was going to report everything I told her. So I'm in it up to my neck. However, this is definitely the lesser of the two evils.

If me speaking out leads to Jon being sent to prison for murder, it will be worth the risk I've taken in telling Cassie. I never thought he'd come back here but now he has, I'll do *anything* to get him out of my life.

From the research I've done, I'll be *very* unlucky to get sent to prison – not after all these years. They're hardly likely to pass a prison sentence, especially when I've got my mother so dependent on me.

Yes, I perverted the course of justice but they'll see the main villain as Jon. I've often thought of getting proper legal advice about this but any solicitor would have been duty bound to report me to the police, so up until Jon returning to Tolbeck Cottage, I've kept quiet.

With hindsight, prison might not have even been a credible threat when I was being blackmailed by Jon's father – I was, as the court might have seen it, young and impressionable. But at the time, I believed Jack's threats and the consequences of telling the truth.

A violent slam echoes through the air, jolting me from my thoughts. I rise to my feet and slam my own door before dialling three nines as my breath comes in rapid gasps. No matter what, that little boy needs me to do something.

I need me to do something.

The operator tells me to stay on the line and keep talking until the police get to us. She asks me to keep an eye on their house and provide her with a running commentary. They're taking this seriously. Of course they are – a child's safety is caught up in it.

I recount last night's events to the operator, my voice quivering, desperate for her to understand the danger we're in. She reiterates the importance of me staying on the line. She tells me to double-check the doors are locked. As I head towards the front door, my mother starts wailing. Wailing, wailing, always wailing. It's a dreadful sound, like an animal in a slaughter line.

It drives me insane. But this is my life. It's probably all I deserve.

'I'm going to have to hang up,' I tell the operator. 'It's my mother – I need to sort her out.'

'I really think—'

'I'm OK. The doors are locked. The police are *definitely* on their way, aren't they?'

'Two units have been dispatched.'

My mother becomes louder. She's always been hyper-intuitive. Even while bedridden and a shadow of the woman she used to be after her stroke, she's still got a nose for when something's going on.

And something's definitely going on.

Of course there's still Amelia. Jon should have kept his hands around her scrawny neck for as long as it took. I wish I knew what the odds were with her – the real reason I tried ringing the hospital. If she were to recover, she could be a serious fly in the ointment. After all, she also knows that every word of my testimony ten years ago was a fabrication.

I'll never forget the look on her face as she stood shaking her head in the witness box while I was cross-examined. She will, no doubt, do whatever it takes to hurt me and ruin my life as much as she can if she survives.

She's got real skin in the game, unlike Cassie, who'll no doubt just want to look after Teddy and take Jon for every penny she possibly can and get on with her life. That's if she still has one, after what I've just heard from next door.

I sit beside my mother, a placatory hand on her arm as her terror ebbs away. Once things were the other way around, especially during the bad dreams that followed firstly my father's death, then Jade's.

My father's death was a cruel twist of fate and I was helpless to prevent it. But Jade's was different.

I wasn't lying to Cassie when I told her about Jon adding white powder to Jade's drink.

But what I was lying about was the fact that I'd never thought of him as anything other than the boy-next-door. I knew he was going to bed with Amelia.

But he was also going to bed with me.

FORTY-SEVEN
BECCA

Serious time and money had gone into my appearance that night. My wild, wiry curls were meticulously styled at the hairdresser's, and my new wrap-over dress hugged my figure, making me feel like a completely different person. As I looked at myself in the mirror, I barely recognised the image staring back at me. I felt a mix of excitement and anxiety, hoping that Jon would finally feel proud to be seen with me.

When I'd been round at his house a couple of days prior, he promised me Amelia wasn't invited and said Jade was only coming because he'd already invited her. He assured me things had cooled between them, and that he only wanted me from then on. Then, as always, we'd had sex in his bedroom while his parents were at work.

Clearly he'd only told me what I'd wanted to hear, to get what he wanted out of me.

When I arrived at the party, he barely glanced at me as he opened the door. He snatched the bottle from my hand with a nod, and quickly averted his attention to the lads coming up the steps behind me.

'Hey, guys!' he exclaimed, the fact that he was genuinely

pleased to see them evident in his voice. I felt about as wanted as a debt collector. To begin with, I was gutted. Then the rage took over.

The thumping music reverberated through the room, laughter and chatter filling the air as I nursed a glass of cheap wine in a dimly lit corner. I looked on as a shriek of girls ogled Jon's best mate while another boy who'd appointed himself as the DJ rifled through a pile of CDs. Some other friends of Jon's laughed as they studied the old photos of him.

Then something else caught my attention. As he rested his hand in the small of her back, Jon spoke into Jade's ear and she smiled. After a moment he pulled back and winked at her. I might as well not have existed. With each passing moment, my fury intensified as he cosied up to her. This anger became a knife twisting in my gut, the hurt giving way to an over-whelming desire to make him pay. And her.

I wasn't the only one standing alone, watching – Amelia was doing exactly the same, observing the interactions between them like a bird stalking its prey.

Nobody would have guessed in a million years that he was having sex with me. With my frizzy gingery hair, buck teeth and piggy eyes, I could almost understand him wanting to keep our relationship a secret. If it could ever have been called *a relationship*. I loved Jon with every fibre of my being and had always clung to the hope that he'd eventually see me as more than just a convenient fling. I craved the validation of being officially known as his girlfriend.

Amelia was far prettier than me in those days, but nowhere near in Jade's league. No one was in Jade's league. Eventually, I went over to speak to Amelia, where it soon became clear that she knew *nothing* about me and Jon. Her only competition, as far as she was concerned, was Jade. It was also clear that my only use to her was as his next door neighbour as she pummelled me for information. She wanted details such as how many times I'd noticed Jade coming and going from his house and how recently.

Frustration, anger, and sadness swirled in my gut, making me want to rip my new dress off and stuff it in the dustbin. I felt like yanking out my earrings and ramming them down Jade's throat. I wanted to stand in the middle of the room and scream that it wasn't fair. This soon gave way to wanting to hurt Jon – to do something – anything that might wipe that self-assured smirk off his face.

He hadn't looked at me. Not once. I was no match for Jade with her stick-insect figure, large eyes and glossy blonde hair. And I never would be.

Eventually, it all got the better of me. When Jon managed to tear himself away from her, I took the opportunity to get him on his own. I didn't have a clue what I was going to say to him or whether he would even listen but I had to try *something*, so I followed him from the room.

I was telling the truth when I told Cassie how Jon had grinned when I saw him adding the powder. I was also telling the truth when I repeated the words he'd said – *this will make the evening more interesting.*

But I told a whopping lie when I told Cassie I'd thought the drink was for him; I knew he would *never* have put anything in his football-committed body apart from the odd pint of beer. He never went near spirits, smoked weed or anything else for that matter. He was as clean as cut glass.

Then I sensed someone behind me and realised Amelia had followed us too. I wasn't the only one who knew what he'd done.

It wasn't until the news reports came out that I discovered what the powder was. But even to this day, I have no idea how he laid his hands on it.

But what I knew all along was exactly *who* that glass was meant for.

I was just about to tell him how he'd made me feel when there was a crash from outside, followed by a load of shouting.

One of his mates burst in. 'They're scrapping in the garden,' he told Jon. 'A couple of the pots have been smashed.'

'Shit. My mum'll kill me.' He brushed past me as though I was invisible, leaving me standing there, alone with the glass he'd prepared, along with the knowledge of where he'd stashed the bag containing the rest of the powder. Amelia turned and hurried after him.

I peered around the door as they ran through the conservatory, knowing this could be my big chance. Before I could change my mind I tipped more of the powder into the liquid.

Scrunching the still quarter-full bag back where I'd got it from, I stirred the drink with a pen. I dropped it into my bag, leaned towards the glass and sniffed. All I could smell was Coca-Cola, probably with a vodka or three slipped into it. I slopped a bit more in. After all, vodka is tasteless.

What I'd added to it would be more than enough to ensure that *I'd* be the one in Jon's bed tonight, not *Jade*.

But I didn't think it would kill her.

FORTY-EIGHT

BECCA

The ensuing angst from the whole experience nearly brought me to my knees. Each catastrophic incident pursued the previous one as though dominoes were knocking into one another.

Pretty Jade didn't die a pretty death. There was vomit all over the place when she collapsed to the floor clutching her stomach. There were cries of *ugh* and *gross*. From what I could gather, everyone assumed she was badly drunk. Only one person went over to her – surprisingly, it was Amelia.

She apparently told police she'd been trying to help. But that's not how everyone else saw it. Personally, I only saw opportunity – *Amelia* could take the blame for what I'd done.

I couldn't have planned it any better – what's the saying? *Two birds with one stone.* I had, in one hit, eliminated all competition. Jade was heading six-foot under, while Amelia was heading for a prison cell.

After something so dreadful happening at his party, Jon would be drawn to me – he would lean on me for support – after all, I'd always been available to him until that point. And with what I knew, I could ensure he would *always* want me; I wouldn't give him any choice – after all, I was the only person who knew about him spiking Jade's drink in the first place and I planned never to tire of reminding him.

After Jade's body was carted off in the private ambulance, the dominoes continued to fall. One by one, everyone at the party spoke of Amelia's jealous obsession with Jon.

But nobody will have embellished their statement as much as I did. I told the police how I'd noticed Amelia constantly hanging around his house – at all hours of the day. I repeated her warning that *Jade was going to get everything that was coming to her.*

I'll admit I felt more than a few pangs of guilt, but that wretched bubbling in the pit of my stomach for a few days would be more than worth it for Jon's undivided attention beyond that.

Except I didn't get it. Instead, in the days that followed, Jon hid himself away. I tried calling round when his parents weren't there but he wouldn't even come to the door. Nor would he take my calls. This was the main reason I accepted his dad's invitation into the house when he stopped me in the street – in the hope I'd finally get to speak to Jon.

But after that horrendous conversation, where I was given no chance to reject what was being demanded of me, I barely saw Jon again. Other than him getting into the car to be packed away to a relative's house by his grim-faced father – at least that's what Mum told me. He only returned to testify at Amelia's trial.

We didn't speak that day either – and he brushed me off when I tried. He and I had been so close, yet he wouldn't even look at me.

But then I was, as far as he was aware, the *only* other person apart from Amelia and his parents who knew about him tipping powder into Jade's glass.

What he didn't know and will *never* find out was that it was *me* who spiked it even further, adding enough to have actually killed her.

I'm jolted into the present by a thumping on the back door.

FORTY-NINE

BECCA

'I'll be back soon Mum.' I let go of her arm and bolt to the top of the stairs. Thank goodness the police have got here so swiftly. Whether Cassie has reported Jon or not, I'd better tell the police exactly the same as I told her.

At least I'll be free when it's all over – I can get on with my life instead of everything hanging over me. It's not my fault – it's *his.* Sleeping dogs could have continued to lie, but Jon had to balls it all up by moving back into next door and subsequently inviting Amelia back into our lives.

I swipe at the keys from the kitchen counter to let the police in. No sooner have I twisted the key in the lock than the door bursts open and Jon charges at me.

I shriek as the icy steel of his golf club presses across my neck, and we land against the fridge. It's the closest I've been to him for ten years.

'Why the fuck did you have to spill it all to my wife?' His voice is a snarl and his spittle flies into my face.

'The police are on their way,' I manage to say, though my voice is a gurgle. But I hear sirens wailing in the distance.

'It'll be too late for you by then.' As the weight of the metal grinds into my throat, I have no doubt that he really means it. The taste of fear fills my mouth, making it difficult to breathe. 'Do you really think I'm going to allow you to carry on while I rot in prison?'

'It's – no – less – than – you – deserve.' My survival instincts kick in – I have to fight back to stay alive until the police get here. Drawing on every ounce of strength, I drive my elbow into Jon's side, causing him to loosen his grip. Seizing the opportunity, I rake my nails into his hand, hoping to break free as the echo of sirens becomes closer.

'You fucking bitch.'

The force of the golf club against my neck slackens enough for me to get my arm free and be able to drive my fingers forward, deep into his neck. I always knew the self-defence class I took would come in handy one day.

He lets me go completely, his own breathing now disrupted as he staggers back to the sink.

'Always the big shot, weren't you Jon?' My words pump out in gasps. 'Well not anymore.'

A thundering of footsteps up the garden path tells me I'm safe. Then more sirens, presumably for next door.

I don't know what sound to tune in to, the word *Mummy* echoing from the house, the splintering of wood as their front door is broken down, or Jon's snarled words as four police officers wrestle him to the ground.

'I'll fucking kill you for this.'

'It's over,' one of them says as another snaps handcuffs on him. 'You won't be *killing* anyone.'

FIFTY

AMELIA

'Thanks for seeing me. I wasn't sure if you would.' Cassie loiters in the doorway. She looks exhausted. It's the first time I've ever seen her without make-up and perfect hair. 'Do you mind if I sit down.' She gestures to the chair next to my bed.

I nod.

'I hear you're being discharged tomorrow.' She perches at the edge of it and looks at me. I can tell her eyes are drawn to my throat, just like everybody's are since I've had the tube taken out.

'No thanks to you.' It's still sore to speak. However, I've defied the doctors with my road to recovery. At first I was warned that speaking would always be a struggle but bit by bit, my throat's healing.

'Look Amy—'

'Amelia,' I correct her.

'Amelia – I was never responsible for my husband's actions.'

'You wouldn't give me the time of day though – in your conservatory that day – you wouldn't even hear me out.'

'We could go around the houses all day about this, couldn't

we? The bottom line is, though, that you survived, I survived and Jon's finally where he should be. Can't we put all that behind us?' She looks at me with hope in her eyes.

I stare back at her. She's spot on, of course she is. My resentment towards her is hugely misdirected. After all, she did the right thing in the end and told the police what I'd told her as well as coaxing a confession out of Becca. And for all this, she nearly ended up as one of Jon's victims. Now she's on her own in life. For all the envy I once had towards her and her lifestyle, she's now the same as me.

'How are you?' I relax as my initial hostility on seeing her again leaves me.

'Getting there, I suppose. I'm just trying to focus on Teddy.'

I lean against the pillows. Here I am, being funny with *her* after what I put her through that day.

'I'm sorry. Really, I am.'

'I know you are. This is why I've come to see you. There's been so much that's happened, that we kind of need to lay it all to rest.'

I turn my head away. I can't tell her how much it hurts me to have her in front of me. She's as much a reminder of everything that I've struggled against as the scar on my throat. All I want now I've been cleared of Jade's murder is a fresh start.

'I think it's better if this is the last time,' I say to the window, rather than her. 'It's not personal, it's just...' My voice fades away.

'I know. You don't have to explain anything. I'm just glad you can start again now. He can't hurt either of us anymore.'

'That's one of the reasons I was hanging around your houses, you know. I'm sorry I scared you.'

'At least I know now.' It's her turn to look away and fix her eyes on the constantly blaring TV at the end of my bed. I never really watch it but I like the company. If I've got voices around me, I don't feel quite so alone.

I turn back to her in time to notice the tears which have filled her eyes. Tears which I can't provide comfort for. I need to focus on myself now. I just need to get out of here and move forward with my life. 'I think we've said all that needs to be said, don't you?'

She fumbles in her handbag. 'I found this.' She passes an envelope to me. 'The other reason I've come here today.'

'What is it?'

'A National Savings passbook. I think Jon's mum must have opened it quite some time ago. I found it in a filing cabinet.' She looks puzzled as she hands it to me. 'I was quite surprised to find it actually.'

I slide it from the envelope and open it. 'She wasn't lying to me then.' I have to rub my eyes at first as I look down at it. There, in black and white, is a similar amount to the bank statement I once found at Tolbeck Cottage.

'Who wasn't lying?'

'Your mother-in-law.'

'I'm not being funny but why on earth would she leave you that sort of money?' There's no malice in Cassie's tone. No suggestion that I *shouldn't* have it.

'She came to see me in prison not long before she died.'

'Elsie did?' Judging by her expression and the rise in her voice, this is all complete news to her.

I nod slowly. 'She'd started a letter to me, she said, but then decided that wasn't enough. She wanted to see me.'

'Why? How long before she died?'

'She paid one of the hospice volunteers to bring her. She wanted to say sorry. As if that could ever be enough.' The figures on the letter blur before my eyes. I'll never know poverty again but nor can I ever get the time back that's been robbed from me.

I'll never forget how frail Elsie Hemingway looked when she was wheeled into that prison visiting room. I'd had sleepless nights in the run-up to her requested visit, wondering what it could be about.

'Sorry for what?'

'She'd spotted the transaction from Jack to Becca on a bank statement he'd tried to hide from her.'

'Elsie knew what Jon had done?' Cassie's voice is almost a squeak.

I nod. 'Jack eventually owned up to what he'd done, that he was paying Becca Thorpe off to protect their son's future and their own reputation.'

'But she didn't do anything?'

'By that time, I'd already been sentenced. She told me she was too scared of going against Jack at the time.'

'Oh my God.' Cassie's hand flies to her mouth. 'No wonder she was so distant from us.'

'She still left me to rot in there.'

'It's no wonder she insisted Tolbeck Cottage should be Teddy's as well. We were only ever allowed to live in it until he was old enough to own it for himself.'

'Anyway, she decided she couldn't take what she knew to her grave. She told me that guilt had eaten her up for years and she wanted to say sorry to me. She also wanted to check that I'd accept the money she'd put aside when Jack died.'

'It's certainly enough money to completely set yourself up.'

'I'd have rather she could have spoken up and helped me clear my name.'

'Presumably you said this to her?'

'Of course I did. However, she wouldn't agree to it.'

'And this was just before she died?'

'Days. Her argument was that Jon had his own family. She couldn't do it to him – or to her grandson. She'd keep his secret if I'd keep her money, she said. She said, if I'd accept her apology, she'd get the account book lodged with her solicitor and write to me with the details.'

'Which, clearly, she didn't?' Cassie looks even more worn out than she did when she first arrived.

'Except she died within a couple of days of that conversation. And every solicitor I've contacted since my release won't deal with me.'

'Why not?'

'Data protection. They've all said that they can only divulge information about a person's estate to beneficiaries or executors.'

'And you never knew *which* solicitor she might have been using?'

I shake my head. 'I might have had a chance if I did – this is one of the reasons I wanted to get inside Tolbeck Cottage to see what I might be able to find.'

I'll never forget how Elsie Hemingway had looked at me with tears in her eyes in that visiting room as she told me how dreadfully sorry she was. She was the only living person, other than Becca and Jon, who knew I'd taken the entire blame for someone else's actions. But sorry was a bittersweet word. It was too little, too late.

I press the passbook between my palms. I have no qualms about accepting this money. A hundred thousand pounds for every year of my incarceration. As well as the knowledge that Jon's going to serve at least double the time that I did. He'll be nearly fifty before he's eligible for parole.

'I hope the money helps you start again.' Cassie's voice breaks into my thoughts. I'd almost forgotten she was here for a moment.

'Thank you for coming in,' I say, my voice cracking. I've been told to use it minimally and I've totally overdone it. Though I'm aware I'm lucky my voice has come back at all. I'm lucky to still be here. 'Good luck with everything. I hope things turn out well for you.'

And I do mean this. I may not wish to be friends with Cassie when I'm discharged tomorrow but I do wish her well.

Becca too. If they hadn't spoken up against Jon and for me in the end, I could have ended up right back where I started.

Instead, I've got money, I've got my freedom, but mostly importantly, I've got my reputation.

EPILOGUE

CASSIE

I try to ignore the lump in my throat as I lock the door of Tolbeck Cottage for the final time. I'd thought we were embarking on a happy and exciting fresh start as a family – I never imagined Teddy and I would end up compelled to live with my mother and having to start again.

I'm lucky to be living at all.

By the time the ambulance got to me that day, I was in a coma. But thank God they were able to give me something to reverse the effects of the insulin and give me a chance at continuing to bring up my son. I've no idea how much he heard or saw that day and can only hope his memory fades as he grows older. When they broke into the house and found me, he was apparently curled into my side.

The psychologist has said it's unlikely he'll have a clear memory of being this young as the years progress, and they're working hard to help him recover from all he's been through.

At first, he asked for his daddy constantly. Now he seems to have accepted that he's not coming back. To start with I told him he was working away but now, following the psychologist's advice, I've had to tell him that his daddy has been bad and had to go to prison. That's all he needs to know for now – he's far too young to understand *why*.

The judge gave Jon the severest sentence he could, not only for Jade's murder, but also for the attempted murder of me and Amelia.

The judge said he believed Jon poses a grave danger to society and wouldn't be leaving prison for the entirety of his sentence. He was also found guilty of causing actual bodily harm towards Becca. His final conviction was perverting the course of justice.

I trudge down the steps from the front door for the last time, grateful I was able to leave Teddy with my mother today. Coming back here after all these months would have only confused him even more.

'Hey.' Becca emerges from her gate, wearing her yoga clothes as always. 'How are you doing?' Her hair's grown since I last saw her and she's wearing it in a ponytail. She looks better than when I last saw her – somehow lighter and less angry.

'I'm getting there,' I reply. 'I've been discharged from the outpatients now so that's something – they said I've been really lucky.'

'How about Amelia?' A weird look enters Becca's eyes and I know it's because she doesn't *really* like her all that much. 'How's she getting on?'

'Oh, you know.' I think back to the last time I saw Amy just before she was discharged from hospital. She'd made it clear she didn't want to see me again and just wanted to move forward with her own life. 'I've been told she left the approved premises straight away and has been helped to find somewhere new.'

Becca gives me a knowing look. 'Is she going to move away from here?'

I shrug. 'Why should she? She's been cleared.'

'Mud always sticks, that's the problem.'

'Hopefully not,' I reply. 'Even though Amelia's been completely cleared of all wrongdoing, she'll always be scarred by what she's been through.'

'You mean her throat?' Becca points to her own throat and I'm reminded of the awful bruising Jon caused to it with his golf club.

'I was thinking more of the emotional scarring. But yeah, that too – she apparently needed another operation, even after the emergency tracheotomy.'

'At least she'll get some compensation for it all.'

'I suppose so – it can't buy all those years back though, can it?'

I pause, deliberating over whether to tell Becca about Jon's mum and the fact that she'd also carried the secret for years. Then I decide against it. I'm not going to blacken Elsie's name any more than she'll have blackened it herself while wrestling with her conscience.

Maybe she feared Jon as much as I did in the end. Though I suspect the real reason is that she didn't want to ruin his life by speaking the truth earlier like she should have done. Perhaps she died believing she'd done as much as she could do for Amelia. All I know is what's done is done and we've all got to move forward. It's a shame really that Amelia and I agreed that the hospital visit would be the last time we would have anything to do with one another. When I met her, I saw a potential friend. Clearly, in me, she saw something entirely different. A way to get to Jon. A way to clear her name. And she nearly got us both killed while trying.

As Becca and I chat, I can't shake the feeling that the past isn't entirely buried. There's still an uneasiness in the air, like something is lurking in the shadows, waiting to resurface. But I push the thought aside; I have to focus on the present now and get well away from here.

'At least he's serving his sentences consecutively.' Becca's words cut into my swirling thoughts, which is probably a good thing. I do far too much thinking these days. I wish I could completely let go and move on but it's difficult.

'I know.'

I was warned the judge might order the sentences to be served concurrently, in which case Jon would have been out before Teddy even reaches adulthood. As it stands, with his sentences for all his convictions added together, Jon will be a much older man before he's free again. Though after what he's done, he'll *never* be truly free. I can only hope his conscience keeps him awake each and every night.

I can't help but feel a degree of anger at both Elsie and Becca for keeping the truth to themselves and the near-fatal result this had for myself and Amelia, and even Becca herself, if the police hadn't got to her when they did. But at least, in the end, their consciences got the better of them, and some might say that they, themselves, were victims. Certainly of my father-in-law and his nasty threats.

And, as Mum keeps saying when I try to heap the blame onto Becca, it was *Jon* who added the ketamine to Jade's drink, not *her*. So I was relieved when Becca got a community order, as from what she told me before, it sounds as though she's already served her time. Being held hostage throughout her years in that house, caring for her mother is hardly living a life.

I nearly ask how her lengthy stretch of unpaid work is going, but perhaps that would rub too much salt into the wounds.

'Anyway, I'd better be getting back to Teddy.' I start towards the car, aware this will probably be the last time I'll see Becca as well.

Deep down, I know that nothing good can come of keeping in touch with either Amelia or Becca. It's probably for the best that we all have a clean slate just to get on with the rest of our lives.

As I drive away from Tolbeck Cottage and out of Cherry Tree Lane, I don't look back. I will never come near this place again.

A LETTER FROM MARIA FRANKLAND

If you want to keep up to date with all my latest releases, just sign up at the following link. Your email address will never be shared and you can unsubscribe at any time.

www.bookouture.com/maria-frankland

It was a throwaway remark to my editor that sparked the idea for this novel. I'd joked about how some of my ideas are sparked from being nosy – from eavesdropping juicy-sounding conversations and glancing through semi-lit windows when I'm walking the dog in the evening.

Thankfully, that's where my similarity with Amy ends but I hope you enjoyed getting to know her and Cassie, and are happy with their outcomes. The loneliness and yearning for company that drove Cassie to naively trust others in the story is all too common, as is the jealousy that drove many of the other tensions.

As with all my novels, some dubious internet searches were required so I hope you'll vouch for me if I ever have to answer for them!!

I'd love to know your thoughts on the story and would hugely appreciate a review on Amazon or Goodreads, or both if you're feeling generous. Or even better, come and find me at one of the following places:

KEEP IN TOUCH WITH MARIA

mariafrankland.co.uk

facebook.com/writermariafrank

instagram.com/writermaria_f

BOOK CLUB QUESTIONS

1. How did the prologue set the tone for the rest of the book?

2. What are your initial impressions of Cassie and Jon as a couple? How do their interactions change throughout the story?

3. Discuss Cassie's decision to invite Amy into her home. What were her motivations, and how did this decision impact her life?

4. Amy's past is revealed gradually. Did you sympathise with her character, or did you find it hard to connect with her given her actions?

5. What do you think drove Amy to be so obsessed with Cassie's life and her house?

6. How does the author use the setting of Tolbeck Cottage to build tension and suspense in the story?

7. Teddy is just a child, but he witnesses and experiences a lot of tension and turmoil. How do you think the events in the book will affect Teddy's development and well-being in the long run?

8. Discuss the significance of Becca's character. How does her involvement in the events of the past and present impact the story's outcome?

9. Cassie's background and her experiences of feeling watched and unsafe are crucial to the story. How did her past influence her decisions and reactions to the events in the present?

10. Amy's past is intertwined with a murder that took place at Tolbeck Cottage. Were you surprised by the revelation of her connection to the crime? How did this revelation change your perception of her character?

11. If you were in Cassie's position, how do you think you would have reacted to the situation with Amy and the secrets surrounding Jon?

12. Do you think Amy's time in prison and her encounter with Cassie and Jon will lead her to make positive changes in her life, or do you believe she might continue down a darker path?

13. The book highlights the consequences of secrecy and lies. How do you think the characters will approach honesty and trust in their relationships moving forward?

ACKNOWLEDGEMENTS

Thank you, as always, to my amazing husband, Michael. He's my first reader, and his opinion is vital with my editing process for each of my novels. His belief in me means more than I can say.

My next huge thank you goes to Susannah Hamilton, my editor at Bookouture. It has been amazing to have her input into the story and we make such awesome progress by chatting the ideas around together. This book wouldn't be what it is without her! I'd like to also acknowledge the hard work of Laura, my copy editor, and Becca, my proofreader, as well as David Grogan for his amazing cover design.

A special acknowledgement goes to my existing community of wonderful readers, especially those in my FrankFans reader group, who give me so much support and encouragement.

I will always be grateful to Leeds Trinity University and my MA in Creative Writing tutors there, Martyn, Amina and Oz. My master's degree in 2015 was the springboard into being able to write as a profession.

And thanks especially to you, the reader. Whether you are new to my work or have read every book, thank you for taking the time to read this story. I really hope you enjoyed it.

PUBLISHING TEAM

Turning a manuscript into a book requires the efforts of many people. The publishing team at Bookouture would like to acknowledge everyone who contributed to this publication.

Audio
Alba Proko
Sinead O'Connor
Melissa Tran

Commercial
Lauren Morrissette
Jil Thielen
Imogen Allport

Cover design
Head Design Ltd.

Data and analysis
Mark Alder
Mohamed Bussuri

Editorial
Susannah Hamilton
Nadia Michael

Milton Keynes UK
Ingram Content Group UK Ltd.
UKHW041903120324
439302UK00005B/250